A Legion Archer series and the associated books are the creation of J. Clifton Slater. Any use of *Salvation of Exile*, in part or in whole, requires express written consent. This is a work of fiction. Any resemblance to persons living or dead is purely coincidental. All rights reserved.

When I write, my mind is full of story, history, and the ancient environment. In short, it's a jumble of information, and much like clothing in a dryer, they tumble around without purpose. Thanks to Hollis Jones for guiding my wandering mind as I wrote this book. She kept me on the path, adjusted the structure, identified rough spots, and called my attention to overly long descriptions. Because of her, *Salvation of Exile* exists.

And, I'd like to extend my sincerest 'thank you' to you. My readers are the reason I can spend my days doing research and writing stories. Rendering a hand salute to you for being there for me. Ready, two!

If you have comments, contact me:

GalacticCouncilRealm@gmail.com

For a list of books and series, or to sign up for my monthly newsletter and receive articles on ancient topics, go to my website:

www.JCliftonSlater.com

Act 1

The defeat of Hannibal at the Battle of Zama left Carthage as a subject state of Rome. Taking advantage of the war in Africa, Iberian Tribes revolted. And while Cornelius Scipio was winning the honorific Africanus against Carthage, Proconsul Manlius Acidinus conducted operations to settle Iberia. Both Roman Generals returned with vast fortunes for the treasury. Beyond the riches from two lands, the Legion victories established Rome as the prevailing force in the eastern Mediterranean.

But to the west, across the Adriatic and Ionian Seas, the richer, more cultured, and collectively more powerful Greek city states eyed the affluence and influence of the growing Republic. The only thing holding the Greeks back from following the lead of King Pyrrhus and Hannibal Barca, and invading the peninsula of Italia, was the lack of a dominant leader.

The tribes in the Po River Valley didn't have that problem. While Rome controlled most of Italia, in the north, one of Mago Barca's Lieutenant Generals remained among the tribes. Adding a Carthaginian to the incendiary mix of Boii, Cenomani, Salassi, and Insubri warriors ignited a threat to Rome much closer than a sea voyage from Greece.

For one man, there was no escape from duty. For another, there existed a salvation of exile. If he could survive long enough to realize the dream.

Welcome to 200 B.C.

Chapter 1 – For One Man

"Lo Africanus," a shopkeeper shouted. "Come partake of your midday repast at my restaurant."

From across the street, another shop owner disputed, "Not there, but here. For mine is the finest eatery in this section of Rome."

"If that dingy snack place is the finest, I'll eat your tunic," the first challenged.

Cornelius Scipio laughed and replied to both men, "My household staff insists that I eat before I leave the villa. Unfortunately for you, despite your warm invitations, I'm still full."

The Roman General and his bodyguard continued along the sidewalk.

Once out of hearing range, Sidia Decimia whispered, "If you ate at one, the restaurant would thrive for a year off the reputation of feeding the hero of Carthage. And you could eat there free, forever."

"Yes but it would put the other eatery out of business," Cornelius told him. "Caution limits my public exposure."

"Lo Africanus, thanks to you, I have a shipment of raisin wine from Carthage," a vino seller shouted. "Come taste a sample."

"I need a clear head for the peoples' business," Scipio replied. "It'll be a long afternoon in the Senate, if I begin sampling vinos."

Sidia suggested as they passed the wine shop, "Most men would cash in on your fame, General."

"Optio Decimia, I don't want to be the King of Rome or the richest man in the Republic," Cornelius responded. "I'm a citizen like my father and his father before him. That's all the prize I need in life."

"Lo Africanus," other merchants solicited the victor of Zama.

Cornelius Scipio Africanus waved to each but didn't pause or speak. A block later, he and Sidia left the market street and entered the Forum. Across the wide venue, two men stood on a wooden stand. Around them, a crowd watched quietly. Cornelius and Sidia stopped behind the audience to listen.

"The Twelve Tablets of Law compose all the laws Rome needs," Sextus Paetus announced, "or will ever need."

"They call you The Clever based on your studious approach to the law," Tribune Porcius Laeca countered. "But would a clever man close his mind to the needs of the citizens of Rome?"

"The Twelve Tablets make provisions for a citizen's property rights," Sextus asserted. "If ownership is established and protected by the law, the law has fulfilled its purpose."

"Yet, one breach of a rule and a citizen can be whipped as if he was a common slave or a non-citizen," Porcius Laeca explained. "Or sentenced to death without recourse by a magistrate or a Legion officer."

"A Legionary is under orders and those can't be questioned in times of war," Sextus told the crowd. "Because each heavy infantryman must be a citizen, you can see where law and discipline could easily be at cross purposes."

"Suppose the law simply allowed for a citizen to appeal a verdict," Porcius offered. "Or a Legionary to ask for the judgement to be reviewed by a superior officer."

"There are many sample cases and ways to stretch the logic of the law out of reason," Sextus described. "For example, what if a citizen was found guilty of murder and sentenced to crucifixion? Would the review reduce the killing to a fine? What justice would be served by a pay-for-murder clause?"

"Let's examine the case as you defined it," Porcius argued. "Taking a life for a life is retribution and accepted by Greek and Roman citizens alike. But what is the purpose of the sentence? Is it not to keep the accused from endangering other citizens? Suppose the law allowed a convicted citizen to relinquish his property, surrender his citizenship, and go into exile? Wouldn't that vengeance by the state be equal to dying on a cross?"

"Perhaps they should start calling you, The Clever," Sextus Paetus concluded. "I'm beginning to see your reasoning. And thusly, good sir, I declare you, Tribune Porcius Laeca, the victor of this debate."

The two orators bowed to each other and extended their arms to the crowd. They left the stand to polite applause.

"What do you think, General?" Sidia inquired as they walked towards the senate building.

"If I sentence someone to death," Cornelius answered. "I expect them to die at dawn. And not to bother me for a second opinion."

"Lo Africanus," Sidia muttered.

"I heard that Optio," Cornelius teased. "Don't forget, you are not a citizen. None of that debate affects you."

"I am the bodyguard for the most popular man in Rome," Sidia pointed out. "If I have to kill an assassin to save you, that should count for something."

"I'll be sure to volunteer to defend you," Cornelius offered. "But don't worry, as soon as I can secure a Proconsul position, we'll be leaving Rome."

"Back to campaigning," Sidia summed up. "It is a simpler life, General. Only the enemy wants to kill you and you can see them coming."

Walking fast to avoid drawing a crowd, they crossed the Forum.

***

In the senate building, Caecina, the President of the Senate, hammered his fist on the podium.

"Gentlemen, if you please, settle down. We must select a pair of Censors today," Caecina announced, with an emphasis on today.

Censors weren't politically powerful, having no legislative leverage or direct effect on trade or laws. But the two Censors would have their names spread throughout the

Republic. Popularity created the ability to sway the crowds, and that was a formidable power in itself. Caecina feared the debates for the positions would go on all afternoon.

"I nominate Cornelius Scipio Africanus as Censor for the next census," a voice boomed from a section of the chamber. Heads snapped around. Not because of the abrupt nomination. Although rude, it wasn't rare. The surprise came because the speaker was a known adversary of Cornelius Scipio.

"The Senate acknowledges, Senator Marcus Cato's nomination," President Caecina allowed. This will be an easy vote, he thought before asking. "Do I hear a second?"

From a seat near Cato, Titus Crispinus sealed Cornelius' fate. "I second the nomination of Africanus as Censor."

Those who loved and supported Cornelius, and those who despised him, all signified their approval.

"The motion carries." The President accepted the unanimous vote before asking, "And for the second Censor, do I hear a nomination?"

"Aelius Paetus," Cornelius announced. His choice was a man he trusted.

"Do I hear a second for Aelius Paetus?" the President inquired.

From Cornelius' side of the chamber, three voices confirmed Aelius.

"The Senate calls for a vote on Aelius Paetus as a Censor of Rome," the President announced.

"If it pleases the Senate," Cato demanded, "I nominate Titus Crispinus for Censor."

"Do I hear a second?" Caecina inquired. He hoped there wasn't more support for Crispinus. With opposing factions nominating their own man, the long debate he feared was developing. Yet, he couldn't see a way out of a tortuous afternoon.

"I second the nomination of Titus Crispinus for Censor," Valerius Flaccus stated from his seat near Cato.

A man squatted beside Cornelius and touched his arm to get his attention.

"Senator Scipio, the knives are out for you," the assistant to Aelius Paetus warned. "If Crispinus is elected, Senator Paetus fears there'll be discrepancies in the census."

It seemed that Marcus Cato, Titus Crispinus, and Valerius Flaccus were far ahead in planning moves to discredit Scipio. Cornelius sighed at the unexpected attack.

"And I'll be tried for incompetence," Cornelius offered. "I didn't see the assault coming."

"Pardon me, sir?" the assistant asked, confused by the statement.

Cornelius didn't explain the military nature of being the target of enemy's surprise maneuver. Rather, he inquired, "Does Paetus have a plan?"

"Yes, sir. But you may not like it," cautioned the assistant. "You insist that as a field commander, you have deficiencies in your administrative abilities. And insist that you need Senator Paetus by your side to assure the accuracy of the count."

"When an enemy exposes himself during an ambush, first you destroy his protective screen of spearmen," Cornelius remarked. Then, with a smile, he instructed, "Tell Senator Paetus to protest every accusation I make."

"Protest you, Sir?" the aid asked.

"Every inflammatory statement. It's for his own protection."

"As you wish, Africanus."

The aid had just left when Cornelius jumped to his feet and bellowed, "Maniple. Advance."

Most of the Senators had served in a Legion during Hannibal's war. More than half had the honor of qualifying as heavy infantrymen. Involuntarily, they hammered their left hand outward as if performing the first move with a shield. They laughed at the reflex action and the memory of days and months perfecting the drill.

"It's good to see you haven't lost the skill," Cornelius congratulated them. "Now I'm going to call on you to defend the General who's been assaulted in this chamber."

"Who has been assaulted?" a Senator demanded.

Cornelius didn't answer. Instead, he left his seat and walked to the front of the chamber.

"President Caecina, I ask for the floor," he requested.

"The Chamber recognizes Senator Scipio Africanus."

***

As he had done at other times, Cornelius allowed his face to go blank. Expressionless, he said, "I fought underhanded snakes in Iberia and chased vipers into their dens. In Africa, I dodged war elephants and battled a man who defeated every man in this chamber, your fathers, uncles, and brothers included. And now, when I've come home to rest, and do my civic duty, I find snakes here in this chamber."

"I protest the accusation that we have serpents in the Senate of Rome," Aelius Paetus blurted out.

"Mister President," Marcus Cato called. "Mister President, I protest."

"What do you protest, Senator Cato?" the President asked. "Are you saying there are snakes in the chamber?"

Before Cato could answer, Cornelius raised his voice, "Thank you Senator Paetus for pointing out my impudence. Allow me to rephrase. I returned victorious, bringing wealth and peace with me. But here today, I meet criminals."

"President Caecina, I must object to the idea that any Senator of Rome is a criminal," Aelius Paetus said in full voice.

"Again, I stand corrected," Cornelius declared. "In Iberia and Africa, I held the power of life and death in my hands. But here today, I am being vilified by Godless…"

"Surely, we can confirm that no one in this chamber doesn't respect the Gods," Aelius Paetus shouted.

"My language describing foes, I fear, is better suited to a Legion marching camp than to the Senate of Rome," Cornelius admitted.

Before he continued, one of the Consuls stood. He waved to be acknowledged and demanded, "President Caecina, allow me to make a statement."

"The Senate recognizes Consul Sulpicius Galba."

"I believe what Scipio Africanus said is the truth," Galba insisted. "He has been at war and gone from Rome for many years. It's obvious as the Censor, he'll need a partner to work closely with him. Not only for the census but for the celebration of the Gods after the count is finalized."

"Your point, Consul?" Caecina asked.

"Aelius Paetus has shown the courage to interrupt Scipio and to correct him. I believe that is the type of character we need in a Censor to balance the passion of the warrior Africanus."

"All in favor of electing Aelius Paetus as the second Censor of Rome," Caecina proposed, "raise your hand."

The logic of the Consul's argument carried the vote for Paetus. Most of the Senate was excited to have the vote for the Censors behind them, except for one sector. Around Marcus Cato, grumbling and angry gestures dominated their conversations.

"The Senate will come to order," Caecina stated. "We have…."

But the President of the Senate stopped to watch a courier, dusty and exhausted, march into the chamber. The courier might have a message for any of the Senators, perhaps a death notice or a birth announcement. But accompanying the courier were two Tribunes in Legion armor. It was the escort by active duty Legion staff officers that halted Caecina.

The three hurried to Consul Aurelius Cotta, where the courier handed over a scroll. After reading a few lines, Cotta waved Galba to his side. Both Consuls of Rome read the message together. Then Aurelius Cotta walked to the podium.

"If you don't mind Caecina, I'm taking control of the Senate."

"As is your right, Consul," the President allowed.

Caecina backed away while the Consul studied the men who ruled Rome.

"Senators, I hold in my hand a report of rebellion in the Po River Valley," Cotta disclosed. "Three and a half days ago, savages from the Boii, Cenomani, Salassi, and Insubri tribes attacked Placentia."

"Placentia has defensive walls," a Senator informed the chamber. "They can hold out until the garrison from Remini arrives. What's the problem?"

"Scouts report as many as forty thousand spearmen from the tribes have taken up arms," Consul Cotta told him. "And they're under the command of Lieutenant General Hamilcar, one of Mago Barca's commanders."

"Carthaginians," Cornelius exploded. "Consul Cotta, make me a Proconsul and give me Legions. I'll put down the rebellion."

"Censor Scipio Africanus, your duty to Rome is here," Cotta reminded Cornelius. Then to the Senate, he explained.

"I'm dispatching my Legions from Fiesole and placing them under the command of Praetor Furius Purpureo at Rimini. He'll contain the rebellion while I raise another two Legions. Provided, it's the will of the Senate?"

Every voice called for the execution of Cotta's plan. Especially enthusiastic were Marcus Cato, Titus Crispinus, and Valerius Flaccus. While their scheme to undermine Cornelius had failed with the election of Aelius Paetus as second Censor, the strategy of holding Cornelius Scipio in Rome had worked.

"We didn't get everything we wanted," Marcus Cato preached to his confederates. "But we did prevent Africanus from gathering to his breast more glory, fame, popularity, and riches."

"Under our watchful eyes," Valerius Flaccus declared, "there will never be a King Scipio."

"Never," the other leaders of their section agreed.

Chapter 2 – Echoes of Hannibal

Five days before the election of the new Censors of Rome, Lieutenant General Hamilcar stood on a wagon bed. A mile to the south, the Po River flowed toward the sea through thick forests and fertile farmland. Bathed in the light of a full moon, the Carthaginian General addressed a gathering of Tribal Kings and their War Chiefs.

"Someday soon, Hannibal will land and march up the Po River Valley. When he arrives, the footfalls of his war elephants will shake the earth. The winds from his swift light cavalry will scatter pollen far and wide. And his heavy infantry will sweep the valley clear of Roman Legions," Hamilcar projected. "However, before the great General returns, we must prepare the landscape."

"You mean capture towns for his headquarters and the comfort of his staff," B'Yag, King of the Insubri, offered. "From what my war chief tells me, Hannibal will need a place to lick his wounds after the battle with Scipio."

"What are you getting at King B'Yag?" Hamilcar demanded.

The Carthaginian bodyguards stiffened and adjusted their spears. Not intimidated by the armor and steel spearheads, the Insubri guards expanded their chests and glared at the soldiers.

"We don't need a promise of a savior or a higher purpose," B'Yag answered. "We all hate the Latians and the settlements they've forced onto our lands."

"Then we're in agreement," Hamilcar told him. "The towns of Placentia and Cremona must be captured."

"And cleaned of Latian scum," the King of the Boii added. "And stripped of gold and silver and slaves."

Cheering greeted the statement.

B'Yag pulled his son close enough to whisper in his ear, "War Chief, keep us out of the middle of the fighting. If the Boii are on fire for conquest, they might start on our side of the battle line."

With Milan, just thirty-five miles north of the riverbank, the Insubri couldn't afford to get weakened by the Romans and give the Boii Tribe an opportunity to conquer Insubri land. A sneak attack during the battle wasn't beyond the aggressive Boii Tribe.

"I'll keep us away from them," Brocc B'Yag assured his father. "And you're right, Hannibal has no chance of showing up for many years. We watched his defeat in Africa as we marched away."

"Once we have control of Placentia," Hamilcar continued from the wagon, "we'll sweep the defenders from Cremona and build walls. This section of the Po River Valley will forever be land belonging to the Gaul."

"But first, we have to take the cities," mentioned the King of the Cenomani.

"How could you doubt it? Look around at the army we've gathered," Hamilcar encouraged. "At dawn, we'll reclaim the stolen lands. For now, go prepare your warriors."

"Bíois. Bíois," the tribal leaders cheered.

Brocc B'Yag fell in step with his father as they left the planning session.

"Did I miss something?" Brocc asked. "Did the General present a plan of attack?"

"No. But he gave a rousing speech," King B'Yag mentioned.

Behind them and their bodyguards, the other tribes cheered Bíois, Bíois, in the old language. *Life* seemed a strange war cry, but many would die in battle, and it made sense to wish each other *Life* before the fighting began. Plus, the chanting bolstered the spirits of the weaker spearmen.

"Bíois," Brocc B'Yag said as they entered the campsite of the Insubri.

***

The reason the Carthaginian officer hadn't disclosed his plan was he didn't have one. This dawned on Brocc B'Yag as he kicked and swam while pushing a small reed raft across the river. Accepting the discomfort of the cold water, he continued towards the far bank.

Hamilcar had called together kings, and each leader had summoned their clans. With no command structure, the General was nothing but a figurehead. A carved post in a town square with no purpose except to gaze down on the citizens.

Shivering, War Chief B'Yag kicked and fought the current to keep from being washed too far downstream. It would be embarrassing for the War Chief of the Insubri to emerge from the water under a Cenomani, Salassi, or Gods forbid, a clan banner of the Boii.

A soft pink in the sky provided enough light to show thousands of heads and small reed rafts crossing the Po River. Brocc reached the far shore, scrambled out of the water, shook to sling off the dampness before taking a bundle of clothing, linen armor, and weapons from the reed mat. While he dressed, a dying cry reached him from the east. Following that, shouts of men in pursuit signified warriors running after fishermen.

"And there is the flaw in not having a command structure," Brocc sneered.

"What?" one of his spearmen asked.

"While the Salassi are busy chasing fishermen, let's get to the walls of Placentia," Brocc B'Yag replied, ignoring the question. "Maybe we can get over the wall before the defenders wake up."

Without real control, Hamilcar lacked the ability to send warriors across the river to silence witnesses to the crossing. No king wanted to volunteer their spearmen for the dangerous and heartless mission of murdering anyone who approached the river at dawn. The killing seemed justified during the actual attack.

The Insubri clans clustered around War Chief B'Yag. After he counted twenty-five banners, Brocc shouted, "Bíois."

"Bíois," the spearmen responded.

While screaming the war cry of *Life*, they jogged in the direction of Placentia. Farther away, but hidden by thick trees, the other tribes chanted as they ran the half-mile to the ill-fated town.

***

Wooden logs and boards gave the town the look and feel of a small village. The low walls used the same building material, meaning the defenses could have been more substantial. But as a collection point for local farmers, herders, and regional craftsmen, Placentia needed to be accessible for trade from all sides. The walls were designed to keep animals in and packs of predators out. Many small gates to facilitate trade made the town almost indefensible.

In the early morning of that fall day, an army of Galic tribes with a Carthaginian General screamed their war cry as they ran from the woods. The fastest warriors leaped and grabbed the top of the walls. They scrambled over and vanished. Not to be outdone by his spearmen, Brocc jumped, hung for a moment before hoisting himself up and over the wall. Landing, he looked for threats. But the swiftest Insubri warriors had killed the city guards.

"Open the gates and let our slower brothers in," Brocc instructed. "And set a defensive line on each street."

From different parts of the town, war cries announced the arrival of the other tribes and clans.

"If we wait here, the other tribes will get all the spoils," one of his clan leaders whined.

"Did you look at the size of Placentia from the top of the wall?" Brocc asked. Then he realized the clan leader was a heavy man who couldn't have climbed the wall. So he described. "It's ten times bigger than your largest village."

"Not as big as Milan," another clan leader mentioned.

"Nor as well defended as our capital. Or we would have lost warriors," Brocc told him. "But that's good. I never want to sacrifice warriors for profit. Besides, there are plenty of spoils for everyone. We'll wait until we have more men."

Getting four thousand Insubri over the wall and through the small gates delayed the plundering. But when they did move into the trading center, the warriors of the Insubri were a powerful force.

"I declare this sector of Placentia as Insubri territory," Brocc exclaimed after moving several blocks into Placentia. "Seal the streets. No one gets out and no one gets in."

"No one?" a clan leader inquired.

"Not a guardsman, a potential slave, or a warrior from another tribe crosses our lines."

Armored and spear carrying city guards appeared. They jogged from down the street, heading for the Insubri.

"No one gets into our area. Kill them," Brocc directed.

With a wave of his arm, he sent the spearmen forward.

"Bíois. Bíois," his warriors shouted as they charged into battle.

Although Brocc had criticized Hamilcar's lack of leadership, the War Chief's technique didn't display much more control than the Carthaginian's style.

With thousands of tribal warriors scaling the walls and a few hundred guardsmen trying to defend the town, Placentia fell by midday. But while the battle for the walls ended, the fight for the streets and the valuables continued.

**

Lines of warriors carrying silver plates, golden statues, copper pans, cured hams, and sacks of grain, along with captives, flowed from Placentia to the river and back. And while the Insubri clan leaders ogled the wealth they were getting from the town, War Chief B'Yag rushed from street to street, checking on his spearmen. They had stacked furniture and carts to block the streets. At one intersection, a cluster of Boii warriors rushed towards the blockade.

"We've got trouble," a warrior cautioned.

While Brocc had enough men to stop the Boii, he worried because they carried lit torches.

"This is Insubri territory," Brocc told them when they got closer. "Turn around and get back to your tribe."

"You Insubri are arrogant, and ignorant of the ways of war," the leader of the mob said, piling on the insults. He appeared to be speaking more to the tribesmen around him than to the spearmen at the barricade, "and you're greedy. You aren't the only tribe with the right to raid these businesses?"

"We captured them," Brocc answered. "Just as the Boii captured other blocks of the town. But enough talk, get out of my space."

The leader turned as if to leave. But he grabbed a torch from one of the mob and tossed it into a linen shop. A flash revealed the fire had lit a bundle of loose fabric. Flames appeared in the window and a moment later fire crawled up the wooden frame.

"Keep your bounty," the Boii sneered, "or what's left of it."

The mob fled. Brocc motioned for his warriors to get back and ordered, "We're done here. Retreat to the gates."

"But there's so much more to get," a warrior noted.

"Look. The flames have already spread to the other buildings," Brocc pointed out. "Now, do as I say."

While the tribesmen retreated to the gates, Brocc B'Yag raced to the other intersections to warn those men about the fire. By the time the War Chief passed through the gate, the entire section claimed by the Insubri burned fiercely. But not as hot, or as angry, as his feelings about the Boii Tribe for their interruption and destruction of a prosperous raid.

***

With a backdrop of smoke from the burning town filling the sky, Brocc climbed up the far riverbank. A pair of legs at the top of the embankment stood in his way.

"Scouts from the Boii tribe said the fire started in the Insubri section. And General Hamilcar is incensed about the loss. Apparently, we burned Placentia to keep other tribes from gaining wealth," King B'Yag proposed before asking. "Did we burn the town?"

Brocc climbed up and stood beside his father. After wrapping robes around their shoulders, they watched the smoke boiling above the trees.

"It's a lie spread by the Boii scouts," Brocc answered. "They started the fire when we wouldn't let them pillage from our area."

The King exhaled through his nose, pushing out exasperation along with the air. Then he explained, "The first to tell an insidious falsehood wins the contest. The Boii have seized the initiative. Anything we say in our defense will sound like a pathetic excuse."

"But we have the truth on our side," Brocc pushed back.

"In your opinion," B'Yag told him.

"It's the truth," Brocc insisted.

"Not in the minds of the other tribes or the Carthaginian," the King stated. "For that reason, we're leaving. The Insubri will protect our borders and care for our people but will not seek expansion."

"Then the Boii win," Brocc spit out.

"That's one way to look at it," King B'Yag offered to his son. "The other is we're preserving our warriors to protect Insubri land. It's late in the year and soon frost will visit the lowlands and snow will come to the highlands. Send the clans home, we're leaving Hamilcar's army."

***

King B'Yag and his clans turned north and marched for Milan. Farther downstream, General Hamilcar and the remaining tribes forded the Po. Lightly loaded with spoils, the Insubri marched quickly for their capital. They were miles away while Hamilcar's forces were still floating two hundred wagons of stolen goods and guiding three thousand prisoners across the river. It would take the slow-moving caravan and undisciplined army six days to reach the walled stronghold of Cremona. By then, King B'Yag would sit in Milan, his warriors out of the conflict, and his clans intact. The affair was over as far as he was concerned. Unfortunately for the leader of the Insubri Tribe, others thought differently.

Chapter 3 – Ready and Able

Eighty-five miles north of Rome, the four Legions of Consul Cotta guarded the northern border of the Republic.

Beyond the infantry, the four consular legions had twenty-four hundred cavalrymen under their banners and three thousand auxiliary skirmishers. Three days after the election of the new Censors of Rome, eighteen hard-ridden horses climbed the final hill to the town of Perugia.

Colonel Furius Crassipes, the Battle Commander of one Republic Legion, and acting commander of the second, split off from the riders. His command staff raced with him to their headquarters.

Colonel Marcus Caecilius, the Battle Commander for one Roman Legion and acting commander of the second, and his staff, galloped for his command villa.

The final set of riders continued to the stables of Perugia. Colonel Valerius Flaccus and his staff needed to be on the road to Remini before dark. And by the time the infantry packed their marching gear into wagons and took to the road, the vanguard of the cavalry would be halfway to the Governor of Cisalpine Gaul.

"First Centurion. Set up relay stations," Flaccus directed his Centurion of Horse. "Make sure the squadrons, when they arrive, get pointed towards Remini."

"Yes, sir," the senior combat officer replied.

After the First Centurion left, Senior Tribune Arnza asked, "Colonel, do you know Furius Purpureo? Is the Governor qualified to command Legions?"

"Ten years ago, Praetor Purpureo served with General Claudius Marcellus," Flaccus told him. He patted the scroll on his hip. "He understands the logistics of Legions. As far as command? The Senate of Rome is handing him the authority. That's good enough for me. Get your staff on the road, Senior Tribune Arnza. I'll catch up with the squadrons stationed in Perugia. The rest will be along with the infantry."

Messengers rushed from the headquarters of the Roman Legions and Republic Legions to towns and hamlets where the Legionaries stood guard over the northern border. Tribune of Horse Arnza issued travel orders to his staff. And while the cavalry began the ride to Remini in a day, assembling eleven thousand heavy infantrymen and their support wagons would take slightly longer.

***

At Remini, Governor Furius Purpureo waited at the gate. His pacing had created a groove in the dust beside the stockade entrance. When a single rider came out of the tree line, Purpureo braced and waited.

"Has Cremona fallen?" he demanded of the rider.

"No, Praetor. They closed the gates before the tribes arrived. The garrison commander has every citizen on the walls. He's armed them with spears, stones, bricks, slings, and bows," the scout told him. "I believe they can hold for at least a couple of days, sir."

Furius Purpureo's heart skipped a beat and his stomach soured. Earlier, scouts reported that over twenty-five thousand tribesmen with a Carthaginian commander had attacked and burned Placentia. Now the barbarian army was heading for the walled city, and Cremona's only hope was relief from a Legion force. But after Hannibal's defeat by General Scipio, the Senate decreed a reduction in provincial forces. The order left Praetor Purpureo with only a few thousand Legionaries to govern all of Cisalpine Gaul.

While walking away from the gate, he pondered, "Is the sacrifice of my Legionaries worth the attempt to save a city?"

Inside his office, he stopped and looked over his staff. Young faces, soft and easily sunburned, and old faces, weathered from years that took their youth and muscle mass, looked up when he entered. Neither the old nor the young would survive combat against an army of the Gaul. But he couldn't allow another Carthaginian to establish a new reign of terror in the Republic.

"Orders, sir," an older clerk asked.

"Instruct the Tribunes to ready the garrisons. We march for Cremona in the morning," Furius Purpureo replied. "And have an aid set out my armor."

"Are we going to war, sir?" a young clerk inquired.

"There are two ways to deal with an invading army," Purpureo told him. "Pay the commanders to go away. Or kill them. And I'm fresh out of gold and silver coins."

"We are going to war," the clerk uttered with a quiver in his voice.

"We are going into combat," Purpureo breathed out the confirmation. His brash statement to the clerk was meant to show disdain for the challenge. Yet, it sounded flat, considering the reality that they would die in defense of Cremona.

Furius Purpureo left the office. Now that he'd committed to helping Cremona, he expected to feel relief. He didn't. Instead, foreboding curled the hairs on the back of the Governor's neck.

***

Where marching Legions never fully unpacked their gear and were ready to continue the march, a permanent garrison tended to sprawl and collect goods. In the morning, only half his Legionaries, light infantrymen, and cavalry were ready to travel.

"Praetor, we are behind schedule," Senior Centurion Laetorius admitted. "Our wagons are only half loaded. The Centurions are sorting out the equipment from the baggage."

"I can see that," Purpureo said. He scanned the empty ranks and growled. "If I send a message to Cremona, do you think General Hamilcar will delay his attack on the walls until we get there?"

Caught between the painful truth and the sarcasm, the senior combat officer remained silent. During the quiet, an Optio at the gate bellowed, "Riders approaching."

"Merchants or tribesmen?" Purpureo asked.

"Legion cavalry, sir," the NCO replied. "Columns of four and, Governor, the riders are still coming through the tree line."

"Standdown your Centuries, Senior Centurion," Purpureo instructed. "Let me see who the Senate's put in charge of the cavalry."

Colonel Valerius Flaccus trotted to Praetor Purpureo. After halting his mount, he saluted.

"Governor Furius Purpureo?" the Battle Commander asked.

"I'm Praetor Purpureo, Colonel."

Flaccus opened his heavy robe, pulled the scrolls from his belt, and extended it. "By order of the Senate of Rome, Lieutenant General Purpureo, you are granted command of the Legions of Consul Cotta. Until he arrives, you are the supreme Legion commander in Cisalpine Gaul. Orders sir?"

Furius Purpureo scanned the scroll. And while he finished quickly, he kept his eyes on the parchment as he thought. From a governor with command of garrisons and no chance to save Cremona, he had been elevated to the head of four full Legions, auxiliary skirmishers, and twenty-four hundred Legion cavalrymen.

"General, the infantry should be here in a day or so," Flaccus offered. "It might be best to wait for them."

"There's no time to wait, Colonel Flaccus. Bring your staff to my headquarters," Purpureo instructed. "Your riders can rest while we form a plan of attack."

"Yes, sir," the cavalry commander acknowledged.

***

Two and a half days after Colonel Flaccus rode into the stockade at Remini, his cavalrymen and half a Legion of mixed infantry reached the south bank of the Po River. From the exertions of a hard march, their breaths sent steam into the chilly air.

Scouts who ranged ahead appeared on the far side of the river. As they swam their horses across, Lieutenant General Purpureo trotted forward to where the cavalry commander waited.

"I could almost get a message to Remini by having Legionaries hand it back along the line of march," Purpureo remarked.

"Sir, it's not like they aren't rushing," Flaccus said, defending the infantry. "The Centuries were garrisoned in different towns. It's a wonder Colonel Crassipes and Colonel Caecilius could arrange the movement at all."

"I'm not unappreciative of their efforts, Colonel," Purpureo assured him. He pointed backwards at the groups of straggling infantrymen and added. "What we have, so far, outnumbers my original Centuries. And for that I am grateful."

The scouts rode out of the shallows and raced up the riverbank. River water flew from their mounts and clumps of dirt from their hooves created a loose brown arch behind them.

"Sirs, the tribes are away from their camp," one described. "Their wagons. Their horses. And their spoils are lightly defended."

"General, I've been a Legion scout for ten years," the other rider mentioned. "In all those years, I've never seen an enemy camp more deserted than the one across the river. It's like they're begging to be attacked."

Valerius Flaccus stiffened and clamped his mouth shut. Beside him, Senior Tribune Anza held his breath. The report from two of their trusted scouts dangled a tasty morsel in front of the newly promoted General. Purpureo had every right to take advantage of a careless enemy and order an attack.

"Where are their warriors?" Purpureo asked.

"Some are at the walls of Cremona and others are cutting trees for ladders," the first scout answered. "But most are drinking and celebrating west of their camp."

"A quick strike, sir, and we could burn the plunder," the second scout proposed. "That would strip the Carthaginian of his finances. And take away the rewards for the clans. It might prevent a battle."

"If the Gauls left," Purpureo commented, "we could avoid a fight."

He paused to think. While they waited for the Lieutenant General to collect his thoughts, Senior Tribune Anza shifted his eyes. Coming off the road were hundreds of weary infantrymen. They would fight if ordered to, but many would die in the shield wall from not being rested.

"Is it worth pushing exhausted men into a running attack?" Purpureo asked, as if he read Anza's mind. Then he answered his own question. "We're here for more than breaking a siege. The Senate gave me four Legions to punish the Gauls. If they run off, it'll take a year to track them to their homelands and administer justice. We'll wait for tomorrow. Then we'll attack and break this Carthaginian and his allies."

"Very good, sir," Colonel Flaccus agreed. "We'll begin the layout of the marching camps."

"Cross the river first," Purpureo told him. "I don't want to struggle across the Po and advance into tribal spears to reach the other side."

***

"Bíois. Bíois. Bíois," the cry echoed off the walls of the Legion stockade.

Sentries peered into the black of night, but the lack of light hid the spearmen.

"They could be right outside our gates," the duty Legionary mentioned. "I wish they would stop the stupid noise. Life, I'll take their life and see what they have to shout about then."

"Don't ridicule the war cry," his Optio told him. "If they didn't scream Bíois, we wouldn't know they were coming."

"Should we report them to the Centurion?" the sentry inquired.

"Report what? That thousands of Gauls, trying to hype themselves up for an attack, are screaming us awake?" the Optio scoffed. "Or trying to intimidate us with their ferocity?"

In each of the Legion marching camps, horns and drums called the infantrymen to formation. As the Optio noted, being screamed at by twenty-five thousand warriors woke the Legionaries, the Velites, the allied light infantry, and the cavalry. Compared to the yelling of the squad leaders, Tesserarii, and Optios of the Centuries, the drums and horns were a formality.

From his compound in the center of the camp, Battle Commander Marcus Caecilius studied the response of his Legionaries. Although they were mostly shadows in the early morning light, he judged how efficiently they assembled on the lanes of the camp.

"We need readiness drills," he instructed a gaggle of Junior Tribunes. "Too long in garrison weakens the preparedness of the Centuries. Remember that when you command a Maniple."

The young noblemen watched wide-eyed as the Legionaries began lining the lanes between rows of tents. For the twelve junior staff officers, it was the first time they witnessed two entire Legions of infantrymen in one place. Their prior experience was limited to an assembly of a few Centuries garrisoned in one town. The light of the rising sun reflected the awe in their faces.

Their hands shook from the frightening cries of the Gauls. "Bíois. Bíois. Bíois."

Caecilius interrupted their thoughts and reminded them, "A response is customary in the Legions of Rome."

As a group, the twelve youths replied, "Yes, sir."

"Senior Tribune Philia, I need a status report," Caecilius informed his top staff officer. The Colonel walked away as if casually observing a drill. While the Gauls continued to scream Bíois from outside, more and more hearty Rahs arose from the Legionaries.

"Attention, Junior Tribunes," Philia barked out the instructions. "Gather a report from the Maniple Tribunes and report back to me. You have your orders, go, go."

Sprinting away, the Junior Tribunes separated and raced for the twelve Tribunes assigned to the Maniples. While running through the streets, lined with big shields and armored men holding helmets and spears, some of their fears lifted.

"Will they perform under pressure?" Caecilius asked.

"They're good boys," Philia answered. "And we've drilled them enough."

"Enough to overcome that?" Colonel Caecilius questioned while tapping an ear.

Both officers listened for a moment. "Bíois. Bíois. Bíois," came from over the stockade wall.

"They have to be ready, Colonel," Philia assured Caecilius. "They are the future of Rome."

"And if we fight today, the key to victory," the Battle Commander insisted.

A pair of horses approached the Colonel's compound. Guards from the First Century stopped the riders. A moment later, Lieutenant General Purpureo and a Senior Centurion rode up and dismounted.

"Colonel Caecilius, I'm sorry we didn't have more time to speak last night," Purpureo greeted the Battle Commander.

"I realize arriving late was an imposition," Caecilius acknowledged. "But the stragglers needed heavy encouragement to finish the march with a cold swim."

"I understand. My Senior Centurion Laetorius didn't meet everyone either," Purpureo conceded. "He was overseeing a forward guard to be sure we weren't interrupted by Gauls while we built the marching camps."

"Sir, I have to ask," Caecilius requested. "Are we going to wait for Consul Cotta and the other Battle Commanders?"

"That would depend," Purpureo disclosed. "Is your command staff competent?"

The blunt question in reply to a sensible inquiry gave the Colonel pause. In the regulations, each Legion had a Battle Commander. But in the hurried assembly and march to Cremona, Furius Crassipes commanded two Republic Legions and Marcus Caecilius had the two Roman Legions. If the other Colonels had left Rome, they would be days away and traveling with Consul Cotta.

In the interlude between the question and a reply, a majority of his Junior Tribunes sprinted to the compound. Marcus Caecilius looked over the faces of his junior staff officers.

Ignoring the General's question, he faced Senior Tribune Philia and demanded, "Report."

Philia turned to the Junior Tribunes assigned to the Algea Legion. "Report."

"First Maniple, Algea Legion is ready and able to march with twelve Centuries, sir."

"Second Maniple, Algea Legion is ready and able to march with twelve Centuries, sir."

"Third Maniple, Algea Legion is ready and able to march with twelve Centuries, sir."

After an accounting for the Legion honoring the Goddess of Pain on their banner, Philia turned to the Junior Tribunes assigned to the other Legion.

"Reports from the God of Mad Rage."

"First Maniple, Furor Legion is ready and able with twelve Centuries, sir."

"Second Maniple, Furor Legion is ready and able with twelve Centuries, sir."

"Third Maniple, Furor Legion is ready and able with twelve Centuries, sir."

Philia snapped a cross chest salute and informed his commander, "Colonel Caecilius, both Legions are prepared to carry out your commands."

"Thank you, Senior Tribune," Caecilius acknowledged. Turning to Purpureo, he stated with confidence. "General, I have the best command staff in the entire Republic. And I have utter confidence in them. Your orders, sir?"

The twelve junior staff officers forgot to listen to the Gauls' war cry. Filled with confidence at their Colonel's words, they focused on the answer.

"We could wait for the Consul and a full complement of senior officers. But that would give the tribes an opportunity to slip away," Purpureo explained. He seemed to forget the alternative where the super number of tribesmen overwhelmed the Legions. Instead, he suggested. "Right now they're massed just outside our gates. It appears to me we have been handed a gift from the Goddess Bellona. And so my orders are we form up, march out, and provide a lesson to the tribes of the Po River Valley."

"Prayers to Bellona, the Goddess of War," one of the junior staff officers shouted.

"We'll give her a worthy offering," Senior Tribune Philia proclaimed.

Act 2

Chapter 4 – Ready to Travel

Colonel Crassipes received instructions to extend his combat line by moving Centuries from his Second Maniple forward to the assault line. The formation reduced the ability of the Republic Legions to rotate out the First Maniples if the battle became a protracted fight.

Crassipes argued against the change in strategy for a few moments. But Purpureo held the position of Lieutenant General and, in the end, Crassipes agreed.

The benefit of having only two Battle Commanders for four Legions became apparent immediately. When Purpureo sent the Republic Legions forward, Colonel Crassipes put his Senior Tribune in command of one and placed his Senior Centurion in command of the other Legion. Because the three staff officers had worked together for several years, the Maniples linked up quickly despite being a mixture of First and Second.

Before Hamilcar and his Gauls could coordinate an attack, the Legions formed a double wall of shields nearly twenty-three hundred feet long. The farmland that divided the Gauls from the Republic Legions wasn't much wider. A short expanse of open ground stretched from the wings of the Legions to the trees. Beyond those near the unoccupied ground, forest defined three sides. To the west, the walls of Cremona topped the branches and men stood watching the coming battle.

Behind the Republic Legions, Marcus Caecilius and his Roman Legions waited as reinforcements. To the rear of the Legions, Lieutenant General Purpureo faced an angry Valerius Flaccus.

"We should be on the flanks," Colonel Flaccus insisted. "Not back here, standing around adjusting our saddles straps and scratching our backsides."

"Suppose I want our flanks open?" Purpureo questioned.

"Then you'd be inviting an envelopment by the tribes," Flaccus told him. "And that would be stupid."

"Would it, Colonel Flaccus?"

In his passionate argument to be at the forefront of the fighting, Valerius Flaccus had neglected to address Purpureo properly. By all rights, the Lieutenant General could have Flaccus grounded and removed from command of the cavalry.

"Sir, I apologize," he begged. "I was…"

"Be silent," Purpureo ordered while waving him off. "Laetorius. What are you seeing?"

The Senior Centurion nodded as if agreeing with himself after an internal struggle. "Sir, they're going for the center of the Republic Maniples. Just like you thought."

"Nothing on the edges?" Purpureo asked.

"No sir. It looks like the Carthaginian wants to punch through the Legions," Laetorius offered. "And a good thing too. They outnumber us. If they round either wing, we're done."

Twenty-five thousand voices screamed, "Bíois. Bíois. Bíois."

The war cry rolled over the four Legions in a deafening roar. In response, eleven thousand heavy infantrymen shouted, "Rah." Adding to the counter battle cry, seven thousand Velites and auxiliary light infantry gave their voices to the Rah.

Once excited enough, the tribal spearmen raced forward. When faced with an all-out charge by the Gauls, auxiliary skirmishers retreated through the ranks of heavy infantrymen.

Next, resembling the sound of a rocky avalanche, the shields of the Gauls and the Republic Legions clashed together. And as Senior Centurion Laetorius noted, the attack concentrated on the center of the Legion line.

"Sir, I want to apologize," Flaccus began again. And again Purpureo waved him down.

"Laetorius? Are you seeing that?"

"They're shifting left," the Senior Centurion warned.

"Have Colonel Caecilius split his Legions," Purpureo instructed a Junior Tribune. "One far left and the other far right. Extend out assault line but not to the tree lines."

"Yes, General," the youth said before galloping forward.

Resembling a fast moving rainstorm across a plain, the Gauls began to flow left, carrying the fight and warriors along the right side of the Republic Legion. But as they approached the end of the shields, Algea Legion appeared and began delivering pain. On the left, Furor Legion brought mad rage to the other end of Purpureo's Legions.

With the fighting stretched over a combat line three thousand feet long, Laetorius and Purpureo, studied the fighting. They rode apart, judged the rotations of the Legionaries, the shape of the infantry lines, and trotted back to converge at the command post.

"While trying to get around us, Hamilcar thinned his center," Laetorius pointed out. "Sir, a push will split their assault line in two."

Purpureo waved Flaccus to his side.

"At the Battle of Cannae, the Carthaginian managed to get his cavalry behind the Legions," Purpureo told Flaccus. "I want to return the favor. Go break their reserves. And Colonel, those tribesmen massacred citizens of the Republic and burned Placentia. Non capimus!"

"Understood, General. No prisoners!"

Colonel Flaccus split his cavalry. He sent half to the left and the other half to the right. As they thundered away, Purpureo instructed a Junior Tribune.

"Tell Colonel Crassipes, the middle of the Gauls' line is sparse and only three ranks deep. I want to see his Legionaries standing on the baggage train before the sun reaches its zenith. Go."

The Senior Centurion bent from his horse and suggested, "General Purpureo, you were outnumbered and fighting a force that was prepared for you. But you've won, sir. Congratulations."

"Not yet, but I'm praying really hard," Purpureo admitted. "I promised Jupiter, if the God granted me victory today, I would build a temple to his glory."

The cavalry easily sliced away any tribesman attempting to round the Legion line. Then the advances of the Republic Legions began. With every shield smash, gladius thrust, and step forward, the heavy infantry chewed through the center of the Gaul's attack line. With their wings clipped and their center broken, the warriors attempted to break contact. But Colonel Flaccus and his cavalry, as if harvesting grain, cut them down as they ran from the Legionaries.

***

Lieutenant General Purpureo walked his horse through the carnage just as the sun reached the top of the sky.

"We captured seventy clan banners," a jubilant Centurion called out.

Purpureo saluted, and a few paces later, he passed a pile of dead men in blue armor. He didn't stop to gloat at the last stand of Hamilcar the Carthaginian.

Closer to the camp of the Gauls, he saluted the Legionaries of Colonel Crassipes. They were posed on top of a baggage train made up of two hundred wagons.

On the other side of the wagons, he met a squadron of cavalrymen. They were conversing with their commander.

Colonel Flaccus saluted and told him, "About six thousand Gauls escaped. But the rest died on our lances or were cut down by Legion gladii."

"Total victory was what I prayed for. Extend my appreciation to your cavalrymen."

Purpureo continued across the camp of the Gauls, heading for the walls of Cremona. Before he got close to the city, Colonel Caecilius and his staff intercepted him.

"General, we discovered who burned Placentia," Caecilius informed him.

"I assumed it was vengeance by the Carthaginian against the Republic."

"No sir. A dying warrior from the Boii Tribe told me. The Insubri set fire to the town to keep the other tribes from collecting more goods and taking additional prisoners," Caecilius stated. "With his dying breath, he cursed the selfishness of the Insubri."

"General, are we going to punish the Insubri for their crimes?" Senior Tribue Philia asked.

"It's too late in the year to be marching into the mountains. Besides, Cisalpine Gaul is settled," Purpureo answered. "For me, as the Governor, that's enough. I'll leave the punishment of the Insubri for the Senate to decide."

"What now General?" Caecilius questioned.

"Now? I'm riding to Cremona and demanding, as payment for saving their city, a feast. A celebration worthy of this victory for the officers of the Legions and the cavalry who fought and won the battle for Cremona."

***

In the heart of Insubri lands, King B'Yag walked to the top of a hill and looked down at a farming village. Winter had come early to the mountains, but he liked it cold. Few raiding parties from neighboring tribes would venture out in the frigid weather. Until spring, the boundaries of his kingdom would be secure.

A light dusting of snow covered the empty fields. Despite the weather, several foremen had laborers out, picking rocks from the farmland. Footsteps alerted the King to the approach of an individual.

"Cold this morning," Brocc B'Yag noted as he draped a robe over his father's shoulders.

"I often wonder if keeping slaves is worth the grain needed to feed them," the King mentioned. "Yet, I have to admit, everyone down there is working."

"They're working to earn their food and moving to stay warm," Brocc suggested.

"Except one," B'Yag pointed out. "He's strapped to the rock sled but neither stomps his feet to keep the blood flowing nor bats his arms to stay warm. It's almost inhuman."

"That's the Roman Colonel my son captured in Africa. Tasco calls him his Latian Dog," Brocc told his father. "He's addled, and unfortunately, pulling a sled is the only thing he's good for."

"All my people and slaves work at whatever chore needs to be done. We've no reason to feed a man when a mule can do a better job," B'Yag declared. "Get rid of him."

"As you wish father," Brocc confirmed. "I'll have the foremen tell my son when he returns from the hunt."

***

Another light dusting of snow the night before added thickness to the frost. The white crust rested on top of the short weeds and brown grass. Although a long way from planting season, and a cold day, the farm foremen had men in the field digging and pulling rocks. As they dug up one, they placed it on a sled. Harnessed to the load was a muscular man in threadbare woolens. He had long unkept hair, like most of the poor and enslaved. But while they could pick up rocks, the Latin man pulling the rock sled could not. His fingers were curled in a claw-like fashion. Also, unlike the other workers who talked as they picked rocks, the man attached to the sled had his head down and his eyes closed.

Tasco and two warrior friends, excited from a successful hunt, rode off the trail and dismounted. They stood beside the field and watched the slaves as they dug up rocks. The son of War Chief B'Yag pointed to one of the work crew.

"I call him my Latian Dog," Tasco bragged to his friends. "He was at one time a bowman and, get this, a Legion battle commander."

"No, really," the smaller Insubri said in shock. "A Legion Colonel?"

"Sure was. When a spear took him off his horse, I crushed his fingers, and kept him as a trophy," Tasco bragged.

"If he was a battle commander, where's his armor?" the other friend asked.

"That's my one regret from Carthage," Tasco admitted. "I lost his armor when we retreated from Zama."

"It would be fun to see a Latian Dog pulling a rock sled in Legion armor," the first friend offered. "Does he ever talk about those days?"

Tasco laughed and waved at Jace.

"Come here, Latian Dog," Tasco called. Then to the pair, he remarked. "He's so addled, unless you use his full name, he doesn't know you're talking to him."

Jace located the sound of the voice before walking in that direction. The cold weather and snow made pulling the sled easy. Only once on the way did Jace glance up to adjust his course.

"Watch this," Tasco alerted his friends when the rock sled arrived. "Look at me, Latian Dog. I said to look at me."

With his chest heaving and his limbs shaking from hesitation, Jace lifted his face, but his eyes remained shut.

"Here we go. Now watch this," Tasco invited his friends. "Latian Dog. Look at me!"

Jace opened his eyes and tried to perceive details within the bright glow surrounding the shape. For a moment, he noted arms, legs, and a faceless head. Then a blinding white light stabbed into his eyes. With pain beyond reason, his arms and legs locked up, and his eyes slammed closed. Jace fell to the snow with his body jerking.

"Pretty great isn't it," Tasco declared. "He'll be like that for a while before he can get back to work."

"Tasco B'Yag. Do I have to tell your father that we stopped work in the middle of the day so you could do party tricks?" the foreman asked.

"We were just leaving," Tasco told him.

"While I have your attention," the foremen advised. "Your father wants the Latian Dog gone. He's only good for pulling the sled. He eats too much and can't clean or wash himself. Nobody wants to be near him. Lord B'Yag said to tell you by week's end."

Oblivious to the Latian Dog's discomfort, Jace twitched on the cold ground, as the Insubri tribesmen talked.

***

At sundown, Jace shook off the harness and shuffled to a small supply shed. A little moonlight filtered in through slits in the siding boards. But while it gave enough soft light for Jace to open his eyes and locate his bedding, the gaps between the boards let the cold in. Wrapped in two thin blankets, he shivered and waited for food or for morning, whichever came first.

In his mind, storm clouds rolled in billowing rotations. A yelp of fright escaped his lips. Not a conscious sound, it was more an animal's involuntary utterance. Streaks of lightning crisscrossed black clouds. But when white clouds pressed through and presented themselves, the flashes stopped.

The Latian Dog began rocking back and forth. For when the lightning stopped, the voice began. And the voice always demanded that he hurt himself.

"Massage your fingers. Pull them. To fix broken bones they must be straightened."

"No. Please no," the Latian Dog begged. "Pain. Pain. Pain."

In his mind, the black clouds rotated forward, the lightning began, and during the flashes, the Dog relaxed. Wrapped in two thin blankets, he shivered and waited for food or for morning, whichever came first.

***

At the hut of his father, Tasco B'Yag stood dejected.

"Really, I don't know what to do with him," Tasco told his father. "He follows directions if you're specific. And he's strong. But with his hands broken, he's not good for any kind of labor."

War Chief Brocc B'Yag crossed his arms over his chest. Bronze armlets stretched as he flexed his muscles.

"Your uncle's widow, M'anta, lives east of Credaro," Brocc mentioned. "To get water, she has to walk to the Oglio River. Then hike back with a bucket. Do you suppose your Latian Dog could pull a cart for her?"

"It's one of his only talents," Tasco confirmed.

"I've got a patrol heading that way in the morning," Brocc told him. "Be sure your Dog is ready to travel."

"He'll be ready," Tasco assured his father.

Chapter 5 – The Innocent

Inflated by fifteen spearmen who had traveled to Milan at the request of the King, the patrol grew to resemble a war party. The men from border villages trudged home from Milan, with a few coins in their pouches but no glory. B'Yag's warriors, who traveled to enforce the King's laws and secure the boundaries of Insubri territory, gladly accepted the tagalongs. Controlling the men and the route, patrol leader Earnán ruled with big fists and a long staff.

"What is that?" Earnán demanded. Tasco B'Yag guided a shaggy beast with two thin blankets on his shoulders for warmth. The patrol leader noted. "It's got rags for shoes and a dirty tunic for clothing."

"He's my Latian Dog and my aunt needs a puller for her water wagon," Tasco said, as if the transfer was his idea. "She needs him in Credaro."

Earnán sniffed and bent back.

"Is he not allowed to bathe?" the patrol leader asked.

"I'm not sure he understands the concept," Tasco responded. He tossed the lead rope to the ground and instructed. "Latian Dog. Go with the patrol leader."

"Is he blind?" Earnán questioned.

"No, he has a problem with light," Tasco coached as he backed away from the patrol. "Just don't make him open his eyes."

Tasco B'Yag strutted away. He realized, getting rid of the Latian Dog was a relief.

"Can you follow?" Earnán questioned the Dog. "Or does someone have to guide you?"

Although Jace didn't reply verbally, he reeled in the guide rope and wrapped it around his arm.

"Keep up or you'll die in the forest," Earnán warned. "Patrol, move out."

Where some spearmen had walked close behind Earnán to reach the valley, with the Latian Dog following the patrol leader, spearmen kept a distance from the unwashed Dog.

Earnán wasn't immune to the stink. As they followed the winding trail up a hill, he kept repeating, "Two days to the Serio River. Two days to the Serio River."

The rear of the patrol stretched out to avoid the stink.

***

Two and a half days later, they spotted towering trees from the top of another hill. The growth identified a major water source. After the patrol descended the slope, they pushed through thick branches and came to the bank of a river. Clear water, fed directly from the mountains, rushed between sandbars. In the spring, when the snow melted, the water would fill the river from embankment to embankment. An early winter crossing was easier, but not simple. Between the sandbars, deep channels of swift water raced downstream.

Earnán and the Latian Dog climbed down to the first sandbar. The rest of the spearmen followed, taking positions south of the patrol leader.

"Dog, get in there and scrub yourself," Earnán ordered.

An aware man would squat on the sandbar and scoop water from the river to wash. Numb to his surroundings, Jace stepped into the channel. Water swept his legs from under him. Instantly, his shoulders hit the water and his face submerged. With no sense of self-preservation, he reflectively waved his arms in the manner of a dying animal.

"Grab him," Earnán shouted.

The last two spearmen reached into the water and seized Jace. One held an arm, and the other hooked a leg. Together they fished the Latian Dog from the cold water.

"He doesn't smell as bad," the warrior holding Jace's arm announced.

For the first time during the voyage, the Latian Dog shivered and his lips turned blue.

"He's as near frozen as my cousin Fial," the man holding Jace's leg observed. "He fell into a lake in winter. The next morning, we found Fial as stiff as the coating of ice on his robe."

Earnán rushed to the men and looked at the Dog.

"Get a rope to the other side of the Serio," he directed. "We'll camp there tonight and see if the Dog survives."

Locking arms, the spearmen supported each other until they formed a living bridge. One man reached the far bank and tied a rope to a tree. Once he tossed the end back, one by one, the members of the patrol crossed to the far bank.

Earnán hoisted Jace onto his shoulders and carried the unconscious man to the far side.

"Would someone lend him a pair of woolen trousers and a shirt," the patrol leader requested. While digging in his pack for a pair of old sandals, he added. "I'll see that you get them back."

A pair of pants and a shirt were tossed over by a pair of spearmen. Not surprising, both donors offered, "Keep it."

Around several campfires, the patrol warmed and dried the legs of their trousers. As they settled in for the night, the Latian Dog sat up, hooked his arms around his legs, and began to rock.

***

In his mind, storm clouds rolled in and the Latian Dog yelped in fright. Streaks of lightning crisscrossed the black clouds. Only when white clouds parted the rolling black clouds did the flashes stopped. The Latian Dog shivered and continued to rock.

When the lightning faded, a booming voice spoke to him.

"Still your breath so your hands are steady. Calm your heart so your eyes are clear. Focus your mind on the task."

"No. You go," the Latian Dog begged.

Respecting the plea in his mind, the black clouds rotated forward, the lightning began, and during the flashes, the Dog relaxed in the chaos. Once the loud, insistent voice left, Jace sat numb, waiting for sunrise.

***

Two days after crossing the Serio River, the patrol took a well-worn path through a gap. On the far side of the hills, they approached a curve in another river. Unlike the low flow of the Serio, even in early winter, water at the new river flowed from bank to bank.

"The river to our right is the Oglio," Earnán announced to his party of warriors. "Up ahead is the village of Credaro. The second safest location in all of Insubri territory."

"Care to explain that," a spearman urged. "We are close to the border."

"The Oglio is fed from Lake Iseo so it's always flowing, providing a barrier from raids by the Cenomani. No one wants to swim a river to attack a hamlet. Lake Iseo separates the Cenomani in the east from the mountain clans of the Veneti. And Insubri is situated west of both tribes at the point of Lake Iseo."

"And second safest?" another spearman inquired.

They neared the corner of a dilapidated rail fence. Some posts, rotten at the base, barely stayed upright, while other posts succumbed to the rot and sprawled on the ground. Some cross rails floated off the ground because they were supported by weeds and bushes.

"Only Milan, with its stone walls and spearmen," Earnán declared, "is safer than Credaro with its natural barriers."

Beyond the pitiful fence, a woman stood from her gardening and addressed the patrol leader.

"Earnán. You give that speech every time you come through Credaro." She was middle-aged. A gaunt, sunburnt woman with a voice as coarse as a saw blade cutting through a dry pine log. "I believe you do that to excuse why your patrols don't stay very long in the hamlet."

"You've a sharp tongue, M'anta," Earnán scolded her. "But even though you question my leadership, I brought you a present from Tasco."

"And what does my pompous, rooster of a nephew have for me?" M'anta sneered.

Earnán reached back and pushed Jace out of line.

"He doesn't say anything, barely opens his eyes, but he's strong enough to pull your water wagon," the patrol leader answered. "Don't know his name but Tasco calls him a Latian Dog."

A squeal came from the other side of the woman.

"A dog?" a little girl of five years appeared from the other side of M'anta. Her long auburn hair hung down her back, but a cloth band held it back from her small face. She inquired. "Where is the dog?"

The spearmen in the patrol assumed the little one would be disappointed when she saw the shaggy man with the lowered head and closed eyes. But the girl raced around the overgrowth, heading for an opening in the broken fence.

"Sucaria, get back here," M'anta demanded. But the little legs churned as the girl rounded the fence and bounded towards the patrol. M'anta repeated the order. "Sucaria, get back here."

Not knowing what the Dog might do, two warriors lowered their spears. The tips hovered close to Jace's back as the little girl approached.

"I'm Sucaria," she introduced herself. As if she was an experienced animal trainer, the little girl reached up and gripped one of Jace's curled fingers. "My but you are a mess. Come with me. We'll see about shearing you later."

As docile as a lamb, the Latian Dog followed the little girl to the garden.

"Patrol forward," Earnán ordered.

"And just what am I to do with a half-wit?" M'anta demanded.

"Don't ask me," the patrol leader replied as he marched away. "I was only directed to deliver him."

M'anta glared at the spearmen as they passed. She held her opinion of the warriors because her mind was on the Dog.

"What am I supposed to do with him?" she muttered.

Then from behind, the little girl instructed, "Bend your elbows. That's very good."

M'anta turned and watched Sucaria place a woven basket in the folded arms. Then, the little girl reached high into the air and dumped a pair of parsnips into the basket. The child stooped and pulled two more of the root vegetables from the ground.

"I guess he can carry crops and keep the girl company," M'anta answered her own question.

***

In the morning, Sucaria directed Jace to load two barrels on a cart. After M'anta dropped a leather line over his shoulder, the little girl took his finger. With a gentle tug, she guided the Dog, the cart, and M'anta away from the barn.

They traveled a quarter of a mile to the banks of the Oglio River. Once there, Jace stood by the cart as M'anta dipped a bucket, carried it up to the cart, and filled the barrels. While she worked, Sucaria stood in the weeds. She turned over rocks, squatted down, and investigated the exposed bugs. Once the barrels held more water than they had since her sister died, leaving Sucaria an orphan, the three left the riverbank.

That afternoon, M'anta poured water into a large copper pot. After a fire heated the water, she dumped the water into a bucket. An armload of raw wool went in and she began scrubbing. Manure, hay, dirt, and other objects washed free, leaving the wool clean and ready for brushing and spinning.

Away from the washing, Sucaria strolled around Jace. With her little fists on her hips, she pronounced, "You are a shaggy dog. Sit down."

A gentle pull was all she needed for Jace to lower himself onto a log. A neighbor woman came over with an armload of dirty wool. She scanned the girl and the long-haired man.

"Do you have enough water to wash a little more?" she asked.

"Thanks to the Latian Dog, I have more than enough to wash your wool and mine," M'anta told her.

"Latian Dog?" the neighbor inquired.

"Sucaria hasn't been this happy since my sister died," M'anta answered. "She's taken with caring for that half-wit."

The women dumped the dirty water. Next, they filled the copper tub and stoked the fire.

While waiting for the water to heat, Sucaria called to the neighbor, "Gobnait. Can you shear the Dog?"

"Child, do you mean give him a haircut?"

"Yes, ma'am, he's a shaggy dog," the little girl pointed out.

"I don't see why not," Gobnait agreed.

She went to her barn and returned with a long-bladed knife and a honing stone. As she walked up behind Jace, she ran the blade back and forth across the stone.

What she didn't notice were the muscles rippling down the Dog's arms and across his back with each stroke of the blade. When she got close, the rasping of steel on stone got louder. In a move quicker than the little girl or the woman could perceive, the Dog leaped from the log and rolled across the yard. He came up in a crouch, turning his head from side to side as if listening for a threat.

"I don't think this is a good idea," Gobnait stammered. She started back to the barn. On the way, she mentioned to

M'anta. "You need to get rid of that animal. I don't know if he is human. I've never seen a man move that fast."

Undaunted by the violent acrobatics, Sucaria walked toward Jace.

"No," M'anta shouted. She threw a handful of wet wool on the ground, took half a step, but froze in mid-stride.

Sucaria stood beside the man, petting the side of his head while saying, "there, there, it'll be all right. I understand. When my mother got sick and died, I didn't want anyone to touch me either."

In a slow and gentle move, the Latian Dog lowered his head and placed it under the little girl's hand. They remained like that while M'anta and Gobnait finished washing the wool.

"I still don't like it," the neighbor complained.

"After my sister died, every evening I listened to Sucaria cry late into the night," M'anta explained. "When I went over to comfort her, she shied away, not wanting to be touched. That's the first time she's shown any kind of human affection."

"Well, I still don't trust the Latian Dog," the neighbor insisted.

***

That evening, snow fell on the village of Credaro and the temperature dropped. In the cottage, the fireplace took the bite out of the cold in the single room.

With a wool blanket pulled up to her chin, Sucaria asked, "Do you think the Dog is cold?"

"He has a blanket," M'anta replied. "It's enough."

In the barn, Jace lay on the ground, shivering and waiting for the clouds.

***

The storm clouds rolled in and the Latian Dog yelped in fright. Streaks of lightning crisscrossed the black clouds. And a moment later, the white clouds forced their way through the rolling black haze. An instant later, the flashes stopped.

The Latian Dog sat up and placed his curled hands under his chin for warmth.

"Your bow is but a tool. Your mind is the true weapon. Often, you'll be charged with protecting an innocent. And that's a harder contract than taking the life of an evil man."

"I don't understand," the Latian Dog whined. "What do you want?"

"I want you…" But the last part was drowned out by thunder and then the lightning flashed as the dark clouds returned. Laying on the frozen ground, Jace tried to think of what he heard, but the very act of trying to focus hurt. Going numb, he relaxed and waited for dawn.

***

The little person brought him a bowl of grain with tiny vegetables resembling miniature carrots. Using a hand, he scooped up the grain and chewed slowly. As he ate, Jace ventured a peek through the slits of his eyes. The little girl stood very close, searching his face.

"You need a haircut and a shave," she announced while rubbing his forehead.

"Sucaria?" M'anta called. "Where are you child?"

"In the barn, feeding the Dog."

"That was your food," M'anta scolded.

"But the Dog needs his strength if he's going to pull the cart."

"Sometimes I think you're wise beyond your years," M'anta said. "Come into the cottage. I'll fix you another bowl."

The girl and the woman left. In the haze of his mind, a single word drifted through the nothingness. For the most part, the Latian Dog didn't understand. But every few heartbeats, he grasped, if only for an instant, the word - *Innocent*.

***

The dusting made the footing slick. But the Dog ground his feet into the pathway. Bent to the task, he followed the little girl, plowing the cart through the snow. At the riverbank, he dropped the line and waited for the woman to fill the barrels.

Eyes closed, he heard the pails of water being added to the containers. With a rhythm, she made the trips regularly from the river to the barrels. Then, the rhythm stopped. Moments passed, and the Dog bent his head to listen for her climbing the embankment.

"Sucaria," M'anta screamed. "Sucaria. Where are you?"

Downstream, a pair of splashes and a tiny helpless cry was the only reply.

"Stay with me," the voice from his nightmares urged. "*Still your breath so your hands are steady. Calm your heart so your eyes are clear. Focus your mind on the task. Tell me of General Xenophon's archers.*"

The words didn't make sense. But the emotion of sitting in icy water filled his heart. Along with the feeling came three words. And the Dog bellowed, "Protect the innocent."

Sprinting downstream, he chanced a peek, searching for the little girl. The light spiked his brain and he stumbled. But he closed his eyes tightly and fought off the effect. Listening as he ran, the Dog searched for a sound beyond the rippling of water along the riverbank.

Then not too far ahead, little arms splashed. Not much more than the flutter of a water bird ruffling its feathers, the out-of-place sound drew the Dog off the bank. He dove into the cold river. Underwater, he opened his eyes and swam towards the memory of the weak splash.

The body was small and floating down the river just below the surface. Jace swam under her and lifted the small child out of the water. Then he rolled onto his back, and as he kicked for shore, the voice in his head instructed, "*Compress her torso and release the pressure. Feel the air fill her lungs. Compressed and released.*"

When the Dog reached the shore, M'anta snatched Sucaria from his arms. The little girl was coughing up water and wheezing.

"Can you find your way to the cottage, Dog?" she asked while walking away. "If so, bring the cart."

With the wet and cold Sucaria cradled against her breasts, M'anta hurried down the path, leaving Jace alone on the riverbank.

Chapter 6 – Insubri Surgeon

Late in the day, a dusting of white covered the ground. M'anta came out of the cottage to find the cart and barrels in the yard. She noticed unsteady footprints, showing where the Latian Dog had staggered from the cart to the barn. Gusts of cold wind and a slate gray sky warned of a storm coming off the mountains. After a glance at the low clouds that hid the high peaks, she went back into the cottage.

Jace shivered and rocked in his wet clothing. Sitting on the blankets, he lacked the presence of mind and the strength to swaddle in the wool fabric. Outside, the wind blew through the trees. The sound resembled a group of people sweeping a stone floor in uneven strokes. Footsteps approached the barn, and Jace stopped rocking to listen.

"Sucaria is the last of my bloodline," M'anta whispered. She placed a large bowl of stew in Jace's lap. "Two days after my sister died, neighbors found the child hugging the body. When they pulled her away, she fought them off, broke free, and ran back to the body of her mother. Not until you arrived did she stop brooding and become interested in her surroundings. I don't know who you are, but you brought back the curious little girl she had been. And now, you've saved her life."

A rustle of fabric preceded the pressure of a heavy fur robe as it settled over Jace's shoulders.

"It was my husband's," M'anta told him. "He said that when he wore it into the mountains, the thick fur was his shield against the elements and against the teeth and claws of predators. If he had taken it to Africa, he might be here today. But he's not, and you are."

She left the barn and vanished into the snowstorm. Under the heavy fur robe, the Latian Dog thawed, drank the stew, and although he didn't comprehend the words, he felt the warmth of M'anta's sentiment.

Outside, the wind howled and blowing snow whipped around. The world blurred into swirls of white. In the cottage, Sucaria hugged M'anta as they huddled under blankets. For the Latian Dog in the barn, the night passed without a visit from the black clouds, the lightning, or the voice.

***

By dawn the storm moved on, leaving the cottage, barn, and items in the yard capped in a coat of fluffy white. Sucaria appeared in the doorway and greeted the bright world with a howl of joy.

"It's beautiful," she gushed. "I'm going to check on the Dog. He saved my life you know."

"I know," M'anta admitted before instructing. "Put on your cloak before going out in that mess."

A moment later, the little girl crossed the yard while kicking snow and laughing. At the entrance to the barn, she paused to allow her eyes to adjust to the dim interior.

"Dog, are you here?" she inquired.

No answer came, but a mound of fur moved, identifying Jace's location. With a scream of joy, Sucaria raced into the barn and jumped on the fur. As she snuggled into the soft pelt, an arm lifted a corner of fur and folded a section of the warm robe over the child.

Responding to the scream, M'anta sprinted from the house. Her heart beating wildly in her chest, she raced into the barn.

"Sucaria? Sucaria, where are you?"

A flap of fur robe moved and the small face, beaming a smile, peered at her aunt.

"I'm here. The Dog covered me."

"That's nice dear," M'anta acknowledged, as if finding a child being protected by a half-wit was an everyday occurrence. "I'm fixing breakfast. Come in and eat. And afterward, you can bring your Dog a bowl."

Sucaria wrapped her arms around a small area of fur and hugged Jace. Then she ran for the cottage.

From a pot over the fire, M'anta dished vegetable soup into a bowl. When she placed it in front of the little girl, she proposed, "Your Dog needs a haircut and his beard trimmed."

"He doesn't like to be touched," Sucaria reminded her.

"Not by most people. But if you hold his face and talk with him, I'm willing to try. How about you?"

With soup dripping down her chin, Sucaria smiled and nodded her acceptance of the plan.

**

When the sun was high overhead, and the air not nearly as cold, Sucaria brushed snow from a log and directed Jace to sit.

"Now relax," the child urged, while placing her little hands on each side of Jace's face. "Aunt M'anta is going to cut your hair. But you must remain still. Do you understand?"

A nod of the Dog's head let her know he understood.

"Ready," she announced.

M'anta took a handful of hair and chopped it off. Then she grabbed another length and cut that. Working around the head, she trimmed the hairs without any reaction from the Latian Dog. Because Sucaria maintained a constant dialogue, the haircut went quickly on three sides.

"You were at the cart and M'anta was carrying water from the river. My feet slid on the grass so I stayed up high and away from the river. I turned over a rock but there were no bugs. So I went to a bigger rock. It took two hands to turn it over. But when I did, a snake jumped out at me. Or was it a big spider? Anyway, when I stepped back, my foot slid on a rock. I fell into the water. Dog, I was so scared. When I tried to yell, water got in my mouth."

M'anta collected strands from the left side of the Dog's head without a reaction. But when she pulled it straight for cutting, Jace jerked away.

Undeterred, Sucaria extended her hands higher up on the sides of the Dog's head.

"It's going to be fine," she assured him. "You're looking better already."

Although she was young, when her fingers touched a bulge under his hair, she knew it was out of place.

"He has a bump on the side of his head," Sucaria described. "Do you think it hurts him."

With Sucaria distracting the Dog, M'anta cut the last long strands. Then, carefully, she reached out and cupped the left side of the Dog's head.

"It's not a recent injury," M'anta observed, "or it would be warm to the touch. But you're right, the injury must hurt him."

"Can a doctor fix him?" Sucaria asked.

"I'm not sure if a physician can fix a bump," M'anta submitted. "But when Clan Chief Garos comes for his winter visit, we'll ask his doctor to look at the injury."

***

The ten cottages of Credaro represented a small village. Once each hut housed a spearman. It made the settlement an important part of the defense of the Insubri border. But war and the years had stripped Credaro of its warriors and with them went the village's status. Next, conflict with the Latins shifted the defense from cross-border raiding to battling

Legions. Yet, for services rendered in the past, the Clan Chief called on the hamlet during the winter. And with his court came a physician, who after a meal, would review the health of the people in the village.

"Will the Clan Chief stay with us?" Sucaria inquired.

"No child. He's an important man and needs to see many villages," M'anta answered. "Once they eat and the doctor checks everyone, they'll move on."

"But what about the Dog?" the girl pleaded. "He must see the Latian Dog."

"I'll tell you what. We'll make an extra batch of honey cakes and bribe him."

"What's a bribe?" Sucaria asked.

"In this case, it's honey cakes in exchange for a medical opinion," M'anta explained.

***

On the border of three tribes, with the center of Lake Iseo as the point of conversion, any assembly in the summer was seen as an act of aggression. In the shortest and darkest days of winter, no one feared an attack by a neighboring tribe.

Clan Chief Garos led a group of warriors through the hills. They hiked along the Oglio River and entered the village of Credaro. Forewarned of the Clan Chief's course by a runner, the citizens of Credaro placed beeswax candles in their windows. The lights, spilling from every hut, gave a warm welcome to the chief. The residents came out as he entered.

"Winter is a time to rest," he exclaimed. "And to eat. Do you have food enough to share."

"We do," the residents replied. Then each invited the Chief. "Come to my cottage and enjoy my hospitality."

The entourage gathered behind the Clan Chief. After Garos decided where he would dine, the others would pick a hut to host them. Among the group, Physician Dubnorix stood back. Once he ate and while Garos raved about the cooking, the doctor would look over any medical ailments.

A small hand tapped Dubnorix on the arm. The physician glanced down to see a girl of about five years.

"Can I help you?" he asked.

"We have a bribe," Sucaria told him. Her eyes grew wide, and she whispered. "We have honey cakes for you."

Dubnorix dropped to a knee and inquired, "a bribe usually means a trade of some kind. If I get honey cakes, what do you get in return?"

"My dog has a lump on the side of his head," Sucaria answered. "It's hurting him."

"I usually reserve my treatments for humans," Dubnorix informed her.

"Yes," Sucaria said, nodding in agreement with the doctor's statement.

Chuckling, Dubnorix indicated his preference for dining at the little girl's cottage to the Clan Chief.

"I see the widow of an old friend," Garos announced. "Gobnait, are you still the best cook in Insubri?"

"There's none better," she replied. "Would you honor my late husband by dining at our cottage."

"I accept," Garos declared.

While the warriors went to different huts, the doctor and his assistant followed the little girl to M'anta's cottage.

"I hear you have honey cakes," the doctor told M'anta. "And a sick dog."

"We do, but it's not what you think," M'anta warned. "Come, honor my late husband by dining at our cottage."

"We accept," Dubnorix stated.

With the formalities completed, the doctor and his assistant were ushered to M'anta's hut.

***

They dined, and indeed, there was an abundance of honey cakes. After the meal, Dubnorix observed, "You two appear healthy. Are there any complaints?"

"My Dog has a lump," Sucaria insisted. "He's in the barn."

"As an animal should be. But tell me, does he bite? Is he dangerous?"

"Not if Sucaria is near him," M'anta told him. "But you should see for yourself."

They left the cottage and strolled to the barn.

"Dog, come here," Sucaria ordered.

From the shadows emerged a big man in a bulky fur robe. His hair was medium length and his beard neatly trimmed. The only sign that something was amiss, his eyes were closed and his head bowed. And when he exposed a hand, the fingers were curled.

The child took a finger and guided the strange man to a log.

"The physician is going to look at your bump," Sucaria explained. "If you want him to stop, he will."

M'anta grasped the hand of the doctor and placed it on the left side of Jace's head. A moment later, Dubnorix used his fingers to probe the raised area.

"Run and get my medical kit," he instructed his assistant. Then to M'anta, he ordered. "Go tell Chief Garos that I'll be staying in Credaro an extra day."

"For the honey cakes?" Sucaria guessed.

"Partly," Dubnorix admitted, "but also to perform a surgery."

***

Most of the furniture had been shoved to the outer walls of the cottage, except for the dining table. That table, they shifted to the center of the room.

"Don't move Dog," Sucaria encouraged.

"Warn him that this will hurt," Dubnorix instructed. When his assistant finished shaving Jace's scalp, the doctor selected a small, sharp steel blade. When the bump lay hairless and rinsed, the surgeon directed. "Hold him tight."

Sucaria's hands were on the sides of the Dog's face. Because the patient reclined on the tabletop, the little girl, with her waist twisted for leverage, stood on a chair and squeezed.

"It'll hurt Dog, but it's good for you," Sucaria assured him. Dubnorix cut Jace's scalp by drawing a long line across the bump. Blood ran down Jace's face and over Sucaria's hands. Showing courage and affection beyond her years, she urged. "Stay Dog. Stay. It's nothing. We'll be okay."

In his addled mind, Jace wanted to jerk away from the sting of the blade. But the soft voice and the pressure of the little hands held him rigid on the table.

Dubnorix sliced a line diagonal to the first cut. Using the blade, he carved under the four corners until he could peel back four flaps of skin. His assistant slowly poured water over the exposed skull to flush the wound.

From his kit, the doctor pulled a pair of tongs. Slowly, he extracted splinters of bone from Jace's skull. He held one up. "These slivers of bone are from the injury and why the bump never went down."

"Is he all better now?" Sucaria inquired.

"Not yet. I'm about to start the delicate part of the operation," Dubnorix told her. "But your Dog won't feel anything."

From a mug of melting snow, the doctor took a small brass pipe. On one end, tiny teeth had been filed to create a serrated edge. Placing his hands on either side of the pipe, he lowered the cutting edge to Jace's scalp. Then he rotated the pipe back and forth by rolling it between his palms. All the while, the surgeon's eyes studied the scalp. Once he had a defined circle drilled into the bone, he placed the pipe back in the cold water.

"The metal heats up," Dubnorix said. "We don't want to cook the dura."

"Dura?" Sucaria questioned.

"Under the scalp and beneath the skull bone, the meat of the brain is protected by a thin sheet of tissue called the dura," Dubnorix described. "I don't want to cook his dura with the hot brass or cut into it and expose your Dog's brain to air."

He pulled the chilled brass tube from the mug. Once he fitted the cutting teeth into the circle, the doctor began rolling the pipe again. Under his manipulations, the tiny teeth drilled into Jace's skull. As if saw dust collecting around a saw blade, particles of bone collected around the pipe. Then, a gush of blood from the hole washed away the bone dust. Dubnorix lifted the drill from the hole and handed it to his assistant.

"I've released the blood trapped in his skull," he said while studying the flow. "If it begins to run black, I'm afraid your Dog will die."

"Then don't let it run black," Sucaria pleaded.

"I'm an Insubri surgeon, not a God, child," Dubnorix responded. "Your Dog's life, at this point, is in the hands of the fates."

Act 3

Chapter 7 – That Rotten Fence

In the middle of the night, he became aware of his surroundings. A tap with the fingers of his right hand informed him of a bandage on the left side of his head. Curiously, the fingers were stiff and it hurt when they moved. The linen head wrap, he understood. It meant an injury and some form of treatment. Although he appreciated the heat from the embers of a hearth, the warmth seemed unfamiliar. He couldn't place the last time he awoke near a stone fireplace. And while his right hand flexed as if he'd slept on it, two fingers on his left hand angled inward and refused to move at all.

As he lay on the table, trying to remember how he arrived in a small cottage, surrounded by sleeping people, a voice crept into his mind, *"If you're captured or wounded and wake up among strangers, don't move or call attention to yourself. See how others react to you and be guided by their expectations."*

"Who are you?" he whispered to the voice.

In the quiet of the cottage, the words seemed loud to his ears. Yet, only one of the sleeping bodies stirred. He believed he'd avoided detection. But from the corner of his eye, he noted a short person rise and crossed the room. Walking on the balls of her feet, she reached the table, climbed onto a chair, and laid down beside him. She shivered, and without thinking, he covered her with a section of his blanket.

"Thank you, Dog," the little girl said.

He might have questioned her, but she folded her arms, curled up against his chest, placed her head on his arm, and went to sleep.

"My name is Dog?" he pondered before drifting off.

***

"Sit up," a man instructed.

Not knowing who was being addressed, he remained still. The little girl poked his ribs.

"Sit up, Dog," she encouraged.

Following directions, the Dog rose to an upright position. During the movement, the blanket jerked and the girl tumbled over the edge of the table. Face first, she fell towards the floor. Before making contact, an arm swung down and caught her in mid fall. Completing an arc with the girl in hand, the Dog lifted the child and gently deposited her on the end of the table.

"That's more agility and awareness than we witnessed yesterday," Dubnorix noted. "What's your name son?"

He knew the name Dog. But it sounded incomplete, so he remained silent.

"The Dog was sent to me by my nephew," M'anta volunteered. "The only name, and may the Gods bless me, it is all the information I have on him. They called him, Latian Dog."

"And he's a good boy," Sucaria declared. "He saved my life."

"I don't know about that," Dubnorix pronounced. "But he is certainly a healthier boy this morning. We're leaving. As for a prognoses, you can expect improvement for about a week. After that, the Latian Dog will be the best he'll ever be."

"It's the injury to his mind," the doctor's assistant volunteered. "We can relieve the pressure, but we have no way to tell if the mind suffered any damage."

Dubnorix and his apprentice declined breakfast and left the cottage.

"Sucaria, send your Dog to the barn," the woman ordered.

"But Aunt M'anta, can't he stay with us until he's healed?"

"I'm afraid not child. It's unseemly for a grown man to be living with two women he's not related to," Aunt M'anta insisted. "Take him to the barn."

"Yes, ma'am," agreed a dejected Sucaria. "Come on Dog. You have to go to the barn."

He didn't feel like leaving the warm cottage. But having an opportunity to sort out the situation in peace appealed to him. The Dog started for the door.

"Latian Dog, you forgot something," M'anta scolded.

Believing he did something wrong, the Dog turned to face the woman and hung his head.

"I don't see any change," M'anta grumbled. She picked up the big fur robe from the back of a chair and carried it to the Dog. After draping it over his shoulders, she stated. "It's cold out there."

Sucaria latched onto one of his fingers and guided him out of the cottage. They started across the yard, heading for a dilapidated barn. Constructed with wattle and daub walls and a thatched roof of straw, the barn offered minimum shelter. After a few repairs, the barn would provide a strong wind break and protection from the weather.

The Dog's problem was how much of the repairs could he do and still hide his recovery. And he needed to hide. For the name, Latian Dog still seemed incomplete. But it was the only name he had, and that was more than he knew about his history or an actual name.

"Go inside, Dog," Sucaria instructed. "I'll bring you dinner this evening."

As the Dog walked by a pair of barrels, he noted they held water beneath a layer of ice. Off to his right, a rotten fence line with an overgrowth of weeds surrounded a garden. Once in the barn, the Dog stepped to the side and watched the little girl return to the cottage.

A quick tour showed where the daub matter had separated from the lattice structure. The Dog returned to the barrels, punched a hole in the ice, and filled a bucket. He placed the bucket in the barn and went to collect dead weeds and dirt from under the broken fence.

It took several trips to the barrels and the garden, but by early afternoon, the holes in the walls of the barn were patched with straw and mud. In addition to the new daub, six squares of wet, mud bricks created a firepit.

"It's like this Aunt M'anta," the Dog thought as he used a hatchet to strike a hoe to make a spark. After a few flashes, the kindling caught and he fed the fire. "This Latian Dog needs a few creature comforts."

***

Wrapped in the robe and warmed by the fire, the Dog curled up and closed his eyes.

"A broken bone needs to be straightened," the voice persisted, *"and bound to a splint to keep it straight."*

"No, it will hurt," the Dog protested.

"What in life doesn't hurt?" the voice questioned.

***

Late in the afternoon, Sucaria carefully crossed the yard. Each step threatened to spill stew over the lip of the big bowl. But with her mouth set in concentration, the little one waddled along the snowy path to the barn.

At the entrance, she peered inside, expecting to search the dark for the Dog. Instead, she noticed a fire between bricks and the Dog behind the flames. Next, she screamed.

The Dog held a hatchet over his left hand. Under the bent fingers, he'd placed a board. He swung the hatchet downward and Sucaria cried a long, drawn out, "No, Dog, no!"

Sucaria was shaking in horror when M'anta reached her. Looking over the child's head, she watched the Dog frantically trying to tie his left hand to a flat of wood. With tears of pain streaming down his face, the man fought for control of the leather strap. But his right hand couldn't begin knotting the band.

"Νάροηκα," the Dog said when M'anta reached him.

"I don't understand," she admitted. Pushing away his hand, she began tying the fingers and the hand to the slat. "What have you done?"

"Isióno ostó," the Dog said, grinding out the words between clenched teeth.

"What are you saying?" M'anta demanded.

Part of the answer became obvious. Bruising and blood covered two fingers and the knuckles on his left hand. Lying beside the board, the flat of the hatchet also had blood on the metal.

"Is he, is he?" Sucaria stammered. Despite her anxiety, she held the bowl of stew.

"He's fine," M'anta told her while tightening the strap. "But two fingers on his left hand are broken."

"What did he say?" Sucaria asked.

The Latian Dog repeated in his mind, *"Splint, I made a splint before straightening the bones. Why can't you understand me? I understand you."*

"I don't know," M'anta told the girl. "Give him the food and let's get back to the cottage."

"It's stew," Sucaria announced. "And it's good."

M'anta and the child left the barn. Still in pain and confused why they didn't understand him, the Dog ate the stew and enjoyed the heat from the fire. His broken bones, now straight and tied to the splint, throbbed.

***

A week later, when Sucaria brought breakfast to the barn, she found the Dog gone. Not knowing what else to do, the little girl left the bowl and a loaf of flatbread on a bench. If she had walked behind the barn and followed the footprints and the tracks of the sled into the hills, she would have seen a man exercising. Although she might judge it to be more like torture.

The Latian Dog hung from a branch. Even as his fingers slipped, and his arms shook from exertion, he tightened his stomach and focused on his grip. Before falling, he lifted his legs and touched his thighs to the other side of the branch. Then he dropped to the ground, breathing hard.

"I better get to work before I'm missed," he said while patting the tree trunk. "Thanks friend for helping in my recovery."

While the big tree was safe, older fallen trunks were cut and chopped into firewood. Once he had the sled full of wood, the other part of his exercise program began. He wrapped the line across his chest, dug in the balls of his feet, and lunged forward. The heavy load broke free of the snow and the Latian Dog began the trip back to the cottage and the barn.

***

A week later, M'anta stood in the doorway to the barn. Delicious aromas from a freshly baked crust drifted into the structure.

"Dog," she told him, "because of your work, we have an excess of firewood. And using the wood, I'm able to trade with the other cottages. While their pantries and root cellars grow empty, our cellar remains full. In the last trade, I got apples, figs, and a bag of spelt-grain flour. So I made us pies."

She walked in, and on the Dog's rustic table, she set a copper pan with a crispy crust covering the top. Beside the pie, she dropped a ladle.

"We have enough firewood to last until spring," M'anta explained. "If you can, I'd like the old garden fence replaced."

"*Tóso kaló óso égine,*" the Dog replied.

"I don't understand you. But I'll take that as a commitment to replace the fence," M'anta guessed.

She left, and the Dog dug the ladle into the crust and brought out chunks of apple and figs sweetened with honey. While chewing, he strolled to the door of the barn and studied the rot on the fence.

"*As good as done,*" he repeated after swallowing.

He couldn't figure out why she didn't understand him. Leaving the mystery for another time, he went back for more pie.

***

Firewood could be harvested from downed trees and dead branches. Wood for fence posts and rails needed to be carved from split logs. For the next week, the Dog chopped down trees the size of his thigh. From trunks of that thickness, he could make two fence posts or four rails. However, the issue for getting them off the mountain wasn't the girth. It was the length of the logs that made them heavy and awkward.

After half a day of work, he loaded the two logs from yesterday's chopping and trimming to the sled and added the tree he cut down that morning. With three logs resting on the sled, the Dog centered the strap across his chest, bent his knees, and dug into the first step. Going downhill, the weight sank the rails of the sled into the snow. But countering the mass, the weight also helped push the load down to a ravine.

At the low spot, the Dog carried each log across the gully to the next slope. After reloading the sled, he strapped in and complained.

"There must be a better way than breaking my back to collect logs for that rotten fence."

Under the strain of climbing the hill, the strange voice spoke.

"You pray to Virbius for the right to harvest from his trees. But next you complain about the Forest God's abundance. Perhaps you should have prayed to the God Silvanus for a treeless field. Then you would have no toil."

Before realizing he was replying to an internal voice, the Dog snapped, "No toil means no fence post or rails. Besides, I don't remember praying and I don't know any Gods."

Irritated at the voice and at himself for responding, the Latian Dog bent, grunted, and harnessed the anger to haul the load to the top of the hill. From the heights, he could see over two more foothills.

Sarcastically, he growled at the voice, "That's how I get things done."

But the voice didn't reply. While resting, the Dog scanned the scene beyond the lower hills. Smoke drifted into the sky from cottages in the village. And while some of the ground was still covered in dirty white snow, bare spots of brown dead grass showed that spring was coming to the lowlands. To the west of the village, he could see a lot of embankment at Lake Iseo. Until the winter snows began to melt in the mountains, the lake and the Oglio River were at their lowest.

Casually, he scanned the Oglio at the straight section that meandered by Credaro. Farther downstream, the bend in the river resembled the top of a shepherd's crook.

"Those logs aren't going to sled to the village on their own," he chastised himself. Before reaching for the harness, he added. "God Virbius thank you for the gift of the trees."

After the prayer to a God he didn't remember, he scanned the edge of the forest across the Oglio River. His blood ran cold at what he saw.

From the trees across the Oglio, five warriors approached the slow-flowing river. Normally a barrier, the water ran low, exposing sandbars.

"Don't," he muttered. "Don't cross the river."

But the five Cenomani warriors dropped to the bottom of the riverbank, lifted their spears and shields overhead to keep them dry, and jumped over a channel to the next sandbar. The only thing of value in the direction they were heading was the village of Credaro.

The Dog didn't stay to watch the rest of the crossing. He snatched the hatchet from the sled and sprinted over the hilltop. On the slope, he careened off trees and grabbed branches to keep his balance, while maintaining a fast pace. He was two hills from the village, placing him farther away than the spearmen who were crossing the river. His only advantage, the Cenomani warriors didn't know the Latian Dog was coming for them.

***

In the yard, Sucaria inspected a stack of fence posts and rails. She had seen the Dog easily lift the heavy posts. Walking to the end, the little girl attempted to hoist one in the air.

When the long piece of wood failed to move, she placed her hands on her hips and declared, "I'll leave these for later."

"Sucaria. Are you all right out there?" M'anta called from the cottage.

A flash of movement caught Sucaria's eyes. Between M'anta's house and Gobnait's, a man carrying a shield and spear appeared, but then vanished. When a second spearman passed by, Sucaria whispered as loud as she thought safe, "Aunt M'anta. Run."

"What did you say child?" M'anta asked from the doorway.

Sucaria put her hands on either side of her mouth and repeated, "Run. Aunt M'anta, run."

When two spearmen came from between the cottages, Sucaria did just that. She spun around and raced for the barn.

"Dog," she pleaded, "help. Help."

A Cenomani Tribesman caught up with her and snatched Sucaria up by the hair. Turning to the second spearman who stood between the cottages, he swayed his arm and rocked the little girl in the air as if she was a newly trapped rabbit.

"Look what I caught," the tribesman laughed, "an Insubri rat trying to scurry away."

While holding his wrist to take some of the weight off her skull, Sucaria kicked her legs, attempting to break free.

"What are you doing?" M'anta shouted as she charged out of the cottage. "Put her down."

The tribesman, holding Sucaria, sneered and said, "What a grand idea. Put her down."

M'anta didn't notice the warrior beside the cottage. Nor did she understand the meaning of the tribesman's words or see the spear. In mid-stride, a sharp pain in her back caused her legs to buckle. A twist of the shaft and a push sent the spearhead into her heart.

M'anta found herself walking in fog along a narrow road. For several steps she felt as alone as the night the King sent news that her husband had died in Africa. But shortly after the feeling started, a figure emerged from the fog and wrapped her in his arms. "We're together again," her husband said. Comforted by the spirit, M'anta died.

"Aunt M'anta," Sucaria screamed.

Between the kicking and the sudden scream, the tribesman dropped her. Running to the body, Sucaria dropped to her knees and rested her cheek on M'anta's back. Thinking the little girl was crying, the Cenomani spearmen laughed at the pain they inflicted.

But Sucaria wasn't crying. She was saying over and over again, "Oh Dog where are you? I need your strength."

Chapter 8 – Can Perform Violence

The population of Credaro consisted mostly of old men and widows. Other than the Latian Dog, the only two youngish males were a pair of herders who lived in the village during the winter. When the spearmen arrived, the youths ran into the hills and scattered the sheep. Once they dispersed the flock to prevent it from being stolen, they raced for the town of Seriate and the home of Clan Chief Garos.

Using their spears and shields, the five Cenomani warriors gathered the remaining residents and herded them to the communal well.

"My brother died at Cremona," one of the tribesman shouted. "If the Insubri hadn't run like dogs, we would have defeated the Legions."

"You accused the Insubri of burning Placentia, so other tribes couldn't collect more bounty," an old man spoke up.

"Our warriors were driven off by jealousy and spite. Not by fear of the Romans."

The spear lashed out as if was a quarterstaff. It clubbed the old man on the side of his head. He fell, and the tribesman stepped forward and drove his spear through the old man's chest.

"You Insubri think you're superior to other tribes," a second spearman shouted. "My father died at Cremona. And I will seek blood for blood."

"I'll kill the next person to move," another threatened.

To prove his intent to murder, a thrust drove his spear into the side of an old woman. He yanked it back, tearing flesh as the spearhead withdrew. A short blur raced across the group to reach the injured woman. There, Sucaria squatted, took the scarf from the woman's shoulders, and pressed the cloth against the wound.

"Look, an Insubri rat," the fourth spearman exclaimed. "I think I'll keep her."

"I saw her first," the fifth Cenomani claimed. "Find your own pet. She's mine."

"We're here for revenge," the first reminded the two bickering spearmen.

"And plunder," the third added.

A light from beside a cottage caught Sucaria's attention. A second flash and she understood. The Dog had arrived. Another bright beam of sunlight off a very sharp hatchet passed across her face. The little girl nodded and braced her legs.

The Dog extended an arm from around the corner of a cottage and waved a come to me motion.

Sucaria stood, walked to the fifth spearmen, and stopped. Extending her arm and a finger, she announced, "I don't like you."

The Cenomani Tribesmen laughed because none of them cared what a child thought.

Rotating, she pointed at the third, and she stated, "but you killed my Aunt M'anta. So I pick you."

Sucaria strolled to within an arm's length of the third spearman.

"See, she wants to be my pet," the third glared at the fifth.

Forgetting the little girl, the two tribesmen scowled at each other. Ignored by the pair, Sucaria ran. She reached the lane between the cottages before the spearmen noticed her. With her little legs churning, she attempted to escape.

"She's yours," the fifth said, relinquishing his claim.

Chuckling, the third spearman jogged after his new pet.

***

Sucaria ran to the back of the cottages, spun to see a spearman jogging after her, and screamed in fear. Then she ran from the lane, moving around the corner of one cottage. With his shield held low and his spear resting on his shoulder, the Cenomani ran around the corner.

"Come here rat," he encouraged.

Before he realized the bundle of fur against the rear wall was alive, the flat of a hatchet impacted the side of his head. Brains scrambled, he flopped to the ground. The Latian Dog bent and placed the edge of the hatchet against the spearman's throat. But he paused before spilling blood. The man's linen armor appeared new.

"During battle, weapons break and armor rips," the voice in the Dog's head advised. *"Many a man has died when he ignored a crack in the shaft of his spear or a cleave in his armor. In battle switch or replace, so you have the best possible gear throughout the fight."*

"Who are you?" the Dog questioned.

No answer came from the voice in his head. The Dog dropped the fur robe, stripped the spearman of the linen armor, and pulled it over his head.

"How do you know about armor?" Sucaria asked as the Dog expertly tied the sections together.

"Go call another spearman," the Dog told her.

"I don't understand you," Sucaria said in exasperation.

With hand motions, the Dog directed her to step into the lane and summon another spearman.

"Walk in single file to hide your numbers," the voice directed. *"Leave no witnesses. If the authorities have no evidence, they can't charge you with the crime."*

"You are so familiar, yet I can't place you," the Dog addressed the voice. He pulled the semiconscious man close to the cottage wall. When Sucaria turned her back, the edge of the hatchet slit the spearman's throat and the Dog offered. "But I understand leaving no witnesses."

***

From the area of the village well, the spearmen paused in their threats.

"What is she doing?" one tribesman inquired.

In the lane, the little girl used the fingers of both hands to wave. When she pointed to the rear of a cottage, one guessed.

"I think she wants to show me something," he announced. "Perhaps my brother has discovered a hoard of silver."

"More likely a barrel of beer," another Cenomani suggested.

The spearman walked into the lane and called out, "where are you? What have you found?"

"Languages are important for understanding while negotiating and for hiding among a people," the voice informed the Dog. *"Beyond the foreign words, matching a dialect sells your authenticity."*

Pitching his voice higher to match the tribesman's tone, the Dog replied in perfect Gaelic, "In the root cellar. Come see. Hurry."

At hearing the speech in her native tongue, Sucaria spun and froze. An armored man stood over the fur robe. With the shield held high only his eyes, and a little of his armor, were visible. For a moment, Sucaria feared the spearman had recovered and bested her Dog.

"Move behind me, and kneel by the body," the Dog instructed. When the Cenomani came around the corners, the Latian Dog blurted out in the tribesmen's dialect. "Look at that."

Using the spear, he pointed to the kneeling girl, the fur robe, and the hatchet. His attention diverted, the tribesman rushed to look at the face of the dead man.

"Who is? No, no," the Cenomani protested.

In the Dog's hand, the shaft whipped in a circle. At the top of the spin, the spearhead descended with a whirl. Capturing the energy of the rotating shaft, the spearhead broke the tribesman's clavicle bone on the way down. It pierced the man's lung before the steel settled deep in his heart.

"No," the tribesman muttered before dropping to the ground.

The Dog extracted the spear and picked up the other shaft.

"Can you count to one hundred?" the Dog inquired.

"How did you do that?" Sucaria asked, her eyes wide and her mouth hanging open. "And you speak."

"Can you count to one hundred?"

"M'anta only taught me to count to fifty."

"That good enough," the Dog told her. "Count to fifty twice then run to the lane and scream."

"But the tribesman will come for me," Sucaria insisted.

"Only for a few steps," the Dog assured her. "Now start. One. Two."

They continued together, "Three. Four."

He picked up the hatchet and slid it into his belt, then took a skinning knife from one of the spearman.

On seven, the Dog, holding a shield and two spears, ran into the hills behind the cottage.

Watching him leave sent a chill through the girl. But after squaring her shoulders, bravely Sucaria counted, "Ten. Eleven. Twelve."

***

Shivers caused Sucaria's arms to shake as she neared the end of the second count of fifty. Cottages away, she thought she heard sheep bleating.

"Forty-eight, forty-nine," she counted. At fifty, and afraid she would freeze and not do it, Sucaria ran between the cottages. And she screamed.

The three spearmen looked down the lane at the little girl.

"Why is she still free?" one questioned.

"I'll go check on the brothers," another volunteered. He started for the lane, ordering. "Stay right there child."

Four sheep appeared at the end of the street. On a normal day, a shepherd would be driving them. But the four were tied together by lengths of rope around their waists. And at the center of each rope, the fibers smoldered and glowed. Trying to escape the smoke and the heat, the sheep trotted forward while pulling away from each other. The odd sight grabbed the attention of the three tribesmen.

"Present a foe with a novel sight and you'll have an extra moment to escape," the voice explained. *"Or it will give you a standing target for your first arrow."*

At the lane, the tribesman, who was going to check on the brothers and capture the child, turned to stare at the burning ropes and the line of sheep. From behind the panicked animals, the image of a warrior materialized. Believing it was one of the missing brothers joking around, he didn't react to the danger, nor did he register the spear throw.

As the shaft arched across the sky, the Dog commented to the voice in his head, "I don't know about the first arrow. But it works for the target of a spear."

Sucaria's vision was filled with the menacing tribesman. She wanted to run, but the earlier episodes in the lane had drained her nerves. Trembling in fear, her legs wobbled as she waited for the man to come for her.

One moment, the Cenomani filled the mouth of the lane. Next, quicker than a bird in flight, a shaft appeared from the sky. In the blink of an eye, the spear swept the tribesman from her view. Free from the immediate threat, Sucaria turned and ran for the Dog's barn. The little girl planned to find a dark place to hide. She would stay there forever.

***

The novelty of four sheep running abreast and the burning ropes lasted until a warrior with a cloth over his face threw the spear. Assuming a defensive stance, the closest tribesman lowered his spear and lifted his shield. But the masked man didn't have a moment to spare for a fair fight.

As he ran around the sheep, the Dog threw the second spear on a low, flat trajectory.

The Cenomani bellowed in pain, collapsed, and folded around his shattered ankle. In a feeble and failing attempt, he tried to remove the spearhead from the fragments of bone and the tendons at the top of an almost severed foot.

***

The last tribesman standing, lowered his spear and his shield to protect his lower legs. He needn't have bothered.

The Dog was fresh out of ranged weapons. Drawing the hatchet, he sprinted at the Cenomani.

"You control the fighting circle by not being in the path of your enemy's blade," the voice coached. "And avoiding being taken off your feet."

A ghost pain stung the Dog's upper back. He didn't know the meaning, but the season for reflecting passed as he approached the last spearmen.

The steel spearhead poked the Dog's shield as if the spearman had little strength. At that moment, the Dog realized this wasn't his maiden voyage into single combat. Ignoring the false attack, he chopped the shaft of the spear at an angle. The hatchet dug into the wood. He allowed the weapon to be jerked from his hand.

"Stupid Insubri," the tribesman sneered at the masked warrior. "You've lost your…"

In an instant, the shields slammed together, leaving no room to deploy the spear. But a skinning knife only had to reach over an enemy's shield and make a shallow cut on the side of an opponent's neck.

The Dog stepped away. With blood pumping from a neck wound, the tribesman stumbled and raised the spear. But the shaft swung from side to side as the Cenomani swayed, trying to keep his balance.

"Fight me so I may die honorably," the tribesman begged.

The masked Dog lifted his arm and pointed at the body of the old man before walking away.

A distance from the bloody man, he stopped at the suffering warrior. A foot on his chest rocked the tribesman onto his back. The Dog relieved the man of his coin purse. For some reason, he felt compelled to collect a fee after the combat.

No one questioned or bothered the masked warrior as he strolled down the lane. The villagers were occupied. Several of them assaulted the dying Cenomani, while others used spears on the one with the missing foot, and near the lane, the rest of the Insubri stabbed and yelled at the tribesman with a spear wound in his side.

***

Shaking as if freezing, the frightened girl hid under a blanket.

"Sucaria. Are you in there?" the Dog asked. He washed the blood off his face, hands, and arms. "We need to talk about what happened."

Her little face appeared in the shadows of the barn. She wiped away a tear and tried to be brave.

"Are they gone? Wait, you can talk," she said, her lips quivering. "And you can fight."

"About that," the Latian Dog remarked. "Can we keep both of those things between us?"

"Like a secret?" she questioned.

The Dog walked in and dumped a shield, a spear, a hunting knife, and a skinning knife on the floor of the barn.

"Let my mastery of your language and my abilities with weapons be our secrets," he offered. "And I'll share my secret with you."

"You have a secret?" Sucaria inquired. Then she bragged. "I can keep secrets."

"I know you can. You see, Sucaria, I don't know who I am," the Dog admitted. "I don't know my name, where I'm from, or how I know combat."

Sucaria raised her arms and stretched up on the balls of her feet. The Dog bent down and received a hug.

"It's going to be fine," she assured him. "I'll take care of you."

***

Late in the day, Clan Chief Garos arrived with twenty Insubri warriors and the shepherds from Credaro.

Advancing on Credaro with spears leveled, they expected a fight. Except, before reaching the village, they found five mutilated bodies on the bank of the Oglio River and a crowd.

"What's this?" Garos demanded.

The Widow Gobnait spit on the stack of spearmen, and asserted, "Fish food."

"They came to kill and rob," an old man told the Chief. "What the Cenomani got was Insubri steel in their guts."

"You fought and killed five of their spearman?" the Clan Chief asked in surprise.

"We lost three, including M'anta," Gobnait added, without giving details. "That leaves a child without family in the village."

"What can we do about that?" Garos inquired.

"Her father is from the Gnato Clan," Gobnait told him. "Give her a donkey cart and let her go there."

"A child of five years?" Garos questioned. "Can't she remain here?"

"No, she can't," another widow insisted. "She can travel. She has him."

"You'd send a mere child across all of Insubri. A journey of over a hundred miles with a dog for a companion?"

Gobnait pointed to the other side of the trail. Away from the villagers and the bodies, Sucaria stood with a hand on the big half-wit's shoulder.

"Give her a travel document and send her and her Dog off," the widow insisted.

The Clan Chief didn't notice, but when Gobnait said her Dog, the villagers trembled and they looked away.

"It's not unusual for people to fear the man who can perform violence in their name," the voice informed the Dog. *"It's best to collect your commission and be on your way rather than trying to convince them not to fear you."*

Garos shrugged as a sign of surrender.

"If that's the will of the village," he agreed. "I'll write a letter to Clan Chief Kentus. With both our names on the document, she shouldn't have any trouble traveling across clan lands."

"I have no doubt she'll be safe," Gobnait assured him. The widow glanced at the muscular physiques of the five dead Cenomani warriors. "Of that, I am sure."

Chapter 9 – Hazardous Crossings

The next morning, Sucaria and the Latian Dog left Credaro. Behind them, fire from the cremation of the three dead villagers roared and bellowed smoke into the air. As he walked beside the horse, Dog considered the heartlessness of forcing the child to leave before the ceremony concluded and her aunt's body had been reduced to ashes. The horse and a cart, provided by Garos, stood in place of a payment for M'anta's cottage, barn, and garden. Per any reasonable exchange rate, the Clan Chief got the best of the deal.

"Is a hundred miles a long way?" Sucaria inquired.

Sitting on top of an oiled skin tarp stretched over a maple log, gave her a solid perch. Under the cover were stored her few possessions and Dog's weapons. Due to the size of the maple log, the child rode eye-to-eye with her protector.

The question took him from reflecting on her mistreatment and he replied without thinking, "If we jogged, we could be at Arona in four days and be ready to fight."

"Who would jog for a hundred miles?" Sucaria asked. "And who are we fighting?"

Dog took a few more steps before admitting, "I don't know. The answer just came to me."

"How long will it take us?" she questioned.

"About seven days if the weather stays fair," the Latian Dog estimated. "Unless we're delayed by obstacles."

Sucaria pointed at the peaks to the north and suggested, "Like mountains."

"The scout told us to keep the mountains on our right and to stay on trails leading westward," he informed her. "We'll stay out of the mountains."

"That's simple," she declared.

For half the day, the mountains were to the right and the trail firm underfoot. The horse and cart traveled easily. In the distance, tall trees alerted them to a river.

A traveler, coming from the other direction, informed them about the next river.

"The Serio River is low this period of the year," he offered. "You'll have no trouble crossing."

Sucaria thanked him while Dog remained quiet.

Not much farther down the trail, they arrived on the riverbank of the Serio. Sandbars extended from the banks on both sides, allowing for a shallow channel down the center. The horse walked forward with Dog. When the wheels and cart dipped and water splashed up from the river, Sucaria giggled. The crossing proved as easy as described by the traveler.

They camped outside the city of Bergamo, avoiding the people and questions. At dawn, they passed beneath the walls of the city. When the sun topped the mountains behind them, they followed their shadows.

Counting steps let the Dog know they traveled four miles before reaching another watercourse. He pulled the horse to a stop, dropped to a knee, and studied the smooth surface.

"It's like the other river," Sucaria ventured. "Only wider."

"See the ruts on this bank and the wheel and hoof marks on the other side," Dog pointed out. "They tell us the handlers were driving the animals hard to get out of the water."

"Water monsters?" she asked. Turning her head, Sucaria prepared to leap from the cart and run away from the river.

"Most likely it's a steep riverbed," Dog told her. "There are no shallows near the banks. That means partway across, the center will drop out from under us. Hold onto the side. If the cart starts to go downstream, stay on. I'll come for you."

"Like you did at Credaro?" she requested.

"Like I did at Credaro."

"Okay," she said, trusting him at his word.

The wide flat surface and the tree branches and weeds drifting south gave a false sense of the danger. Before reaching midstream, the Latian Dog was proven correct.

The horse began swimming franticly. The frightened animal looked back for the safety of the embankment it had just left. A U-turn in midstream would flip the cart and spill Sucaria and the baggage into the river. With powerful kicks, Dog grabbed the harness and pulled as he swam. Once his feet were under him, he hurried up the riverbank. And like travelers before him, the cart's wheels left wet, deep furrows in the soft dirt.

"Dog?"

"Yes, Sucaria?"

"Let's not do that again," she pleaded.

***

Seven miles from the deep narrow river, they topped a rise and looked down on a wide river. Unlike the deceptively smooth river they crossed, the new one had ripples from riverbank to riverbank.

"We'll camp here for the night," Dog announced.

"But there's daylight," Sucaria pointed out.

"We'd use most of it getting down to the river. And lose the light about halfway across," Dog countered. "It's best we spend the night and get an early start."

As the sun set, the cold from the mountains rolled down and swept the Adda River Valley. Chilled air from the highlands collided with land warmed by the winter sun. Being just five miles from the toe of the mountain, Dog and the child spent the night watching snow attempt to bury and extinguish the flames in their firepit.

"It's pretty," Sucaria noted.

Only one eye peeked out from under the fur robe.

"It is, little one," admitted Dog as he stacked more logs on the fire. "It's pretty when you have fire and blankets for warmth."

***

Snow covered the sides of the distant mountain, and as if a flowing gown, the white draped the landscape all the way to the sparse campsite.

"You asked how long we'll be on the trail," Dog mentioned as he tightened the harness and readied the horse. "We're about a quarter of the way to Arona. It's taken us three days."

"Is that good?" Sucaria asked.

Dog lifted her to the top of the cart and wrapped three wool blankets around the child.

"We're not Legion, but everything being equal, we're doing passably fair," Dog told her.

"Is a Legion fast?" she asked. She was bundled so tightly in the blankets, she had to twist her upper body to follow Dog.

He packed the rest of their gear in the cart and moved to the front.

"Truthfully, I don't know," he confessed. Gripping the harness, Dog mentioned. "The idea just came to my mind."

"We're not Legion," Sucaria exclaimed as the cart started forward. Her breath shot vapor into the cold morning air. "But everything being equal, we're doing passably fair."

"I guess we are," Dog commented as he urged the horse and cart down the steep grade to the river.

On a narrow track just above the water, Sucaria remarked, "The river ripples. Does that mean it's not deep."

"Good observation," Dog complimented her. "It is not deep. But the ripples identify rocks below the surface. You can see them in the shallows. We'll go slow but it'll be a bumpy crossing."

With one hand on the sideboard, Sucaria nodded her readiness for the river. Dog stepped off the bank and urged the horse down into the water. The beast stepped carefully, often touching a rock before shifting the hoof to the riverbed. Likewise, Dog gingerly placed each foot to keep from tripping. Wheels, unfortunately, lacked the flexibility to choose a different path. The cart lifted on submerged rocks, dipped to one side and then the other, causing Sucaria to rock as if invisible hands shook her.

On the far side, the cart topped the embankment. Rather than going up the steep grade, Dog turned them north and proceeded along a flat zone. He could tell by the watermarks on the hills, the land under their feet would be deep underwater in the spring. When the flood plain widened, he edged the horse westward onto a goat trail.

By midday, they trekked along the foot of high ground and Dog stopped the horse.

"This is a good spot to unpack and dry out our fabrics and leather goods," he announced.

Sucaria glanced around at the rough trail, overgrown with weeds, the trees around them, and the tall slope to their right. She noticed nothing unique or welcoming in that particular location.

"What makes this a good spot?" she questioned.

"We'll have high ground to our backs," Dog answered, turning to face the woods. "If danger comes from the trail, I'll see them advancing. That means I only have to worry about a threat from the trees to our front."

"How do you know these things?" she asked.

"I wish I knew," the Dog told her.

He pulled everything out of the wagon and spread the items on the ground to dry. When he reached the spear, Dog yanked it up and spun the shaft around his neck. Continuing to loop the spear, he dipped to his knees and sprang up. The shaft flipped under an arm and over his shoulder, then he repeated the moves in reverse. When he noticed the look of amazement on Sucaria's face, he stopped.

"It's as if you're doing a ceremonial dance," she proposed, "but with a spear. Are you a priest?"

"Considering the things I did at Credaro, I don't believe holy man fits my skill set," Dog quipped. "Perhaps I was an entertainer."

"I've seen jugglers when they came to our village," Sucaria remarked. "None of them kicked and knelt while tossing balls into the air. I don't believe you were an entertainer."

"That leaves us where we started," Dog advised.

After digging a shallow hole, Dog place kindling in the depression and started a fire. He collected dead limbs from the ground and snapped the branches off for firewood.

"No, we are not," she said, picking up a green stick. After attempting to snap it over her knee, she told him. "We are far from Credaro. That's where we started."

"Try this stick," Dog offered.

She took the dry stick from Dog and snapped it over her knee. As if a conquering hero, she held the sticks overhead, and marched around the firepit, before tossing the sticks into the fire.

Something about her marching triggered Dog's imagination. And the view of the high ground from the trail tightened his chest. His breath caught in his throat.

"The Cretan march allows us to put more arrows downrange than a cluster of archers," the voice echoed in his mind. *"Again, do the steps, perfect the dance. Cretan counter-march firing alignment. Set the beat."*

In response to the instructions, Dog shouted, "Mártios, mártios, step left, step right, mártios."

"What are you doing and what does mártios mean?" Sucaria questioned. "It sounds like the words you were speaking before. I didn't understand them either."

"Mártios means march. It's Greek," Dog told her. Confused by the knowledge, he ventured a guess. "I may be an archer from the Island of Crete. Or maybe I spent part of my life there."

"You speak Greek?" she asked. "Educated people speak Greek. Aunt M'anta said physicians, and philos. Philos? Deep thinkers, come from Greece."

"Philosophers," Dog filled in. "They question the meaning of life, so in a way they are deep thinkers."

"That's what I said, Dog the Greek, deep thinkers," Sucaria insisted.

"Now I'm really confused," he whined. "How can I be a Latian Dog, and also, Dog the Greek?"

"You should eat," Sucaria encouraged. "We always feel better with a full belly."

"I believe you're right," Dog agreed. "I'll get the pot and grain. You get the water skin."

After the meal, with their belongings dry, and them rested and fed, Dog pulled on the harness. The horse and cart moved with him.

"Maybe you're a Greek philosopher," Sucaria offered from on top of the load.

"I don't believe I'm that deep a thinker," Dog told her. "But you have to admit, I'm a good travel guide."

"You do find trails. Maybe you're a scout."

"Could be," Dog replied.

Four miles from the stop, they reached another river. The water drifted slowly downstream, and the surface ran smoothly. The riverbed turned out to be firm.

On the other side, Sucaria commented, "That was the easiest crossing yet."

"Let's hope the rest of the rivers on this trip," Dog told her, "are like that one."

Two miles later, he guided the horse and cart through a field of wild grass. At the end of the green expanse, they entered a line of giant trees. On the other side of the branches, they stopped. A river, fast flowing and wide, ended their trek for the day.

"We'll need a day to prepare to cross that," Dog announced. He turned the horse and backtracked towards high ground.

"I agree," Sucaria confirmed.

Dog guided them up a draw, and where the ridges came together, he halted the horse. Open ground gave him a view of the forest and the trail below.

"This is a good spot," Sucaria announced. "If danger comes, I'll see them."

"Good, you have first watch," Dog instructed.

He unharnessed the horse, hobbled the legs, and dropped a double handful of grain for feed.

"We need meat," Dog told her as he pulled the spear from the cart. Weighing it in his hands, he frowned. "It feels like this is the wrong tool for the job."

After starting the campfire, stacking extra wood, and installing Sucaria as tender of the flames and camp guard, Dog walked across the cleared area and entered the forest.

***

Unlike his days on the mountain above Credaro, cutting wood and exercising, Dog experienced a heightening of his senses. Kneeling among the tall trees, he listened to the sounds of the forest. Chirping from the branches overhead, identified a variety of birds. Leaves and twigs crinkling and snapping in several locations informed him of tiny paws moving across the forest floor. And most surprising, he sniffed in several directions, sampling the environment.

"Rabbit," he whispered before moving silently towards one of the sounds.

***

At first, Sucaria rotated her head and watched for danger. But she got bored. And when she added wood to the firepit, ashes sparked and a column of smoke rose into the air. The display proved more interesting than scanning walls of trees. She threw another piece of wood and enjoyed the result. Enthralled by the first two, she threw a third, and then a fourth piece into the fire.

"That's a nice horse you've got there, little girl," a man behind her remarked.

Sucaria spun to face the voice. But a hand caught her in mid-turn and clamped over her mouth. Hoisted from the ground, the little girl struggled, but a firm shake settled her down.

"Tie her up while I harness the horse," the man directed.

A woman wrapped a cloth around Sucaria's head and tightened a gag. Next, she wound rope around the little frame of her body until Sucaria couldn't move her arms to fight or flex her knees to run.

Dropped beside the firepit, the little girl watched as the man and the woman climbed onto the cart and snapped the reins. Tears rolled down her face as they rode out of her vision. She cried, not because she was hurt, but from failing Dog the Greek by not keeping watch.

***

Hanging from the spear shaft, two skinned rabbits rocked back and forth. The game was a result of the hunt and the sway from Dog's proud strut. A stag appeared between two trees. The forest creature gazed at him as if expecting a greeting.

"You're in luck," Dog said to the buck. "Today, I don't have my bow with…"

Dog stopped talking in mid-sentence and halted in mid-stride. How could he miss a bow and arrows? He didn't remember owning or using the hunting weapon? Dog and the deer stared at each other for a few moments. When the stag bounded away, it broke the spell. With confident steps but confused by the question concerning a bow and arrows, Dog traced his trail back to the edge of the forest.

Stepping out from between branches, he stopped. At first glance, it appeared the girl, the horse, and the cart were gone. All that remained of the camp was a low burning fire and a bundle on the ground. Panic clamped onto his heart and tightened.

Fearing the child was dead, he prayed, "Goddess Artemis, not Sucaria, please."

In his moment of invocation, the voice in his head returned.

"Cretan Archers only keep one deity," the voice instructed, *"the Goddess Artemis. You must learn the rest, plus others, but understand, the Goddess of the Bow and the Hunt is most precious to an archer."*

In a flash, Dog remembered. The Goddess Artemis cared for all forest creatures and was often associated with the stag.

Why send the memory of a Goddess and the spirit of her in a buck if the child was dead? Hope released his heart and freed his feet. Dog sprinted to the firepit and the bundle.

He arrived and lifted the trussed up child. He cuddled the bound body in his arm and savored, not finding her cold and dead, or bloody from an injury. After resting her tear-stained face against his chest, he untied the gag.

"Are you hurt?" he inquired softly.

"Wait," she insisted.

"It's okay, take as long as you need," he offered, thinking she was distressed by the theft and in need of a few moments to recover.

"You count steps while you walk," she said. "It's how you know miles. And I count each step the horse makes. It passes the day. The thieves, a man and a woman, are five hundred paces to the west and riding the cart."

"What am I supposed to do with that information?" Dog asked.

"It's only a quarter of a mile. Go get our horse and cart back," Sucaria answered. She squirmed in the cocoon of rope. "But first, untie me."

Act 4

Chapter 10 – Emergence of an Archer

Dog assumed he would slow down before catching the cart. It was a logical assumption, as sprinting a quarter of a mile should exhaust any man. When he caught sight of the cart and his breath still came easily and his legs churned effortlessly, he maintained his pace even as he left the old wagon trail. Sprinting through the woods, he felt exhilaration surge through his body. Between dodging tree trunks and low branches, he found the run energizing. Moments later, he passed the cart and horse. Pivoting back to the trail, he emerged from the forest ahead of the rig.

"You can get down and leave in peace," Dog warned the man on the cart. "Or you can die an ugly death."

He caught the bridle and halted the horse.

"Do you know who I am?" the man demanded.

"A horse and cart thief," Dog suggested. "And an abuser of children."

"We never hurt the girl," the woman protested.

"Get down from the cart," Dog ordered. "And trust me, you want to walk away."

The man hopped off the cart and drew a long knife. He stood taller than Dog with wide shoulders to match his height.

"I am Bannus, Clan Chief of Lugus Leno," he boasted. "My people are the craftsmen and harvesters of this forest. Anything here is, by rights, mine."

Dog thrust the end of the spear into the dirt and carved an arc across the trail. After drawing part of a circle, he tossed the spear aside and drew the hunting knife.

"The horse, cart, and child belong to Chief Kentus of the Clan Gnātos," Dog replied before pointing to the curved line on the ground. He couldn't remember why he drew it. But he did understand that he discarded the spear to avoid killing a Clan Chieftain. As for the line in the dirt, he had no idea what it signified. After a pause, Dog finished his argument. "I am her protector. So you can see my problem with your claim on the cart and horse."

As he talked, the woman ran off. Her movements didn't reflect a panicked flight, but a steady lope as if heading for a destination. Dog guessed she was going for help. It limited his options.

"Kentus isn't here and neither are warriors from Clan Gnātos," Bannus pointed out. "I give you leave to return to the girl and travel from my lands."

"With the horse and cart?" Dog asked as he stepped over the line.

"You mean my horse and my cart?" the Clan Chief snickered. "No, little man. On your two feet."

Dog paced forward two steps. The action placed him at the ribs of the horse and closer to the Clan Chief. Bannus braced and held the blade of his knife ready to stab or slash.

In a lunge, Dog jerked forward and Bannus thrust with his knife. Before the blade reached him, Dog squatted and slipped under the belly of the horse. Coming up on the far side, he spoke over the draft animal's back.

"You aren't too bright," Dog asserted. "Were you always a disappointment to your father?"

Following the insult, Dog moved as if he intended to run to the rear of the cart and get behind the Clan Chief.

Not to be blindsided, Bannus, angry at the accusation, spun and raced to the rear of the cart. He intended to confront the man who would challenge a son's relationship with his father. But when he arrived at the end of the cart, the stranger wasn't there.

Dog squeezed between the tail of the horse and the cart. With his head lowered, he ran towards Bannus. A heartbeat later, the top of his head hit the Clan Chief in the center of his back.

As if struck by a battering ram, the air in his lungs expelled and Bannus was propelled into the air. The landing might have bruised the Clan Chief. But he'd fallen in countless fights and gotten up each time to thrash his opponent.

The Dog felt the collision in his neck and down his spine. A fog clouded his mind and instinct, or training, took control of his body. Lifting the Clan Chief overhead while driving with his legs, he increased the height and speed of the initial launch. Then he stopped and slung Brennus to the earth. Adding to the damage, Dog hammered the Clan Chief into the ground with his head.

As effectively as if someone used a club on him, Bannus sprawled in the dirt semiconscious and unable to move.

Squinting to block the sunlight, Dog rushed to the horse and guided the animal in a half circle. Throbbing in his head grew into a pounding headache. Fighting the dullness and pain, Dog passed Bannus and the mysterious line in the dirt. The Clan Chief could only manage a moan in protest as his cart and horse were reclaimed.

***

When she saw him coming down the trail, Sucaria jumped up and down in excitement. Dog had brought back the horse, cart, and their belongings.

"You did it," she screeched. But as he drew closer, she noticed he held his head down and had his eyes closed. "What happened? Are you injured?"

"Get on the, ah, wagon," he muttered, as if finding the correct words was difficult. "We can't stay…here."

Sucaria scrambled to the top of the cart. Once settled, she began to cry. Her lack of attention has caused the Dog to become ill again.

The Dog guided the horse and cart off the ridge. At the bottom of the slope, he turned right, heading for the river.

"Oh Dog, it's my fault for not being a good guard," Sucaria told him. Then she remembered they needed a day to prepare for the river crossing. Dog hadn't done anything to get ready for the wide river. A deep fear rose in her chest and the child asked. "Are we ready to cross the river."

"I fought the Clan Chief," Dog stammered. "We can't stay here."

"But the river," Sucaria demanded. "It's just ahead."

As if a mindless and terrified herd animal, Dog marched off the embankment, pulling the horse and the cart into the river. They splashed through the shallows. The current, already a weight on the legs of the man and the horse, attempted to wash them downstream. And the deeper they went, the stronger the current. Then, Dog vanished under the surface and Sucaria shrieked in horror.

***

With his mouth full of water and more shoved up his nostrils, Dog struggled against the river. His headache intensified as he sank. Lightning streaked across his mind. He began to thrash about in desperation as black clouds rolled in. But just before the storm reached its zenith and consumed him, hands reached through the chaos and ripped a hole in the squall. A Master Archer emerged and his words thundered louder than the storm.

"*Injured or hurt?*" Zarek Mikolas demanded. "*Because you'll always hurt. From pulling a bowstring a thousand times, chopping wood, suffering the trials of becoming a Cretan Archer, and every day of a contract, you'll feel pain. Emotions like loneliness, loss of love, alienation, hunger, chills, sore muscles, and weariness in your bones are the price we pay to earn our way. If just hurt, you can keep moving. And if you can keep moving, you can reach safety.*"

"Keep moving," Dog thought. He felt the lead line to the horse tug at his arm. "No you don't. We are not going back to shore."

***

Sucaria held on tight as the cart sank. Then the horse angled as it prepared to retreat to the shore. The cart began to tip and water lapped over the side.

"Oh, Dog, please come back," the little girl pleaded. "You promised you would. Where are you?"

Disappointed and afraid, she waited for the cart to dump her in the wide river. Although she has waded in the Oglio River near Credaro, she had never learned to swim. The last heartbeats of her young life pounded in her chest.

"Oh, Dog, help me."

Ahead of the horse, Dog broke the surface. Sucaria held her breath as the cart tipped farther, threating to ditch her in the river.

***

Cretan Archer Jace Kasia broke the surface, put the line between his teeth and bit down. With powerful strokes and kicks, he swam against the current, guiding the horse and the mostly submerged cart across the river.

On the far side, Jace scrambled up the embankment, snapping words of encouragement at the horse. The cart drifted just beneath the surface. Holding onto the rail, Sucaria floated above the water.

Waterlogged, the cart and load pulled the draft animal back when it tried to get footing on the bank.

"Again," Jace shouted as he pulled with the horse. Slowly, the cart appeared. "Again. Pull."

Slipping and backsliding, Jace and the horse tugged the dripping and soaked cart out of the river and onto dry ground.

"I know you're tired. So am I," Jace said to the horse. "We need to get away from the river and into the woods. Just a little farther and we'll rest."

In a valiant effort between man and animal, they hauled the cart, heavy load, and Sucaria off the riverbank and into the forest.

Jace went to the cart and lifted the little girl from the top. She held his face at arm's length.

"I lost faith," Sucaria confessed. "But you didn't. And you saved me."

Then, although she didn't realize it, she hugged her Dog for the last time.

***

To the delight of the horse, an entire sack of damp, moist grain was opened and left as feed. For Jace and Sucaria, they dumped extra wet grain into the pot of water and discarded the rest.

"Wet grain will go bad in a day," Jace explained while wringing out blankets and clothing before draping them over bushes to dry.

"You sound different," Sucaria commented. "Are you feeling okay?"

The leather facing on the shield drooped and dripped. He rubbed a thin coat of goose grease on the surface, then placed it on a tree branch to dry. Carrying the bag of grease to the cart, Jace rubbed gobs of the thick substance on the axle and around the hub of each wheel. When there were no chores left, he went to the cookfire and sat across from Sucaria.

"My name is Jace Kasia and I am a Cretan Archer," he explained. "It's how I know how to fight, to hike, and to hunt."

Sucaria blinked to be sure she was looking at the same man.

"You talk different," she mentioned.

"I may be speaking Gaul with a Greek accent," he ventured. "Is it bad?"

"Only different," she assured with a shrug. Next, she brightened up and said. "Nice to meet you, Jace Kasia."

"Thank you, Lady Sucaria. It is nice to meet you."

***

They spent the night in partially damp clothing and broke camp before first light. About five miles from the big river, Jace eased the horse to a stop. He strolled back to Sucaria.

"I haven't seen any pursuit from Bannus or couriers spreading news about us," Jace reported. "And we need to replenish our stores."

"Store? You mean like visiting a craftsman's hut?"

"Stores is another way of saying food, Lady Sucaria," Jace told her. "But yes, it means we have to visit a farmer's cottage or a village."

"I hope this journey never ends," Sucaria sighed.

"Why is that?"

"Out here, I'm a Lady. In a village, people ignore me," Sucaria answered.

"I'll tell you a secret. You are smarter than most people. When you grow up, people will listen to everything you say. Just don't tell them, yet."

"Let's go find a village," she directed. "It's going to be a good day."

"Right away, Lady Sucaria," Jace agreed.

***

Two miles later, they exited the trail and followed a path to a cluster of cottages. When they arrived, the village appeared empty despite smoke from cooking fires at each residence. After locating the village headman, Jace purchased grain and dried meat. The Archer used the coins he took from the Cenomani Tribesmen.

"A little farther west, you'll cross the Seveso River," the headman informed them. "It's an easy crossing this time a year."

"The information is much appreciated," Jace told him.

Before he could walk away, the villager added.

"But later, ten miles from our river you'll cross the Olona. It's wide and mostly flat. But you'll want to pick your crossing point carefully. The river snakes through the land, and where it bends, the bottom gets gouged out. In one area you'll wade across no problem. At another, you'll sink in over your head. The Olona is tricky. Yes, sir, it's a tricky river."

"Good information," Jace allowed, "Thank you."

He yanked the horse into motion and left the village. They had almost reached the main trail when Sucaria commented, "He was most helpful."

Jace remained silent. He guided the horse and cart onto the main trail. When trees blocked them from sight of the hamlet, he halted.

"Is something wrong?" Sucaria asked.

"There was smoke from all of the huts," he answered. "But we only saw a few people. Where was everyone else?"

"Are we in danger?" she inquired.

"I'm not sure. They could be off cutting firewood or doing a hundred other things," Jace proposed. He pulled the shield from the cart and slung it over his shoulder. Next, he tied on a belt with a sheath and the hunting knife. "However, if they're waiting to deliver justice for Clan Chief Bannus, I want to be ready."

"I can help," Sucaria professed. Then, in what she assumed was a useless plea, the little girl stated. "Give me a weapon."

To her surprise, Jace reached for her wrist and placed the skinning knife in her palm.

"If there is trouble, stay on the cart," he explained. "And if anyone tries to pull you off, slice their fingers."

Once prepared for an attack, Jace nudged the horse and they set out for the Seveso River.

***

A separation in the trees gave Jace a view of the flowing water. The idyllic scene consisted of the green pine trees with low branches, birds in adjacent trees chirping, but no ground creatures scurrying around. As they drew closer, the low jingle of the river added to the harmony.

"Take the reins and keep the horse moving," Jace instructed.

"Even into the river?" Sucaria questioned.

"The horse will stop on the riverbank," Jace assured her.

As the cart rolled forward, he ducked behind the load and, after a few paces, he sprinted into the tall weeds beside the trail.

"Go, horse, go," Sucaria encouraged while shaking the lines.

Obediently, the animal maintained its steady pace, heading for the river.

***

Hunkered down and hidden in the pine branches, two men on the left of the trail, and two men on the right, waited for the cart. When the horse passed between the trees, they leaped out.

"Get down girl," an older man ordered. "We're taking the cart."

Although frightened, Sucaria extended the skinning knife and shook her head, indicating that she would not comply.

"I said get down, we're taking the cart," he thundered.

From behind the thieves on the other side of the horse, Jace Kasia asked, "What are your plans for the bodies?"

The two thieves on his side spun to face the voice of the traveler. Jace greeted one by hammering him to the ground with the shield. The other thief was slow in turning. Halfway around, Jace stabbed upward into the man's gut.

"I asked, what are your plans for our bodies," Jace inquired while standing upright and charging forward. His calm question ran counter to the speed of his assault.

Between the conversational tone and seeing two of his ambush team disabled, the older thief froze. Beside him, the fourth thief appeared confused. He wasn't sure if he should run away or attack.

Jace moved forward, keeping the draft animal between him and the last two thieves. He ducked, using the body of the horse to hide his location for an instant. When he emerged under the animal's neck, the fourth thief lowered his spear, intending to skew the traveler.

With a sling of his arm, Jace sent the shield sailing over the shaft of the spear. Flying flat, the iron edge of the shield slid up the thief's chest and smashed into his throat. He dropped the spear and grabbed his neck. The Archer didn't break stride. He kicked the blade of an old sword aside and grabbed the leader of the ambush.

"You never answered my question," Jace remarked.

His hunting knife rested against the side of the older man's neck.

"Lady Sucaria are you well?" he asked. Even though he spoke to the girl, his eyes remained locked on the older thief's face.

"I am well, Archer," she replied.

Jace inquired of the thief, "where do you put the bodies."

In a reflex action, the man's eyes revealed the answer. He glanced at the flowing river.

Jace used his free hand to untie the man's coin purse.

"Lady Sucaria. Close your eyes," Jace instructed. "Now."

The blade of the knife angled down and away from the man's neck. In a slash, Jace cut a line in his flesh from his clavicle bone to the ribs on the other side. When the older thief bent from the pain, the Archer grabbed his arm and slung the ambush leader into the river.

In two strides, he clamped onto the shoulders of the choking man and tossed him into the water as well.

On the other side of the horse, Jace Kasia ran to the thief, who was just regaining his footing. With a kick to the side of the man's head, the Archer sent him tripping and stumbling into the river.

The last thief standing, held his bleeding midsection with one hand and his spear with the other. Undaunted, Jace took a step towards him. The injured man tossed down his spear, hobbled to the riverbank, and leaped into the water. The fourth vanished downstream, joining his injured compatriots in a life and death struggle for survival.

Jace began collecting weapons.

"Three spears," he reported as he shoved the weapons into the cart. "And an old short sword."

"And a coin purse," Sucaria pointed out.

"It was a good day," Jace remarked as he guided the horse off the riverbank. "I earned a profit."

Chapter 11 – Ferry To Arona

A mile from the river, Jace led the horse off the main trail and into the thick forest. Overhead, the branches created a dark green sky and underfoot, rather than hard backed dirt, old leaves softened each step, creating a hush in the surroundings.

"Why are we in the woods?" Sucaria asked.

"We don't know if the four thieves have accomplices," Jace told her. He picked a direction where the cart could pass between trees. "I don't want to be on the trail if they come looking for us."

"You could have killed them," Sucaria asserted. "Then they couldn't come after us."

Jace left the horse in a small clearing and followed their trail back through the trees. With the hunting knife, he chopped branches and hung them to hide the passage of the cart. Once sure no one could follow their trail, he returned to Sucaria.

"In every situation, you have to decide on the best outcome for you," he explained while lifting her off the cart. "Our best outcome at the river was to get away from the ambushers as quickly as possible."

"But you said they might come after us," the child repeated Jace's words. "Why let them live?"

"It's like this. Taking a life for an archer is part of the job. But the actual act of killing someone takes effort. While I was ending one thief, the others would recover and return to the fight."

"We couldn't run away so you removed the ambush by letting the river take them away," Sucaria concluded.

"And I got the outcome I wanted," Jace summed up. "Now, seeing as we can't start a fire, how about some dried meat?"

"That's the outcome I want," Sucaria assured him. "I'm hungry."

***

Olona, as the village headman had described, appeared to be a slow, meandering river. Except for the dark and light streaks of colored silt in the water, an unwary traveler could fall for the deception.

Jace waded out into the cold water and halfway across the riverbed dropped out from under him. He swam to the shallows and splashed farther upstream. Once there, he felt firm footing all the way across.

By midday, the horse and cart were on a trail heading south. A high embankment forced the change in direction. But the trail eventually banked west as it left the flood plain. A mile from the lowland, the trail passed through a fair sized town.

Not sure if they were safe, Jace called to a man pushing a cart.

"Is this the land of Clan Lugus Leno?"

"Castelseprio is Clan Cilurnos," the man replied. "Lugus Leno ends at the Lambro River."

The man continued down the street, and Jace relaxed. He rested his back against the cart.

"The thieves were not after us," he divulged.

"Jace Kasia, I know I'm young," Sucaria remarked. "But they sure seemed to be after us."

"They were after us, yes. But that's because we were a target of opportunity," Jace stated. "I thought they were from Bannus' clan."

"Can we not be that again," she begged.

"Be what?" Jace questioned.

"Be a target of opportunity."

"That is the third best idea of the day."

"What's the first?" Sucaria asked. "What's the second?"

"Finding a warm inn with hot food for us," Jace replied. "And locating a stable for the horse."

**

Two days after resting, and with clear directions to the crossing at Sesto Calende, they left Castelseprio. A mile outside of town, snow began to fall. For another long stretch, the snowflakes fell gently until the trail lay under a blanket of white. When the wind picked, the swirling cloud of snow limited visibility.

"The inn was warmer," Sucaria remarked.

"Do you want to go back?" Jace asked.

"No. I want to camp and be Lady Sucaria," she told him.

"Your wish, Lady Sucaria," Jace assured her, "is my command."

He guided the horse off the trail and into the woods. The storm intensified and for three days, the snow piled up. Four times a day, Jace left the shelter of the oiled tarp and the cart and brushed off excess snow from their rig.

On the fourth day, the sun came out and Jace packed the cart. They left the camp, kicking snow out of the way, and after a morning of toil, they reached the edge of the forest. Jace stopped the horse and studied what should have been a pristine blanket of snow. But it wasn't.

Hooves from horses and footsteps of marching men created an ugly trench in the snow. Jace might have worried except the marred snow showed the band of men moved eastward. When he and Sucaria turned onto the trail, they headed west.

***

The band of men had packed the snow, making the ten-mile trip to Sesto Calende as easy as if the trail was clear. It also confirmed the origin of the band. As Jace and Sucaria left the plains and hills and descended into the Ticino River Valley, the weather changed abruptly. Off came the big fur cloak and the blankets from around Sucaria. As if it was an early summer day, they traveled the rest of the way to Sesto Calende in comfort.

Along a low defensive wall, spearmen watched as the horse and cart approached the entrance to the lands of Clan Gnātos.

"No visitors," the gate guard instructed.

"What's going on?" Jace asked.

"Rome is preparing to march Legions on Insubri," the guard told him. "We're here to keep cowards from deserting from the other clans."

Jace glanced at the snow on the mountains, and despite the mildness of the river area, he recalled the cold as they traveled.

"You're not likely to be attacked by Rome. At least not yet," he told the guard. "They can't march until late spring after the Legionaries finish the planting season."

"What do you know?" the guard snapped. "King B'Yag put out the call and the Clan Chiefs are sending spearmen to

Milan to defend the capital. Some don't want to go and defend our tribe."

"It's a waste of manpower," Jace remarked. Then he pointed over his shoulder. "See the little girl on the cart."

Sucaria smiled and waved at the spearman.

"I do. What about her?"

"She's a relative of Clan Chief Kentus. And I'm charged with delivering her to Arona. But the gate guard won't let us in. What do I tell the Clan Chief?"

"I'm the gate guard," the spearmen protested. "Come in. You can catch a boat to Arona at the lake pier. It's off to the right."

"Thank you," Jace acknowledged.

As she passed through the gate, Sucaria waved at the spearmen. Then she saw the sprawling streets of low buildings and workshops. Her mouth fell open.

"She's a simple country girl," Jace reported to the guard. "Not accustomed to a big city."

"If she thinks this is big, you should see Milan."

"I have," Jace commented while guiding the horse into the stone wall. A block from the gate, he whispered. "I've seen Milan as a slave. And I have no intention of ever seeing it again."

***

The transition from the end of Lake Maggiore to the start of the Ticino River consisted of a stretch of rapids.

Churning water on the surface identified the point at which the lake narrowed and became a river. From the waterfront road, Jace noticed the disturbance and envisioned a boat being shredded by the hidden rocks. A little farther upstream, the smooth surface of a long lake stretched into the distance. Closer to shore, houses built on stilts extended the habitable land out over swampy areas. On each raised platform, craftsmen worked, and children played, high and dry above the water, mud, and weeds.

"There's snow on the mountains," Sucaria pointed out, "but I don't need a blanket."

Jace shifted from thinking about the flood-proof housing to looking at the towering mountains around the lake.

"If you hiked up there, you'd need more than three blankets to stay warm," he warned her. They arrived at a dock and Jace waved to get a fisherman's attention. "We need transportation to Arona."

"Chief Kentus' boat is at the end of the pier," he replied. "They'll row back to Arona this afternoon."

"Do you think they'll take us with them?"

"How would I know?" the man confessed. He held up a fishing net. "I'm just one man against all the fish in the lake."

After helping Sucaria down, Jace and the little girl walked the boards over the bog to deeper water. Most berths were empty, although at several locations along the pier, they passed occupied fishing boats. None were large enough to hold more than a couple of fishermen and the day's catch.

At the end of the pier, they approached a young man of about fifteen. He stood in front of a large boat with a shield and a spear.

"Don't come any closer," he ordered. "I'm a bodyguard for Clan Chief Samo Kentus. Know that to approach the chief, or his possessions without authority, is a sentence of death."

Jace examined the young man's stance. His feet were in line, meaning any hit to the shield would tip him into the lake. And he held the shaft high, one hand near the spearhead. Employing the weapon from that grip required a delay to reposition his hand. If a fight broke out, the delay could be deadly.

"Are you any good at it?" Jace inquired.

"Good at what?" the youth asked.

"Being a warrior for a clan chief."

Before he answered, from down the dock a man scolded, "Scanlan, put down my shield and spear."

Fumbling the spear and the shield as he rushed to disarm, the youth dropped the spear. The butt end tapped the pier, bounced, and the shaft started to fall. Jace reached out and caught the shaft, preventing it from splashing into the lake.

"Here you go," he offered up the spear.

"Thank you. Urus would beat me if I dropped his spear. He killed a bear with it, you know."

"I hadn't heard," Jace remarked. He studied the spear. While the shaft could have been changed to a long ceremonial pole, the broad and heavy spearhead made the spear unbalanced and unwieldly for hunting. Keeping his opinion to himself, the Archer said. "It must have been a massive creature."

"Scanlan. Put down my gear," Urus ordered. Jace turned to see a big man strutting down the pier with four men trailing behind him. Noticing a man and a little girl at the boat, Urus demanded, "What do you want?"

"It's not what I want, sir," Jace replied. "I am a simple servant. It's what Chief Kentus wants."

"What does the Chief of Gnātos Tribe want?"

Jace pointed to Sucaria.

"His niece, sir," Jace said while lowering his eyes out of respect.

"Is that her cart?" Urus asked.

"The luggage, the cart, and the horse," Jace explained, "belong to Lady Sucaria."

At hearing the title, the little girl beamed a smile at Jace.

Urus directed three men to unload the cart and the fourth to sell the animal and cart at the stables. Jace left Sucaria to go help carry their gear.

"Scanlan, put the girl in the back of the boat," Urus directed the youth. "And try not to drop her in the lake."

At the cart, the three men shouldered most of the bundles. Jace unrolled the heavy fur cape and put it over his shoulders. The trio of porters laughed at the overdressed man when he lifted out a short log. They stopped when Jace continued by to extract three spears, a short sword, and a shield from the bed of the cart. While the four carried their loads to the boat, the fourth man guided the horse and cart away.

When Jace arrived at the boat with the weapons and maple log, Urus inquired, "What kind of servant are you?"

"Lady Sucaria," Jace redirected to the child, "what kind of servant am I?"

"Jace Kasia is my protector," she stated. Next, with all the confidence of a child, she proclaimed. "He is an archer, although at present, he doesn't have a bow. His is a tracker, a good storyteller, and a fair traveling companion. Oh and he is an efficient killer."

Urus, the three men, and Scanlan snapped their heads around and stared at Jace.

"It was a long trip and we ran into trouble," he commented. "Can we get started?"

The fourth man came running down the pier with a coin purse.

"The horse and cart fetched a fair price," he said. "Who gets the coins?"

Urus indicated Sucaria. Any thought of cheating the child fled after the description of her bodyguard's credentials. He handed the coins and purse to the little girl.

***

The boat launched with three of the men and Scanlan pulling oars and the fifth on the rear oar. Sucaria and Jace took a bench near the aft oarsmen while Urus sat up front by himself.

"Your name is Scanlan," the child stated. "I'm Sucaria."

"Together, pull together," the rear oarsman insisted. "Stay with Scanlan. He knows how to row against the current."

Singling out the youth as an expert rower wasn't lost on Jace. He made a mental note to speak with Scanlan when he had the opportunity.

The boat glided along the east bank of Lake Maggiore. When the shore retreated and the craft was exposed, a breeze coming down the lake blew into their faces. Yet, when the shore extended out, the land blocked the wind.

"We'll row a little beyond Arona before crossing the lake," Scanlan told Sucaria. "Then, we'll use the wind to push us to the harbor of the capital."

As they passed settlements on the shoreline, people waved and shouted. The rowers returned the friendly greetings.

"Over there is Arone," Scanlan told the little girl. "Part way across, if you look on the hillside, you'll see the stonework of the chief's house."

"It doesn't look very far," Sucaria suggested.

"Try swimming it," Scanlan said, "you'll see how far it is."

"You've swum across the lake?" she gushed.

"A few times," Scanlan answered, but he grew silent at the memory.

Farther ahead, a man's voice floated across the water.

"Help. Help," the man called.

"There, take me there," Urus instructed.

With little prompting, Scanlan chanted, "Stroke, stroke. Together stroke, stroke."

Different from the causal rowing, the sharp chant and the response of the rowers sent the craft shooting forward.

"Help," a man standing below a giant willow tree shouted. Behind him, a village on stilts spread out within a forest of tall trees. While trails weaved in and out of the trees, in many spots, the solid ground became wet holes topped by water lilies.

The boat raced through the water until it was two lengths from the grassy bank.

"Down oars," Scanlan ordered.

Streams of water rushed over the four oar blades, slowing the boat. Under the resistance, the bow of the vessel tapped the shore where the man stood.

"What's the problem?" Urus asked.

"They came from the hills at midday," the man answered, his lips quivering in anger. "Lepontic warriors just fought their way across my village."

"How much grain did they take?" Urus inquired. Next, he assured the villager. "Chief Kentus will send replacement sacks."

"When you took our spearmen to defend Milan, Kentus said you would be here to protect us."

"And I will," Urus agreed. "I'll come back with a war party and your grain."

"How about my daughter?" the villager sneered.

"Your daughter?" Urus questioned. "They took your daughter?"

"My daughter and Brigid. What about that?"

The villager went from angry to snide. He ended his emotional ride by dropping to his knees and crying.

Three rowers, with cuts and bandages, appeared on the trail behind the villager.

"Brigid heard there was a sick child in Bruschera," one explained. "We rowed her over at dawn to care for the girl. We were getting ready to leave when they came."

Another rower added, "Seven Lepontic spearmen came down the main trail and attacked us. We fought, but they had shields and spears. We had knives."

Sucaria tapped Scanlan on the arm and asked, "Scanlan, who is Brigid?"

"Chief Kentus' daughter," Scanlan replied. After a pause, he said. "That makes her your cousin."

"A cousin? I've never had a cousin," Sucaria cooed.

"I hate to bring you bad news, but the Lepontic Tribe lives deep in the mountains," Scanlan told her. "Once they're out of the valley, there's little chance of you ever meeting your cousin."

A shiver when through her little body and Sucaria turned to the Archer. Placing a hand on his arm, she looked into his eyes.

"Jace Kasia. I'd really like to meet my Cousin Brigid," Sucaria informed him.

"Don't be silly child," Urus scolded her. "There are seven of them. I'll be back this afternoon, and in the morning, we'll go after the raiding party."

Jace stood, and for a few moments, he studied the mountains above the village. Then he peered down at Sucaria and instructed, "Give me a coin."

Chapter 12 – She's Your Cousin

After getting directions to the main trail, the Cretan Archer jogged along a village path. Branches of alder trees and the cascade of willows blocked the sun, cooling the air. It wasn't enough to make the fur cape comfortable. That would come later when he climbed out of the valley.

With two spears in his hand and the shield on his back, other than a helmet, he was well armed for a spearman. For an archer, he lacked a bow and arrows, and the ability to reach out and touch someone at a distance.

The sun casts shadows on the slope. It gave the impression that the trees were thicker as the leaves and branches blended together with the shade. For good and bad, dusk and dark were still a long way off.

"Hunting at night is the most satisfying and challenging stalk," Zarek Mikolas instructed. "In the dark, your eyes demand a clear picture, and your mind obliges by filling in the missing parts. Shadows become wolves, branches the hand of a witch, and your prey, when you look directly at it, is a wavy shape of drifting shadows."

"Then how can we hunt at night?" young Jace asked.

"Your mastery of the bow is the first step," the Archer answered. "After hundreds of arrows, your muscles remember how to put the arrowhead on the target. Now the trick to night hunting is to never look directly at your target. Keep shifting your eyes, sweeping the prey with your vision while picturing it solidifying in your mind."

Jace needed the sunlight to find the trail of the raiders. After that, excitement from a successful raid on an enemy, and loud boasting by the spearmen, would guide him to the Lepontic warriors, even in the dark.

***

High on the first hill, Jace located a branching path off the main trail. Based on the hard ground and landscaping, the trail had once been the route for hauling logs from the mountain. The piles driven into the mud at the lake, the platforms on top of the stilts, and the homes built on the raised surface told of the need for planks, beams, and poles to build the village. Just off the trail, he located broken brushes and trampled weeds.

Jace stooped and used his hands to examine two depressions. A pair of people sitting in the weeds with a view of the main trail had waited there for a period. After climbing higher, he found signs of the rest of the party.

He assumed the two warriors, on the lower slope, were on lookout duty. They had not reclined but remained upright. At the main body of the raiders, he found marks from another pair of sitters. Whether too on edge to relax or also on lookout, he couldn't tell. Next to them, three impressions in the weeds showed figures lying down. Perhaps experienced fighters, conserving their energy before the raid, or possibly older men exhausted from the trek over the mountain and in need of a pre-attack nap. Other than numbers, he had too many variables to define the individual warriors.

Footprints cutting through the old spot showed no sign they stopped on the way back from the raid. Loaded down with two women hostages and sacks of grain, vegetables, and meat, Jace knew one thing for certain. They hadn't rested since leaving the village and they would need to soon. He could use that to his advantage.

As obvious as a Roman road, the logging route cut a swath between trees. Wrapping and coiling up the mountain, the trail presented a unique challenge for a tracker. Following the quarry on the well-marked path required little skill. The test came from not being ambushed, killed or injured by the trail watchers when they knew the direction of anyone pursuing them.

"An easy way to die is to be where the enemy expects you to be," Zarek Mikolas had coached. "Don't be there."

Heeding the advice of the Master Archer, Jace Kasia left the trail and climbed into the forest. High above the logging road, he jogged through the forest, catching stretches of the trail as he moved.

***

The pair were trail watchers and well trained. Both sat concealed behind bushes with their heads down, peering through branches at the lower path. One was armed with a spear and shield and the other had gifts for the Cretan Archer. A hunting bow and a quiver of arrows rested beside the tribesman. From their positions, the Lepontic watchers would see any tracker long before he knew of the danger. Whether the trail watchers would attack or run and warn the rest of the raiders was anyone's guess.

Jace didn't have enough daylight left for guesswork. Jumping from the forest, he landed on the trail behind them. With total focus on the lower trail below, neither tribesman registered the danger approaching rapidly from their rear.

***

"A group can only travel as fast as their slowest member," Zarek Mikolas mentioned. *A young Jace Kasia and Zarek watched a herd of Cretan Ibex scale a rock formation. While the leader reached the peak first, the other bucks and the does hung back to be sure the kids made the climb.* "An unruly herd, like the mountain goats, will leave wounded behind at the first sign of danger. But a tribe or a family will stay with the wounded even to the detriment of the group."

"I don't understand," *Jace admitted.*

"You will in a few years," *Zarek assured him.*

***

The memory of that day flashed through Jace's mind. A half step from the trail watchers, he flipped the spear around. Rather than using the steel tip on the man's neck, he pounded the side of the guy's head with the butt end. Then he jumped on the back of the second tribesman. With his arms tight on the sides of the man's neck, Jace applied pressure until the watcher passed out. Throwing him aside, the Cretan Archer rolled to the dazed man and choked him out as well.

"Now I understand, Master Mikolas," he whispered while cutting the clothing, leg wraps, and sandals off the tribesman.

Once they were naked, he drove the blade of the hunting knife through the calf of one leg and administered the same treatment to the second tribesman. Leaving the injured and bleeding men on the trail, he took their coats, clothing, supplies, and weapons before trotting back into the forest.

***

Five warriors lounged beside the trail. Two held ropes attached to the wrists of the hostages. Not being familiar with the women, Jace didn't know which one was the daughter of the villager and which one was Sucaria's cousin, Brigid. They both looked cold and miserable. Especially the one with dark brown hair. She seemed to be suffering more than the other woman. He wished he had a description. Was his target the one with the dark brown hair or the light brown with black streaks? He either chose or he needed to change the plan.

From the trees above the raiding party, the archer eased the tension off the bowstring and placed the arrow back in the quiver.

"Change of plan," he uttered as the two naked and bleeding trail watchers staggered into view. Weak from loss of blood and limping painfully, they would slow down the raiders, giving Jace a chance to form a new plan.

***

After bandaging the cuts and redistributing clothing to give the wounded a little protection from the chill, the seven tribesmen and their hostages started forward, slowly.

"The Lepontic tribesmen will stay with the wounded even to the detriment of the group," Jace whispered as he strolled ahead of the raiders.

Below, the seven strung out as they tried to keep the injured men in the center of the group and their weapons ready for an assailant. Jace studied the women. Before, if he could isolate Brigid, he could have killed the man holding the rope and freed her. But now the hostages were spread farther apart.

Jace jogged ahead, found a rock outcrop, and climbed on top. Once sure he had a view far ahead of the raiders, he rolled over on his back, drew the fur cape closed, and went to sleep.

***

Darkness didn't creep into the mountain forest. It dropped as if a door had closed on the day. Jace opened his eyes after a refreshing nap and looked at the stars through the tree limbs. In a few months, leaves would form a roof.

But in late winter, the ceiling twinkled with stars and a bright three-quarter moon cast more than enough light.

While squatting on the rock, the archer chewed the dried meat he took from the watchers. A quick scan and his eyes located a campfire. The Lepontic tribesmen had traveled farther than he thought possible. It would, however, be as far as they got from the village of Bruschera with the hostages.

Stalking through the forest, the Archer dropped a spear and the shield at a fallback position. Continuing with the bow and quiver of arrows, he crept to the edge of the forest. Over a line of bushes, the seven tribesmen sat around the fire. Behind them, the women, while in the flickering light, were far from the warmth.

Two of the raiders held their lower legs, moaned, and questioned what black fate brought them to this side of the mountain. They were already weak from blood loss, and out of the fight. The rest of the Lepontic tribesmen were about to reconsider their life choices.

Zip-Thwack!

Number three rolled off the log and into the dark. The arrow's shaft, coming from higher up, angled back with the tilt of his head, making it almost impossible to separate the feathers from the tall weeds beside the trail.

"Quit playing around," the fourth tribesman scolded. He reached for his companion.

Zip-Thwack!

The arrowhead entered the man's back low on his shoulder. And while Jace would rather have a war bow, he was pleased to see the shaft penetrate the scapula bone, break a rib, and as the man spun from the impact, the arrowhead protrude from the side of his chest.

The fifth raider jumped up, with his spear leveled beside his shield.

"We're under attack," bellowed. He had one problem with his stance.

Zip-Thwack!

He faced down the trail. The arrow came from uphill on the side. Before he fell, the shaft entered his neck at the left carotid artery, releasing a gush of blood that continued pumping as the arrowhead cut his trachea. He dropped the shield and spear. Next, he attempted to simultaneously clear his air passage and stem the bleeding. He failed at both.

Frantically, the sixth and seventh tribesmen tried to untie the ropes while dragging the hostages.

Zip-Thwack!

Zip-Thwack!

An arrow in the hip typically shattered the pelvis bone. Positioned a little low and to the outside, a well-placed arrow would break the ball joint of the leg.

The ropes and hostages forgotten, both tribesmen curled up while holding their legs, trying to put them back in the hip socket.

"Take the women," one tribesman screamed into the night. "Take the women and spare us."

Other than the hostages softly crying, the night grew quiet.

***

A man dressed in a great fur cape, holding a shield and spear, kicked through the bushes. In the firelight, he appeared to be a terrible specter. Considering the damage and death he visited on the raiders, he was a demon.

"Which one of you is Brigid?" the man asked.

"I am," the one with the black streaks in her light brown hair replied. "Did my father send you?"

"No, I was hired by your cousin," Jace answered. He drew the hunting knife and cut the rope. Then instructed. "Let's go."

"Which cousin and why not my father?" she demanded.

"I don't know your father," Jace admitted. "I only know Sucaria."

"Who is Sucaria?"

"I told you, she's your cousin," Jace insisted. "Let's go.

"I don't know her," Brigid started to explain before asking. "What about Sonna?"

"Who is Sonna?" Jace questioned.

"Her, over there," Brigid pointed to the other woman. Sonna was pulling on the rope. She would have run off into the night, but the rope held her anchored to the crying man. "The village headman's daughter. Sonna. Weren't you sent after her as well."

"Sucaria didn't say anything about her," Jace stated.

"Who is Sucaria?"

"Your cousin," Jace said.

"I don't have a cousin named Sucaria," Brigid protested.

"You do," Jace assured her.

Brigid walked to Sonna and wrapped her arms around the woman to calm her down.

"It's all right. Hush, now, you're safe. We're going home." Then, with a glance at Jace, Brigid asked. "We are going home, aren't we?"

"It's what Sucaria wants."

"Who is Sucaria?"

"Your cousin," Jace stated.

"You are the most infuriating man I've ever met," Brigid snapped. "Fine. Escort us to Bruschera."

When the big man in the fur robe came at her, Brigid put her body between Sonna and the hunting knife. She bravely stood her ground.

"Excuse me," Jace advised, as he moved her aside with one arm. He cut Sonna free and directed. "Go downhill fifty paces and wait. I'll catch up."

Both women were shivering with cold and shock. Brigid, with her arms around Sonna, led them away.

"Fifty paces," Jace reminded them. He looked around the camp and said. "Now to dispose of the witnesses."

Once they were out of the firelight, the Cretan Archer said, "Goddess Artemis. It was a good hunt. Accept these brave men as sacrifices."

Then, one by one, he used the hunting knife to end the pain of the three suffering tribesmen. He kicked dirt on the fire and followed the two watchers, who were limping away as fast as they could go. After disposing of them, Jace went into the forest. At the rock, he collected the robes he took earlier before heading for the trail to meet Brigid and Sonna.

***

Fifty paces from the slaughter, Jace's sense of direction brought him from the woods to the trail. But neither Brigid nor Sonna were waiting.

"Brigid," he shouted. Knowing they were afraid and cold, he yelled. "Brigid, where are you, woman?"

Far down the hill, Sonna let out a yup sounding much like a frightened puppy.

"I said fifty paces," Jace said in exasperation as he strolled down the trail. "Fifty."

In the moonlight, he noted the pair locked together and tripping. First one, then the other, would pull them both to the ground. Scrambling back to their feet, they hurried a bit father before going down again.

"Brigid," Jace called, "wait."

He was close enough to see both turn to look at him. One more step and they fell over a bush and down a slope.

"Where are you going?" Jace inquired. "Rushing in the dark is dangerous."

"As dangerous as you?" Brigid demanded from the ground.

"Much more. On this trail you could break a leg," Jace warned.

"But you are removing witnesses and offering them to your evil Goddess," she protested.

"You watched me remove the witnesses?"

"And listened to you pray," Brigid accused him. "You sacrificed those men to her."

"Actually, I did it to appease the spirit of Zarek Mikolas," Jace said. He reached down and lifted Sonna to her feet before wrapping a warm coat around her.

"Is he another of your evil masters?" Brigid snarled.

"Funny you should say that," Jace told her. "It is what I thought of him for years."

He reached down and pulled Brigid to her feet before placing a heavy robe over her shoulders.

"You're not going to sacrifice us or silence us?" she asked.

"And suffer the wrath of Sucaria?" Jace responded. "Not on your life. Oh, sorry, wrong choice of words."

"I have a slight problem," Brigid reported.

"And that is?"

"I've twisted my ankle and can't walk," she admitted.

Jace scooped her up in his arms and instructed, "Sonna, grab my robe and stay close to me."

The daughter of the village headman did more than grab a handful of fur. She slipped inside the robe and hugged both Jace and Brigid.

Locked together under the big cape and moving slowly, it would be dawn before they saw the village of Bruschera and Lake Maggiore.

"Tell me again," Brigid questioned. "Who is Sucaria?"

"She is your cousin," Jace answered.

"Whatever," Brigid commented before snuggling against his chest. "I don't mind competition."

Act 5

Chapter 13 – Eagle Eggs

Urus jogged up the logging road with fifteen spearmen close behind. Sweat dripped from their brows and they breathed hard after the run from the village. Around a bend thick with bushes, the chief's bodyguard halted suddenly. Two warriors bumped into the idle figure before realizing he'd stopped.

"Good morning," Jace greeted the spearmen.

From inside the big fur cape, Brigid and Sonna peered out at the rescue party.

As if he'd encountered a three-headed monster, Urus suffered four reactions simultaneously.

Initial fear of coming across a large furry beast triggered the lowering of his spear. The action countered the surprise of finding Brigid and Sonna safe while realizing the rush of gathering a rescue patrol and a sleepless night had been for naught. In the swirl of emotions, the pair that crashed into his back sent Urus into battle mode. He thrusted with the spear.

At the powerful stab, Brigid cried out, Sonna screamed, and both spearmen who bumped into Urus froze in panic.

Inside the thick robe, Jace twisted, carrying Brigid away from the spearhead. As he moved the daughter of Clan Chief Kentus, the Archer grabbed Sonna's arm and dragged the villager's daughter away from the path of the tip. Although no one was injured, the large spearhead ripped a hole in the great fur cape.

"A shield against the elements and against the teeth and claws of predators," Jace remarked, remembering M'anta's description of the fur cape. He added. "And it appears spearheads as well."

No one heard Jace as Brigid kicked free of the Archer's arms and dropped to the ground.

"Urus, what are you doing?" she challenged while standing on one leg. "Are you mad?"

"No, I got confused," he replied. "All I saw was the fur and thought he was a bear."

"With three heads?" she demanded.

"Yes," Urus admitted.

Sonna's father pushed to the front of the rescue party and ran to hug his daughter.

"Are you injured?" he asked.

"No father," Sonna told him. "But Brigid twisted her ankle."

"Bring up the cart," the village headman shouted.

From behind the rescuers, Scanlan Saltare pulled a two-wheeled cart around bushes while weaving between spearmen. He stopped beside Urus. Seeing everyone standing and Urus' spear in the fur cape, he expected the

Lepontic raiders had lightened their load by dropping food and releasing the women. "Where are the grain sacks?"

"Up on the mountain," Brigid responded. She started to hop away from the Archer while explaining. "Along with the bodies…"

Jace yanked her back, which interrupted her description.

"Up on the mountain," he informed the rower turned porter, "where the raiders dropped the sacks before running away. By now animals will have gotten into the grain and meat."

"They didn't run away…" Sonna began when Jace reached out and placed his palm on her forehead.

"You're feverous," he told Sonna, "perhaps you should ride down with Brigid."

"I don't feel ill," she protested.

"You've been through a nightmare experience," Jace suggested. "And in the dark, our eyes can play tricks on us."

"But I saw you."

Brigid hopped to her and begged, "Sonna, please help me to the cart, my ankle is really hurting."

Forgetting her insistence that Jace killed the raiding party, she placed her arm around Brigid's waist and took the injured woman to the cart.

"If you don't mind, Urus," Jace requested, "can you remove your spear from my cape?"

"I thought you were a bear," the bodyguard protested while withdrawing the spear. Turning to his tribesmen, he announced. "Everyone go back to Bruschera. The Lepontic warriors have gone home. And I'm not about to march into their territory for retribution and get us killed."

"Good decision," a tribesman offered.

At the cart, Sonna whispered, "but he killed the Lepontic raiders. They didn't go home."

"I know," Brigid reassured her. "But he seems to want to keep it a secret."

"In that case, I'll never speak of it again," Sonna stated.

Scanlan Saltare listened to the women talk, then looked at the man in the fur cape. How could one fighter defeat seven warriors? As he pulled the cart around to face downhill, the teen decided he needed to learn more about a hero who wanted to avoid fame and notoriety.

***

Sucaria sat on the raised platform and watched the mountain and then the trail heading into the village. Although Scanlan had told her they would be gone for days, the little girl remained fixated on the empty path and the lush mountain side. A bowl of stew sat on the planks beside her, the broth growing cold and the fat congealing on top.

"You should eat, child," a village matron told her.

"It'll settle my stomach, I know," Sucaria replied. "But my cousin and my Dog are up there."

"I don't remember seeing a dog," the lady commented. "I guess you'll eat when you get hungry enough."

She went into the cottage and Sucaria continued her vigilance.

Not long after the conversation, the little girl shrieked. At the high-pitched scream, the matron rushed from the cottage to find the child standing and holding a post. Bent forward, the little girl peered under the handrail at the trail.

As if a procession at a festival, the rescue party followed the cart. In the cart appeared to be two bodies resting against each other.

"Don't look child," the village matron told Sucaria, thinking to spare the little girl.

"Oh, I've seen dead bodies. A lot of them," Sucaria remarked. "But they aren't dead."

"How can you tell? The women in the cart aren't moving."

"Because the Archer went up yesterday. And Scanlan is coming back this morning," Sucaria explained. "Jace wouldn't have let my cousin die."

"Child, people make promises. As you get older, you'll experience disappointment and understand life isn't fair. And people don't always do what they promise."

"I know," Sucaria informed the matron. "My mother said that before she died. And my Aunt M'anta before she was killed. But what Jace promises, he does."

As if her words reached the cart, both Sonna and Brigid separated from their private conversation and sat upright.

"Not dead," Sucaria confirmed. Villagers poured down the ramp and ran to greet the former hostages. The little girl remained stooped as she scanned the returning spearmen. Over and over, she asked, "where are you Jace Kasia? Where are you?"

When the big fur cape came into view, Sucaria ran down the ramp.

"Who is that?" Sonna asked.

"I've never seen the child before," Brigid confessed. "Her parents must be from the north shore. Maybe a relative of Scanlan."

With her little legs churning, she raced by Scanlan Saltare, the cart, Urus, and the spearmen. She ran to the archer.

"Oh Jace, I'm so very glad to see you."

Jace picked her up and balanced the little girl on one of his shoulders. Then, strutting forward, he passed the spearmen and Urus. At the cart, Sonna climbed out and received welcome home hugs from the villagers. The Archer shoved between the crowd to reach the cart.

"Brigid, Daughter of Kentus, I'd like you to meet Lady Sucaria," Jace introduced them. "This is your cousin."

"Give her to me," Brigid instructed while holding out her arms. When the child was sitting on her lap, Brigid directed. "Scanlan, take us home."

Scanlan started forward, pulling the cart towards the shoreline and the waiting boats. As the cart rolled, Brigid encouraged Sucaria. "Tell me about this archer, Kasia."

Sucaria put her head close to Brigid and whispered, "I will, but don't ever call him Dog."

***

Three weeks later, Jace finished repairs on a section of roof connecting a cabin with an attached shed. As a reward for rescuing the clan chief's daughter, Kentus presented Jace with a rundown structure on a piece of craggy land. From the roof, high on the western slope, the Archer had a view of the lake. Pausing in his task, he studied the light reflecting off the lake. Far out on the water, he saw a boat rowing across Lake Maggiore and wondered if it was Scanlan Saltare.

"Jace Kasia," Sucaria said from below, "are you home? We have a gift for you."

"It's not much of a home," he called down as he slipped off the roof.

Walking around to the front of the structure, he found the little girl and Brigid. The chief's daughter held his fur cape draped over her arms.

"We mended the hole," Sucaria announced.

"I appreciate that," Jace acknowledged. Taking the cape, he examined it, looking for the stitches. Even when he noticed them, he continued searching. "Are you sure this is the right cape?"

Sucaria pouted and ruffled the fur until she located the line of fine stitching.

"Right here," she told him. "Brigid showed me how to make tight knots."

"This is a wonderful gift," Jace told her.

"That isn't the gift," Sucaria stated. "Brigid has your gift."

With a smile, Jace faced the woman and raised an eyebrow.

"Add another two rooms to your house and you'll have a cottage," she said with a wink. After pulling a leather bundle from a pouch, Brigid informed him. "I'm told by craftsmen that these are helpful in bow making."

Jace unrolled the bundle and found a pair of chisels, a set of files, and a hand sized plate of steel.

"They are exactly what I need," he gushed. "How did you know?"

"Sucaria told me you have an aged maple log that you brought all the way across Insubri territory," she answered. "You told her there were at least six limbs and three risers inside the wood. She didn't understand and neither did I. But when I told the bow maker in Sesto Calende, he asked if you made war bows."

"I told him, you were a Cretan Archer," Sucaria inserted, "and you missed your war bow on the journey."

"And what did the bow maker say?" Jace inquired.

"He said he would buy every quality war bow you could make," Brigid replied.

"I guess, I'm in business," Jace commented. "Will you stay for dinner?"

"We can't," Brigid responded by taking Sucaria's hand. "My father has village headmen coming for a feast."

"And we are needed to serve the meal," Sucaria added.

The woman and the little girl walked away. Jace watched them until the path turned and they vanished between trees. After looking at the tools, he headed for the shed to begin carving wood to create a war bow.

***

Later, as the sun dipped low in the sky, a whisper of footsteps reached Jace. So soft was the sound, he almost missed it under the scrape of the metal plate on the block of maple wood.

After grabbing a spear, he challenged, "You can continue to play snail or you can show yourself."

With a sheepish look on his face, Scanlan Saltare stepped into the shed.

"How did you know?" he asked.

"You're good at stepping softly," Jace answered. "But you walk with a rhythm. I separated you from the sounds outside by the uniformity of your steps."

Scanlan stared at his feet.

"No one has ever said that," he confessed. "Mostly they're amazed by how I managed to sneak up on them."

"You do that a lot, do you?"

"Ever since I was a little boy," Scanlan told him. "I move like a shadow at night. Soft and unseen."

"Except for me?" Jace inquired.

"You and the headman of my village," Scanlan confessed. "He caught me stealing and sent me away. I came to Arona to become a warrior."

"Instead, you're a rower and a porter."

"Not by choice," Scanlan told him. "Urus won't train me. He said once a thief, always a thief."

"There is truth in that," Jace explained. "When you have a singular skill, in hard times, you fall back on your natural talent for survival."

"I don't steal because I like it," Scanlan protested. "It's the only way I can, oh, I see what you mean. Survive."

"Why are you here?" Jace asked.

"You defeated seven warriors and rescued two hostages," the boy stated. "I want to know how you did it?"

"First, you're wrong."

"No, I'm not," Scanlan snapped. "I heard Brigid and Sonna talking about how you killed all seven."

Jace returned to the block of maple and began to scrape on a limb.

"Say something," Scanlan demanded. "Talk to me."

Resting the edge of the steel plate on the wood, he looked at Scanlan.

"If you steal from me, I will skin you alive. Then leave your body so far up the mountain, that eagles will pluck out your eyes and feed them to their young."

"I'm a great thief, but I don't know how to fight," Scanlan admitted. "Teach me to fight."

Jace walked to a brick hearth and lit a fire against the coming chill of the night.

"Bring me two undamaged eagle eggs," he offered. "If they hatch, I'll train you in the art of war. If the eggs are broken, or cold and dead, I don't ever want to see you again."

"Eagles build their nests on high rocky outcrops or in tall trees above peaks," Scanlan protested. "How am I supposed to get eagle eggs?"

"You claim to be a natural thief," Jace pointed out, "go steal from an eagle."

"And then you'll teach me how to defeat seven men, like you did?" Scanlan asked.

"I tried to tell you, I did not defeat seven men," Jace explained. "I defeated one warrior and did it seven times. Now, go and die on the mountain."

Scanlan left and Jace returned to shaping the limb for a bow. Under his hands, a flat piece of maple began to taper from one end to a narrow blunt point on the other. He would steam it over a pot of water later and clamp it between two pieces of oak to create a curve. While holding up the rough limb to examine the grain, footsteps approached his shed.

"A busy evening," Jace called to the night. "This isn't an inn nor it is a waystation for weary travelers."

"I am neither of those," Brigid told him as she stepped out of the dark and into the shed. "But a simple country girl with a wineskin, slices of meat, and loaves of bread for a hero."

"You should go back to your father's house," Jace suggested. "There's no hero here. Here is but an indecisive bow maker."

"I beg to differ," Brigid countered. She walked to the workbench and placed a cloth over the wood shavings. "Fresh wood smells lovely."

"I'm leaving when the weather gets warmer," he warned her. "I was a nobleman in Rome."

"And did you like being a nobleman in Rome," she inquired. She handed him the wineskin and set a plate on the cloth. "A nobleman? What's that compared to a man with land and a view of the lake. A craftsman with a tool in his hand, and wood taking form on his workbench. Or a man with a pretty girl at his beck and call. How does that balance against wearing a toga and dwelling in a crowded city."

Jace looked at the food, at Brigid's face, and at the black streak in her light brown hair.

"A pretty girl?" he asked.

"I was talking about Sucaria," Brigid answered.

Jace Kasia reached out and pulled her into his arms.

"I wasn't talking about the little girl," he whispered in her ear. "I was talking about you."

Chapter 14 – A Season of War

By the month of Mars, the flooding of the Tiber had receded, farmers plowed fields preparing them for planting, and the Senate of Rome elected the leaders of the Republic for the coming year. To celebrate the event, citizens gathered for the recognition of the Consuls and for refreshments.

"Lo, Lucius Lentulus, congratulations on your ascension to the Consulship," a Centurion greeted Lucius.

Around them, the citizens of Rome enjoyed the feast provided by the new Consuls. Bakers passed out loaves of free bread and merchants provided endless vino from casks.

Spying the medals on the combat officer's chest, Consul Lentulus inquired, "Where did you serve?"

"I was with Scipio in Africa, sir, and in Iberia before that," the Centurion replied.

Lentulus assured him. "know that Consul Tappulus and I are lobbying the Senate on behalf of the veterans of the great war with Carthage. If we have our way, land grants will be awarded to the heroes of the Republic."

"That would be much appreciated, sir," the combat officer acknowledged. Softly, he described the reason. "Many of us have been away from our farms fighting for the Republic for so long, we lost our legacy to debt."

"Which is not right." Lentulus sympathized with him before offering a salute.

As the politician migrated to a group of supporters, an Optio stepped up beside the combat officer.

"What did he say, Centurion?"

"He's making all the right promises," the combat officer told the Sergeant. "Let's hope the new Consuls can get it passed in the Senate."

***

Across the Forum and on the far side of the crowd, workmen dismantled a set of stands. To remove a brace from the temporary seating, one laborer pounded on a stuck rod with a mallet. The sharp noises drove the crowd back from the work area.

Among the people fleeing the loud hammering, Consul Villius Tappulus flowed with the crowd. He got jostled about by the crowd before a Tribune blocked his path.

"Consul Tappulus, the law must change," Porcius Laeca insisted.

"For a year now, you've pestered the Senate with your novel theories on the law," Tappulus responded. "Give me one good reason why Consul Lentulus and I should consider your proposal to change the laws of the twelve tablets."

"Carthage," Tribune Laeca replied without hesitation.

"At the question, you typically deliver a lecture," Consul Tappulus noted. "So I'll bite. What does Carthage have to do with the laws of the twelve tablets?"

"The peoples of Africa and the tribes of Iberia are now citizens of provinces under the command of Rome," Laeca explained. "Add in a few tribes from the Po River Valley and the Greeks on the east coast, and we have a dilution of what it means to be a citizen of Rome."

"A dilution?" Tappulus questioned. "What do you mean by dilution?"

"Years ago, when the Republic threw off the king, the twelve tablets covered every citizen," Tribune Laeca answered. "But now we have citizens of provinces who enjoy the protection of the law. As it stands, a citizen of Rome has no more rights than a non-citizen."

"And you believe this is a disservice to the citizens of Rome?"

"S.P.Q.R." Laeca emphasized each letter. "It's the Senate and people of Rome, sir, not the Senate and barbarians of the Republic."

"If you can convince a senior Senator to champion your cause, I'll present it to the Senate," Tappulus agreed. "Now if you'll excuse me, I paid for half this festival and I'd like to enjoy it."

Victorious in his argument, Tribune Laeca granted, "Thank you, sir. And congratulations on your Consulship."

Villius Tappulus accepted a mug of vino from a supporter and walked away from the legal activist. The new Consul had no idea of the consequences of his decision to pursue changes to the law.

***

The celebration of Lucius Lentulus and Villius Tappulus to the Consulships of Rome delighted half the Senate. Another section held no strong opinions on either man, while a final third seethed at the elections. In another part of the forum, Senator Valerius Flaccus and Senator

Marcus Cato scowled into their mugs of wine as if the beverage represented the new Consuls.

"When I was a young man, all of our vino came from Latin vineyards," Flaccus complained. "This swill tastes of Iberian dirt."

"They are importing more and more vino from Sicily, Greece, Iberia," Cato confirmed. "And do I detect a hint of common sweat in the vino."

Flaccus chuckled at the reference to Villius Tappulus being a plebeian.

"Common sweat from a common man," Senator Flaccus repeated. "You are a clever fellow, Marcus Cato."

"If I was clever, I would have found a way to keep Cornelius Scipio from earning more glory and fame," Cato admitted. "But with the census concluded, he's free to seek a Proconsul position and the Consuls are apt to grant his wish."

"I noticed you didn't use his honorific, Africanus," Flaccus pointed out. "Do you seek to disparage the great general?"

"I see Senator Flaccus, you are employing your own brand of humor," Cato allowed. "And just as you stated, I am indeed disparaging Scipio."

Hardening his tone and bringing the conversation to a more serious point, Flaccus questioned. "How do we keep him off the battlefields of Greece and Macedonia?"

The crowd roared, drowning out Cato's answer. On the road to the Forum, the hero of Carthage arrived in his wife's gilded carriage.

"Oh look, General Scipio is here to bless the Consuls," Flaccus sneered.

"Are you sure it's not the other way around?" Cato inquired.

"You mean, a coronation of King Scipio by the Consuls," Flaccus uttered.

***

As if to confirm Senator Flaccus' fear, both Consuls worked their way through the crowd to greet the conqueror of Carthage. Inside the carriage, Cornelius peeked between the curtains and frowned.

"I need to be with a Legion," he conceded. "The crowds are growing tiresome."

"I concur, sir," Sidia Decimia agreed.

"Optio Decimia, in a Legion camp you barely rest, have to guard me from barbarians day and night, and all the while, you're tending to the movement of my gear," Cornelius listed. "You can't tell me you prefer that to being in Rome."

"All I need to do in war, sir, is guard you from barbarians," Sidia replied. "Here in the city, I can't tell which arm is reaching to embrace you and which arm is reaching to stab you in the back."

"That's a little harsh," Cornelius stated as he reached for the door to the carriage. He opened it a little and looked out. Seeing Valerius Flaccus and Marcus Cato in the distance and the crowd, he glanced back at his bodyguard. "Maybe not so harsh. Ready?"

"Yes, sir," Sidia replied.

In a well-coordinated exit, Corneluis Scipio Africanus stepped on the doorsill of the carriage and extended his body in full view of the mob. They erupted in cheers and Cornelius waved to acknowledge their adulation. After a pause, he jumped to the ground. The crowd surged forward. To the rear of the hero of Carthage, Sidia Decimia hopped down, filling the space behind Cornelius and preventing the well-wishers from surrounding the General.

A moment later, the new Consuls arrived and thanked Cornelius for coming to their celebration. Cornelius' response was gracious and humble.

He didn't mention that his attendance had more to do with an alternate motive than to celebrate the elections. He wanted to command Legions. And Cornelius would show up at any event to further his cause. From the Consuls festivities, to a boring feast with a Senator or a death match between barbarians, he attended any event where he could plead the case for Scipio Africanus to get a command.

***

Two days later, President of the Senate Caecina pounded on the dais to get the attention of the Senators.

"Gentlemen, if you'll come to order, we can proceed with the business of our citizens," Caecina exclaimed. When the chamber settled, he indicated Lucius Lentulus and Villius Tappulus. "We are honored to have both Consuls in attendance today. Soon Consul Villius Tappulus will leave to take command of the Legions opposing Phillip of Macedonia. We can't allow the Macedonian to upset the power balance in Greece."

"Mister President," Cornelius Scipio requested, "in light of the assignment of Consul Tappulus to Greece, I would like to bring up an issue."

"The chamber recognizes Senator Scipio Africanus."

Applause greeted Cornelius when he stood. While the acknowledgement came from most of the Senate, one sector was decidedly quiet and motionless.

"Thank you," Cornelius said before proposing. "We have an outstanding insult and injury to Rome that must be addressed."

Titus Crispinus bent forward and spoke to Valerius Flaccus and Marcus Cato.

"He should have gone into commerce," Senator Crispinus hissed. "His persistence is admirable."

"If only he was but a merchant and not a glory hungry wolf," Flaccus commented.

"Actually, he's too good at persuasion," Cato added. "We must find a way to stop him."

Cornelius didn't hear the remarks, but he could see the three leaders of the opposition huddled together. He ignored them and continued, "Last year the tribes along the Po River participated in open rebellion. They burned a Latin city and besieged another. If not for the quick actions of Senator Aurelius Cotta and the bravery of Praetor Purpureo, the flames of discontent would have grown from a brush fire to a costly blaze across the Republic."

"We all know the history. It was just last summer," Flaccus spoke up. "Can Senator Scipio get to the point?"

His failure to call Cornelius, Scipio Africanus, wasn't lost on the rest of the Senate.

"I appreciate the encouragement for brevity," Cornelius responded, ignoring the open insult and the challenge for a floor fight. His desire for a command overshadowed his personal feelings. Getting to the heart of the matter, he said, "most of the tribes were punished at Cremona by our Legions. Most that is except for one, the Insubri. They were, according to reports, instrumental in promoting Hamilcar the Carthaginian. Yet, they avoided the punishment of the wicked by leaving with their spoils before the battle. The insult to Rome cannot go unpunished."

"What would you have us do?" President Caecina inquired.

The bit of theater didn't fool anyone. It was obvious Scipio Africanus and Caecina had planned the question.

"With Consul Tappulus off to Greece and Consul Lentulus' presence required in Rome," Cornelius answered, "we need Legions to march on the Insubri and remind the tribe that Rome does not suffer rebellion quietly nor peacefully."

"And who would lead this expedition to punish the Insubri?" Caecina asked.

"To assure success, the operation demands an experienced General. One with a record of victories and the ability and the resources to raise and train Legions," Cornelius announced. He lifted his voice at the conclusion of the speech. "I submit my name, Cornelius Scipio Africanus, to lead the Insubri operation."

In the chorus of voices that followed, President Caecina rapped for order before asking, "all in favor of elevating Scipio Africanus to Proconsul and assigning him to Insubri, signify your acceptance."

As the assistants began counting votes, Titus Crispinus leaped to his feet, thrusts his arms into the air, and bellowed, "Hold. I say hold this premature nonsense."

"The chamber recognizes Senator Crispinus," Caecina proclaimed.

"I have watched this blind race to a decision and I feel we have an incomplete field of chariots in the Forum," he told the chamber. "Why vote now when we are so far from the season of war? Many men would embrace the chance for honor and only one has stepped forward. Let us wait and gather a full field of charioteers before allowing this race to continue. We have months before any action can transpire and there are more pressing matters."

"Like what?" a young Senator questioned.

Titus Crispinus lowered his eyes while trying to think of a substitute for granting Scipio an opportunity for more glory and riches. His eyes fell on Senator Sextus Paetus and the staff officer beside him.

"Tribune Porcius Laeca's proposal to change the law," Crispinus announced, plucking the topic from the ether. "His changes would grant citizens of Rome more protection under the law. It's a more pressing matter than the punishment of a tribe in the Po River Valley."

"That makes sense," another Senator declared.

Feeling the emotions of the chamber shift, President Caecina stated, "We will put off the selection of a Proconsul and open a discussion on a change to the laws of the twelve tablets."

Still on his feet, Cornelius also felt the mood shift. And although angry, he sat.

"I call on Porcius Laeca to explain his new laws," Crispinus asserted. "Go forward Tribune and present your case for the protection of the citizens of Rome."

Laeca marched down the steps and saluted the President of the Senate and the Consuls. Next, he faced the chamber and saluted the Senators.

"All of you have heard my plea for revisions to the tablets," he told them. "One thing became clear from the discussions. You don't vote on theories in this legislative body. And so taking heed of your counsel, I ask permission to present two clear changes to the laws of the twelve tablets."

He looked to Caecina and received a wave of the President's hand to proceed.

"To separate Roman citizens from other peoples, I propose we allow citizens to request a review of any sentence or fine imposed by a magistrate," Laeca said, naming one change.

"Who would contradict another magistrate?" a Senator asked.

"A review won't always be successful for the guilty party," Laeca confessed. "But it would put a second pair of eyes on the case with the authority to reduce, suspend, or even double the sentence. The key, gentlemen, is the second magistrate would have the power of Rome behind his review."

"What of capital crimes?" Cornelius blurted out. His intention of remaining mute and holding his temper failed during what he considered a frivolous discussion. He hoped to end the debate by offering an extreme case.

"What is worse than death?" Tribune Laeca asked. "What is worse than death to a citizen of Rome? The answer, Senators, is simple. The loss of Rome, along with the seizure of his property, is worse than death to a citizen."

"You're seeking to undermine the authority of the Senate," Cornelius complained. His intent had changed from silence to being a vocal defender of the Senate. The posture might gain him a few votes later. "You're talking about voluntary exile instead of an execution. Banishment or crucifixion has always been a power in the hands of the Senate."

"I understand your hesitation, Senator Africanus, but we aren't taking anything away from this chamber," Laeca explained. "Rather we are giving each citizen of Rome the opportunity to invoke a right exclusive to a citizen of Rome. The appeal of a sentence is one change and the privilege to avoid death is the other."

Tribune Laeca saluted and went to his place beside Senator Paetus. As he walked the aisle, in an uncharacteristic move, Cornelius Scipio Africanus called out, "I vote no, on both."

A reaction to Scipio's vote brought Marcus Cato, Titus Crispinus, and Valerius Flaccus to full voice as proponents of the motions. With their backing, the Senate of Rome adopted the changes to the laws of Rome. In the future, a convicted citizen could request a review of the case by another magistrate. And a citizen convicted of a capital crime could demand exile with a forfeiture of his holdings in Rome as the only punishment.

Cornelius left the chamber in the afternoon. His plan to win Proconsul authority and gain command of a Legion crushed under the heels of a pair of new laws.

"I didn't win that engagement," he said to Sidia as they left the Senate Building. "I should have kept my mouth shut."

"Sir, you can't win any battles if you don't fight," the bodyguard countered.

"That's true, Optio. But it's painful to lose."

Unknown to Scipio Africanus, the Goddess Adrestia had watched over the proceedings. And as the Senate debated, the deity of equilibrium and balance placed her hands on the scales to position Cornelius. Unknown to him, he was right where the Goddess wanted him to be at the end of the day.

Chapter 15 – Possibly, A Wedding

Arona buzzed with energy. Trees filled out with leaves, grass even on the high slopes changed from brown to a lush green, and wildflowers filled the meadows. But all of nature's spring wonders paled in comparison to the attitude of the town's population.

"Mister Saltare, you'll be late," Sucaria warned. "The sun is coming up."

"I know," the youth agreed, not looking up from his chore. He continued to grind the mash of worms and insects with a grinder until the bottom of the bowl was coated with a fine smear. Using a pitcher of water, he added liquid a little at a time until the mash had the consistency of runny mud. Only then did Scanlan answer her. "I'm almost done. Just one final step. And I've told you, call me Scanlan."

At a cage, Scanlan Saltare lifted the lid and two baby eaglets began high pitched chirps as they bobbed up and down.

"They think you're their mother." Sucaria laughed.

Scanlan extended a scarred finger with multiple cuts and positioned it over one of the eaglets. Seeing the digit, the second eagle began biting the finger with its sharp beak. Ignoring the pain, Scanlan poured the runny feed down his finger and into the little eaglets mouth. After the first had its fill, he moved to the second. Refusing to be snubbed, the first eaglet began biting his finger as the second one fed.

"Jace said, ignoring pain while completing a delicate task is the mark of a great warrior," Scanlan quoted between grimaces of pain. "According to the eaglets, I may be one of the greatest warriors of all time."

"Or the best mother in all of Gaul," the little girl offered.

Scanlan closed the lid, set the bowl on top, tussled Sucaria hair, and picked her up. Next, he ran for a path down to the lake. On the way by the shed, he snatched a spear and a shield without breaking stride.

"Your legs can do one thing while your hands do another," Jace coached. "Like anything difficult, it just takes the knowledge to understand the possibility and lots of practice."

Armed, carrying the little girl, and at a full sprint, Scanlan raced downhill for the drill field and dawn practice. On this day of all days, he didn't expect training to be too rough. How could it? Today might be Jace and Brigid's wedding day.

***

Jace Kasia sat on a bench, carving a new upper limb for a war bow. Behind him, the surface of Lake Maggiore reflected the last vestiges of starlight. Dawn peeked over the crest of the mountain and shadows of spearmen gathered in front of the Archer.

"Jace, we're all here," one suggested. "Should we begin shield and spear drills?"

Scanlan raced up and stopped behind the group.

Acting as if he didn't notice the youth, Jace instructed, "stack your spears and shields."

"It's because you'll be welcoming a bride into your cottage this evening," proposed another tribesman. "Saving your energy for her brothers. Very wise."

Jace placed the knife and maple limb on the bench, stood, and picked up a nearby stick.

"I could drill you until you dropped to your knees from exhaustion," the Archer lectured while dragging the tip of the stick around. "You might get a little better with the shield and spear, but not good enough to face a Legion assault line."

"The Latians were lucky at Cremona," a tribesman told the group. "I spoke with a merchant from the Salassi Tribe. The Legions came at them before dawn and caught their war chiefs unprepared. If not for that, the tribes would have massacred the Latians."

"Unprepared is when a man hits you unexpectedly during negotiations," Jace offered. "Or when you're walking away and he clubs you from behind. Being asleep or drunk, and knowing lines of armored men with big red shields are coming for you is not unprepared. It's weakness."

"How do you figure their war chiefs are weak?" a big spearman questioned. "I've fought against the Boii and the Veneti. Neither are weak."

"Perhaps I misspoke," Jace stated. He completed drawing a circle in the dirt. "I should have said, they are stupid."

Most of the spearmen laughed. But the big warrior stomped forward.

"Are you calling the Gaul tribes ignorant?" he challenged. "Perhaps we're too rustic for a Cretan Archer who has seen the world outside these mountains."

"Katumaros, you must have missed breakfast, because you are irritable this morning," Jace commented. He walked to the center of the circle and addressed the group. "In a combat line, every man has an area of responsibility."

"I asked you a question," Katumaros growled. "Answer me."

"Step into the fighting circle and let's discuss it," Jace invited.

Katumaros kicked away the arc of the circle as he moved.

"I said…" he began when Jace dropped and grabbed the big man's ankles.

In a single pull, Jace up-ended Katumaros. As he toppled backwards, the Archer jumped to the man's head, gathered two fistfuls of hair, pulled the warrior to his feet, spun him around, and kicked him out of the circle. Before walking back to the center, the Archer redrew the smudged part of the arc with the side of his foot.

"In a combat line, every man has an area of responsibility," Jace began again.

As if a bull, the angry spearmen snorted and ran at Jace. Frozen in place as if paralyzed by the ferocity of Katumaros, the Archer waited.

The nine warriors of the Gnātos tribe assigned to Jace by Chief Kentus watched. To see Kasia bested in a fight would be a delight and it might get them out of the daily drills if the Archer was injured. It would be a shame to see it happen on his wedding day, but what could anyone do about it?

Fueled by rage, Katumaros charged into the fighting circle. With his back bent and his arms extended, seeking to get his hands on the Cretan Archer, the big spearman raced forward. Already tasting revenge for being manhandled and kicked, the spearmen lunged and grabbed. But Jace had vanished.

Then, from below, a foot impacted his massive chest and two hands locked onto his upper arms. Katumaros found himself somersaulting through the air. He landed hard on his back.

"That was sloppy of me," Jace complained before vaulting to his feet. Turning, he strolled to the other side of the circle and savagely kicked one of the big spearman's ankles. "I allowed one of his feet to remain in my circle. Can anyone tell me why?"

From behind the group, Scanlan responded, "because the circle is your area of responsibility. And once you've removed an enemy from the circle, you've done your job."

"Be silent boy," one of the spearman scolded Scanlan.

"Yet, the youth is correct," Jace agreed. He moved to the center of the circle and pivoted to look at the remaining nine spearmen. Three were missing.

Two attempted to stop Katumaros. Limping on the bruised ankle, the big man pulled them to his gear, where he snatched up his spear.

"Get off me," he bellowed while throwing the pair aside. "I'm going to kill him."

"You are armed," Jace alerted him. "Stay outside of my circle and you'll be safe."

"You're the one who isn't safe," Katumaros threatened. He limped close to the edge of the circle, stopped, and brandished his spear. Next he promised. "I'll make it fast so you don't suffer."

"I'm sorry, I can't returned the favor," Jace told him. He pulled his small skinning knife and held it up.

At the sight of the mismatched weapons, the warriors laughed.

"He has a spear and you have a tiny knife," one spearman pointed out to Jace. "Just apologize, Archer, and end this."

"Do you apologize?" Jace asked Katumaros.

In response, the large warrior jabbed with the spear and took a step. Jace didn't flinch or more. The toe of the spearmen's sandal rested two fingers' width from the arc of the circle. None of the observers noticed the placement except for Scanlan. Another thrust with the spear elicited no response from Kasia. But when Katumaros stepped over the line, the Cretan Archer did a handspring that launched his body high into the air.

One moment, Katumaros held his spear level. An instant later, the weight of a fully grown man landed on the shaft. It splintered. Disgusted by the broken spear, Katumaros threw it down and began to raise his arms. But Jace slipped around the big body.

"You want blood?" Jace inquired. He had an arm around the neck of Katumaros and the tip of the skinning knife rested on the big man's cheek. "I can spill your blood or take an eye. Choose."

"Archer, Katumaros is disarmed," a spearman pointed out. "The fight is over."

"Are his feet outside," Jace asked, "or inside my fighting circle?"

"Inside," another answered.

"Did I invite him into my fighting circle?" Jace questioned. "Or pull him in against his will?"

"No Archer, he attacked you," a couple replied.

Katumaros shifted as if to fight. Jace snaked a leg behind the big man's knee, tripped the large warrior, and threw him to the ground. The tip of the skinning knife remained just below the man's eye.

"Why is he in my fighting circle?" Jace demanded.

Scanlan pushed between a pair of spearmen and answered, "Because he didn't listen to the warning."

"What warning?" a tribesman asked.

"In a combat line, every man has an area of responsibility," Scanlan repeated the Archer's words. "The fighting circle is Jace Kasia's responsibility. Anyone entering it is in danger. And Katumaros entered it three times of his own free will."

"Does that make him weak," Jace suggested by kneeing the big man in the ribs, "or stupid?"

The tribesmen and Scanlan refused to answer. Who could blame them? Katumaros would get revenge no matter which response they gave. Silence was the best way to handle the situation.

Jace knelt beside Katumaros and whispered in his ear. A moment later, the big warrior flipped over onto his belly and crawled out of the circle.

"In a battle, you can't control what happens to ten men or three men over from you," Jace lectured. He stood and pointed at Katumaros. "But you can control what happens in your circle. Who is next?"

"Next?" asked a spearman.

"Next to step into my circle," Jace answered. "You'll do. Come forward."

The tribesman entered the fighting circle and was swept off his feet. As he fell, Jace shoved him out of the circle. One by one, all the spearmen went against the Archer and were ejected from his fighting space. After he demonstrated different techniques of combat on each, Jace selected a warrior to fight and defend the circle.

Jace watched and offered hints to better an attack or to strengthen a defense. During the combat matches, Scanlan slipped up beside the Archer.

"What did you tell Katumaros?" the youth asked.

"I told him if he crosses me again, I'll take the eye," Jace replied.

"Katumaros is known to hold a grudge," Scanlan suggested.

"So am I," Jace countered.

By early afternoon, the training ended. The spearmen limped away to tend to their duties, and Scanlan followed Jace up the trail to his cottage.

"I'm going to air the eaglets," Scanlan reported. "Care to watch?"

"I would," Jace responded in Latin. "While we walk, tell me what you've read about the Trojan War."

Not only was Jace Kasia training Scanlan to fight, he insisted on lessons in reading, writing, and speaking both Latin and Greek.

***

Near a cliff overlooking the lake, Scanlan slipped on a pair of leather gloves. After opening the cage, he lifted out the eaglets and placed one on each arm. Then he walked wooden steps up to a rock overhanging the drop-off. The youth stepped to the edge and balanced on one foot. Spreading his arms, he exposed the little eagles to the wind. The birds wobbled their wings in the air currents, which threatened to destabilize the youth.

"You've come a long way with your balance," Jace complimented him in Greek. "I can see it in your spear work and your hand-to-hand combat skills."

A gust of wind rocked the birds and they flapped their short wings violently. Scanlan braced against the airstream and the movement.

When he started taking the eaglets to the cliff, they were tiny and held against his chest. His footing required bent knees and a two-legged stance. Now, he felt the strength of his arms from holding up the active birds and had a better understanding of stability.

"They're getting big and harder to manage," Scanlan admitted in Greek. "I imagine one day in the near future, they'll fly off."

When Jace didn't answer, Scanlan looked down. The Archer had gone. Not surprising as it was possibly Jace and Brigid's wedding day.

***

Late in the day, at the stone house of Samo Kentus, the clan chief's two sons arrived with their families. Once their wives and children had gone inside, the brothers cornered their father.

"King B'Yag is nothing but a nervous mare," Attalus offered. "Calling us to battle, before the Legions had marched, was a waste."

"The King of the Insubri has to be judicious and careful of who he offends with his politics. He has to care about all the clans," Kentus said, defending B'Yag. "But your weeks in Milan gave you a chance to drill with the other warriors. Didn't it?"

Abbo, the oldest, spit out, "all we did in Milan was sit around listening to Brocc B'Yag boast. We grew weary of hearing the tribe's war chief tell us how he would personally kill a commander of the Legion."

"Since we got back," Attalus stated, "we've learned more about warfare from working with Jace Kasia when he trains the spearmen."

"You know he's coming here today," Kentus notified his two sons.

"What's the news in that?" Abbo asked.

"The priest of Olloudius is coming as well," Kentus answered.

Attalus shivered and balled up his hands into fists. "No. Brigid is too young to marry."

"Brigid, Kasia, and the God of protectors, healers, fertility spirits, and prosperity might have a different idea," Kentus suggested. "However, by tradition, it's up to her brothers to prevent a breach of tradition."

"We'll stop him at the door," Attalus declared.

"The tradition of hospitality will be honored in my home," Kentus snapped.

"As you wish, father, we'll allow Kasia in, but we'll watch him the entire evening" Abbo promised. Before he could say more, his wife walked into the room and gave him a harsh look. Abbo told his father and brother, "I've been gone so long, my family needs me."

"We'll talk later," Attalus assured him. Before Attalus could address his father, a toddler waddled into the room, took him by the hand, and pulled. Attalus picked up his son and addressed the clan chief. "Father, if you'll excuse me?"

"Go," Samo Kentus encourage. "We'll speak more at the evening feast."

Although happy to have his sons back from Milan and their wives and children at his house, the clan chief remained apprehensive for the evening. He inhaled the aromas of roasting pig and baked fish. Putting aside the uneasiness caused by the purpose of Jace Kasia's visit, he left to check on the preparations and maybe get a sample before they served the meal.

***

Children ran through the house and across the yard, chasing each other in a mad game of tag. And while they had been born in Arona and were accustomed to a mob of cousins and siblings, Sucaria was not. In a room off the main hall, the little girl and Brigid worked at an ancient crafts.

"Why don't you go play?" Brigid suggested. "I can do that."

"They are children," the little girl replied. She picked up a mint leaf and worked it into the weave of the floral crown. At dawn that morning, Brigid had picked herbs, flowers, and visually appealing foliage to build the crown. As Sucaria worked at completing the wreath, she added. "They have no idea that the world is a bad place."

"A few months ago, I might have argued with you about that," Brigid admitted. She paused in her activity. "Until the raiders took me, I helped my father by going alone to care for the sick. I gave no thought for myself when I left to help women when their men had gone to war. And I traveled without thought to my personal safety when making sure no family of the clan went hungry. Now, I'm not comfortable going anywhere without Jace or Scanlan and that thin spear he carriers."

"It's a javelin," Sucaria stated. "The thin spear is called a javelin. Jace said to throw it and it will convince an enemy to rethink their future. I'm not sure what he means."

"I think it's a warning of the danger in attacking a man who has mastered such a weapon."

"Don't you feel safe when Jace goes with you?" the little girl inquired.

Brigid picked up her comb and separated a lock of hair. Once she had a linen band knotted around the strands, she rested her hands on her lap.

"Safe isn't the correct emotion I feel when Jace is near me," she said before combing out a sixth strand of hair.

"I know the feeling," Sucaria confirmed. "With Jace, protected is a better feeling."

Reaching high on the one side of her head, Brigid tied the last bunch and knotted the fabric around the pieces of hair. Next, she picked up the crown of foliage and carefully placed it so the wreath hid the bands holding the strands.

Spinning around, she asked, "can you see any of the cotton ties?"

"No, but I can see rows of hair where they fall out of the maiden's crown," Sucaria told her. "Everyone will know they're wedding strands. Your brothers will know."

"One thing about Jace Kasia. He always finds a way to defeat the enemy, even if they know he's coming." Brigid sighed. She reached for the little girl's hand and asked, "escort me to the summer festival, Cousin Sucaria?"

"It will be my pleasure, Cousin Brigid."

Act 6

Chapter 16 – The Gods Willing

On the stone patio behind the clan chief's house, servants placed chairs around a long table. Anticipating a chill at the higher elevation, they lit a fire before placing couches around the firepit. From the lawn, the view through the trees was limited. But from the patio, the family and their guests had a spectacular view of Lake Maggiore.

The brothers Abbo and Attalus ushered their wives and kids to the backyard. The women clustered together while the brothers sat sipping wine and watching the children play around the firepit.

"The Legion will come," Samo Kentus remarked while limping from the house. He took a chair between his boys. "Jace said in most of the Republic the farmers have finished planting. The Senate can authorize Legions any day now."

"He knows a lot about Rome's military," Abbo noted. "Don't you find that suspicious?"

"I might," the clan chief told the brothers, "if he hadn't trained so many of our warriors. Because of him, our clan is better prepared for war."

"What will you do with him when we take our spearmen to Milan?" Attalus questioned.

"He's not related to the clan," Samo answered after a moment of reflection. "I can't order him to go off to war. I'll probably keep him here for defense against tribal attacks on our borders."

Brigid and Sucaria came from the rear of the house and everyone stopped talking and looked. While Brigid wore a maiden's summer wreath, six separate locks of her hair hung in obvious tresses. Although she hid the linen wedding-ties under her maiden crown, everyone could see the bridal strands.

"He's not a member of the Gnātos Tribe, yet," Abbo suggested while examining his sister's mixed messages.

"And he won't be," Attalus growled. "Brigid is too young and she's needed here to take care of you, father."

***

By late afternoon, guests began arriving for the summer festival. Cerdo, a priest of the God Olloudius, arrived by himself. He entered the doorway, stopped at the threshold, held up his arms with closed hands, and waited.

A servant noticed the priest and ran for the backyard. Acting more as a patriarch than a clan chief, Samo Kentus herded his sons and their wives and children to the hallway. As he limped down the hall, the stoic and stern looking priest gazed at the clan chief.

"Who is he?" Sucaria asked.

"A holy man," Brigid told her. They halted farther down the hallway, satisfied with a view of the priest from behind people. Brigid offered. "I was hoping he would come."

"Why wouldn't he?"

"During this season, all the priests are wanted in every village and town," she told the little girl. "And while there are many priests and many gods, Olloudius pleases me the most."

"Why?" Sucaria inquired.

"Remember how many strands I tied into my hair?" Brigid asked.

"You bound six strands of hair."

"That's right. Now count the priest's fingers."

"I can't," Sucaria told her. "His fingers are folded into fists."

"He'll extend fingers," Sucaria advised. "Watch and count."

Cerdo held the pose for a moment longer. Then he closed his eyes and called to his God.

"Olloudius protect this home and the kinfolks embraced by this family." On both hands, he extended a finger and swept a tight circle in front of his face.

"Olloudius heal this home and the kinfolks embraced by this family." The priest extended a second finger from the fists and made a motion with four fingers that circled his stomach.

Extending three fingers on each hand, he circled his groin with the six digits. "Olloudius guide the fertility spirits to this house and to the kinfolks embraced by this family."

"Six fingers, six strands of hair," Sucaria whispered.

Brigid gave the little girl's hand a reassuring squeeze.

"Olloudius grant prosperity to this home and to the kinfolks embraced by this family." Priest Cerdo extended four fingers on each hand and swung his hands in a wide, all-encompassing circle.

"The blessings of Olloudius are given to this home and to the kinfolks embraced by this family," Priest Cerdo announced. Then he dropped the stern look, stepped into the hallway, and asked. "Can a thirsty priest get a beverage?"

"My family welcomes the priest of Olloudius," Samo Kentus proclaimed. "Come Cerdo, enjoy the hospitality of this house."

The clan chief and priest linked arms and strolled down the hallway with Samo, using Cerdo's arm for support. Behind them, the crowd followed. Unseen, Jace Kasia slipped through the doorway and fell in behind the procession.

***

Abbo, Attalus, and a cluster of men were drinking and discussing the coming war with Rome. An absence of childish cries and screams of play caught Abbo's attention. Looking to the lawn, he noticed the children had stopped running around the firepit. Rather than games, they sat in front of a couch, listening to a man in a pale yellow tunic. Reclining on an adjacent couch was his sister Brigid. It might have been a coincidence, but Abbo knew better. His sister wore a dress of the same pale yellow color.

"Attalus, we have a warning to deliver," he called to his brother while pointing at the firepit.

Walking fast and with purpose, the brothers reached the couches. But rather than disrupt the children, they waited and listened.

"And after the young spearman escaped from the room, he crept through the palace until he located the storage room where his war chief and a young warrior were being held," Jace retold a story he heard from Senator Alerio Sisera. Out of necessity, he took out the Legion references and created a fictional group of tribesmen. Caught up in the tale, the children cheered when the hero located his chief. "Now they had to sneak out of the walled city and get back to their tribe. But the war chief was brave and angry at the way he'd been treated. What do you suppose he did?"

"Fight the militia," one boy shouted.

"Run and come back later," another suggested.

Jace nodded at each as if it might be the right answer before continuing.

"The war chief in his rage picked burning branches from the firepit and threw them on furniture and the curtains. Soon the place was blazing with fire climbing the walls. The flames forced the hero and his chief to leave the hot palace. By then, the entire city was coming to the palace."

"Did they get caught?" a little boy asked.

"Running stooped and bent below the layer of smoke, they raced for the city gate. But, the gate was closed," Jace said, using his hands to represent being stopped. "A squad of militia men coming down the street spotted them. Quickly, our hero guided the chief and the weak spearmen off to a side street. Moving along the wall, they held their noses and approached the city's manure dump."

One of the little girls squealed in disgust.

"That's right, it smelled something terrible," Jace sympathized. "But there was no other way out. The three walked on the crust of the manure. Near the wall, the war chief broke through and sank up to his chest in manure."

By opening his mouth and squinting, Jace made a repugnant face.

"Our hero reached back and took the war chief's hand. He pulled the war chief out of the muck, and together, they climbed the wall," Jace declared.

"What happened next?" a child asked.

"What happened next?" Jace repeated. "Next, their mothers made them scrub with soap to get the smell off them, and they used buckets of water to rinse away the manure."

A youth stood, reached down for a little one and stated, "take my hand and I'll pull you out of the manure pile."

"No. Yuck," the child shouted. He jumped up and ran for the patio.

Jace and Brigid laughed at the antics as the kids duplicated different parts of the story. In mid chuckle, a voice interrupted their mirth.

"Jace Kasia, you'll not have our sister," Attalus informed him. He rested a hand on the Archer's shoulder in a gesture of dominance.

"Mark our words," Abbo threatened. "If you try and leave with her, you'll have to go through us."

Jace looked over his shoulder and remarked to the brothers, "I wouldn't want to do that."

"I'm glad you understand," Attalus commented.

"Because we will not go easy on you," Abbo assured Jace.

Sucaria bristled, stood up, and put her hands on her waist.

"Tell me when," she stated.

"Tell you when, what?" Brigid asked.

"Before we crossed the Olona River, Jace told me to close my eyes," the little girl answered.

"To keep you from being afraid of the water?" Brigid questioned.

"Oh, no. He didn't want me to see him kill the four men in the ambush," Sucaria explained. Then she pointed at the coin purses the brothers carried. "But it'll be a good day. Jace likes to earn a profit."

Brigid blinked at the girl, then rotated her eyes to search Jace's face. Both her brothers stood confused by the easy assurance that Jace could defeat them.

"We're not river scum," Abbo pointed out.

"Neither were they," Sucaria reported. "They had spears and you don't. You'll be dead quicker."

Before it got Jace into more trouble, he pulled Sucaria into his arms.

"I think that's enough conjecture for one afternoon," he hushed her.

"What's conjecture?" Sucaria asked.

"It means guess," Brigid told her.

"Oh, I'm not guessing," the girl assured her. "After the five Cenomani warriors killed Aunt M'anta, Jace killed them. By himself."

Gently, Jace hugged her and swore, "no one is going to die today."

"If you say so," Sucaria stated, before declaring. "We're not Legion, but everything being equal, we're doing passably fair."

"Yes we are," Jace said to the brothers as he lowered Sucaria to the ground. "We understand each other very well."

Abbo and Attalus snorted. Then they stomped back to the men on the patio and the discussion of war.

"A child should not have memories like that," Brigid sighed. "Then again, if it wasn't for you, she wouldn't be alive to have any memories."

"Right place, unlucky man, and right events," Jace told her. "Let's go eat. I'm hungry."

Together, they rose from the couches and walked to the cooking fires.

***

Later, as they sat at the table, someone placed a mug of wine in front of Jace.

"Come on Archer, have a drink with me," the man insisted. He rocked, his balance already impaired by the wine he had consumed. "You've beaten all the spearmen who stayed back to defend Gnātos Clan territory. You must think you are the mightiest warrior on either side of Lake Maggiore."

"I prefer not to," Jace declined, pushing the mug away.

"What, too good to drink with me?" the drunk sneered. Irate at being snubbed, he yelled. "Maybe you bested the weak ones who stayed behind. But I went to Milan with the real warriors. Try that circle garbage on me."

Samo Kentus and Cerdo glanced around to investigate the angry voice. Before the Clan Chief or the priest reacted, Abbo and Attalus waved them down.

"I said," the drunk began again.

"You're bleeding," Jace told him. He pulled a piece of linen from a pouch and handed it to the man. "You must have bumped into a chair or a table. Look at your ankle."

The drunk and Jace peered down at the man's lower leg. As they searched for nonexistent blood, Jace punched him in the side of his throat. Bent forward and choking, the drunk grabbed his neck.

"Goodness," Jace exclaimed as he helped the man to a chair. "Sometimes, too much drink, you know, will come up on you."

Glassey eyed and barely breathing, the drunk spearman forgot about his assignment to start a fight and get Jace ejected from the summer festival.

Once he had the drunk settled, Jace asked Brigid, "May I escort you to the firepit?"

They left the patio as the sun set. Servants brought out braziers and lit them to provide light.

"He doesn't drink wine or beer," Abbo commented. "We can't get him drunk and fighting."

Attalus peered down to the firepit area at the couches where his sister and Jace lounged. "It'll be fine. We'll take turns keeping an eye on them from here."

Between the food, the beer, and the wine, the festival grew loud. Children ran from the firepit to the patio and back in a never ending game of chase. Groups of adults put their heads together and talked. And Brigid's brothers maintained their vigils.

"Fire. Fire on the lake," a woman shouted. "What is it?"

Every attendee of the clan chief's summer festival rushed to the side of the patio. In moments, the children near the firepit arrived and squeezed between the adult to see the fire on the water.

Out on the lake, flames shot into the air. Although too far away to judge the size or the make of the vessel, everyone could see it was burning fiercely. What they couldn't see was the trail of ripples as a body swam away from the flames.

***

Long before the attendees spotted the fire, Scanlan Saltare loaded a raft with straw and sprinkled fish oil on the dry stalks. Standing in the back, he rowed it out onto the lake. Once he could see lights from the braziers at the clan chief's house, Scanlan stopped rowing.

Sparks flew from the steel as he raked the flint down the bar. After three attempts, a few pieces of straw burned, next a few more burst into flames. The new fire quickly expanded to become a floating bonfire.

Scanlan shoved the fire starter gear into a pouch. And although he knew it was too far away for anyone to hear, he shouted up to the house.

"All the best to you, Jace Kasia and to you, Brigid Kentus. May your escape be uneventful."

Then the youth did an elegant dive into the water. He broke the surface, and with powerful strokes, began the long swim back to shore.

***

"It's a big fishing boat," a woman suggested.

"No. It's a barge," a man countered.

"Must be a wife taking revenge on an unfaithful husband," someone offered.

"Or a fisherman taking revenge on an unfaithful wife," said another festival attendee.

Samo Kentus felt a tug on the bottom of his tunic. Looking down, he saw his deceased brother's little girl.

"What is it Sucaria?" he asked.

The little girl held up Brigid's maiden wreath. Samo stared at the crown, remembering the charity of his daughter, her willingness to tend to the families of the clan, and her way with the sick and ill.

"Father, we can't find Brigid," Attalus divulged when he walked up. "We were distracted by the fire on the lake."

"We've looked for her everywhere," Abbo said when he arrived.

Samo held up the crown of foliage, flowers, and herbs. With tears in his eyes, he informed his sons, "Brigid is gone. Gone from this house and onto another home. Gone from our care, and under the protection of another."

"We can still catch them," Attalus proposed.

The priest stepped forward and rested a hand on the warrior's arm.

"In every season there is a transition. Winter doesn't just become summer. There is a period of change we call spring," Cerdo told the father and his sons. "This afternoon, they were two individuals, a man and a woman."

"What are they now?" Abbo asked.

"The Gods willing, they are spring," he answered. Confused, the brothers kicked the patio with their sandals. Seeing the need to offer comfort, the priest advised. "Come sunrise, we'll go to Jace Kasia's cottage and see if the transition to a couple has been observed. Or if a funeral rite is required."

Chapter 17 – Most At Home

Jace and Brigid jogged up the trail, climbing to his cottage. Once on level ground and near the porch, Brigid stopped. Jace missed the cue and took a few steps forward before spinning.

"Is something wrong?" he asked.

In the moonlight, her hair glowed while her face, although mostly shaded, lit up the Archer's heart.

"Have you forgotten something?" she asked.

"Scanlan burned the raft and I had a ladder on the wall," Jace listed. "We left and no one noticed. What did I forget?"

She reached up and touched her head. Then her finger tapped the small bond holding one of the stands of her hair.

"If you want to cut my bands and free my hair," she told him, "you're supposed to present me with a spear."

"I forgot," Jace admitted. "Wait right here."

"I may for a period," Brigid replied. "Or I might return to my father's house."

Toren between leaving her and completing the ritual, or remaining near her, Jace stepped away, stepped back, then raced for his cottage.

Later, through the open doorway, Brigid saw the warm light from a fireplace inside. A shade darkened the entrance for a moment before Jace appeared in the moonlight.

"Be careful it's sharp," he warned.

Brigid reached out and took the shaft of a spear only as long as her arm.

"Show me to your cottage Jace Kasia," she directed by pointing the spearhead at the doorway.

He offered his arm and escorted her to the porch.

***

As the new fire flared in the fireplace, Brigid held up the wedding spear and examined the polished steel spearhead in the firelight. After the inspection, she handed it to Jace.

"You may remove my hair ties," she instructed.

Carefully, he used the razor sharp spear to cut one of the linen ties. As the hair spread, Jace caught the tie and placed the small piece of cloth in Brigid's hand. Then he shifted to the next strand of hair.

There were six in all and he cut them until her hair hung free. After shaking it out, Brigid enveloped his neck with her arms. As she kissed her husband, he dropped the spear. Jace's wife clutched the tiny pieces of linen tightly in her hand.

***

Dawn revealed a crowd on the flat ground in front of the porch.

"Brigid. It's your father," Samo Kentus called to the cottage. "Come home child. We'll dispose of his body."

Flanked by Abbo and Attalus, the clan chief was tempted to allow them to force the front door. But the priest of Olloudius stood beside them, a stern expression on his face.

"Brigid," he called again.

The door opened, and his daughter appeared in the doorway.

"Father, good morning," she greeted him. Her eyes scanned the group, and she acknowledged each individual. Holding up the ceremonial spear with one hand, she extended the other. Unfolding her fingers, she displayed the six pieces of linen and stated. "Welcome to my home."

Cerdo walked to the steps of the porch and examined the pieces of linen.

"Priest of Olloudius, I've said it before and I'll say it again," Brigid told him. "I'm glad it was you who attended my father's summer festival."

Jace came outside and stood beside his wife.

"My presence here isn't by happenstance," Cerdo confided in her. Then loudly, he asked. "Will you invite me in?"

"Priest, for as long as a relative of mine or of my husband's lives, you are welcome in our home."

Cerdo went to the doorway and stood on the threshold.

"Individuals become a couple, and during the transition, they bond as husband and wife," he announced. Then he closed his eyes and prayed.

"Olloudius protect this home and the kinfolks embraced by this family." He extended a finger from each fist and swept a circle in front of his face.

"Olloudius heal this home and the kinfolks embraced by this family." A second finger popped from his fists and he motioned around his stomach.

"Olloudius guide the fertility spirits to this house and to the kinfolks embraced by this family." He circled his groin with the six digits.

"Olloudius grant prosperity to this home and to the kinfolks embraced by this family." Priest Cerdo extended four fingers on each hand and swung his arms in a wide circle.

"The blessings of Olloudius are given to this home and to the kinfolks embraced by this family," Priest Cerdo announced. Then he dropped the stern look, turned to face the crowd, and exclaimed. "We welcome the bride and her husband and wish their progeny well. Samo Kentus, do you have anything to add?"

The group who accompanied the clan chief held their breaths. Samo could deny the marriage and eject his daughter from the Kentus family. Or he could welcome a new son.

"I will add," Samo answered, "welcome to the family, Jace Kasia."

"Father, we are a new household, and as such, have little to offer. Some beer, some wine," Brigid said from the porch. Then with a bemused look she included, "barrels of fruit juice, and vinegar for water."

Her new husband's taste in beverages seemed strange compared to her brothers' preferences.

"Daughter and son," Samo addressed Brigid and Jace, "this calls for a celebration. I will provide a feast to celebrate the union."

Men rushed down the trail, heading for the clan chief's house to collect the food and beverages for another festival.

***

By mid-morning, Brigid's brothers were full of celebration.

"Brother Jace, come here," Abbo called out before walking to where Attalus and their father waited. Jace crossed the yard with a blank expression on his face.

"I'm not accustomed to the term brother Jace," the Archer admitted. "Is it meant as a joke?"

"Let me see," Attalus replied. "There is me. There is brother Abbo. There is our father, Kentus. And there is our brother Jace."

"It appears the men of the family are all here," Abbo offered. "Are we in error, father?"

Samo Kentus reached out and drew Jace into his arms. Then as he hugged the Archer, tears appeared in his eyes. He pushed Jace away.

"Father, why the tears?" Attalus inquired.

"It just occurred to me," Samo told them. "Soon the Legions of Rome will march on us. And now, instead of sending two of my boys to Milan, I'm sending three. The gods willing, all three of you will return safely from the war for Insubri."

Needing a few moments to reflect, Jace separated from the Kentus men. On the far side of the festivities, he climbed the hill, located a spot behind a big tree and sat on the leaves.

"Scanlan Saltare, I know you're up there," he said before the youth moved.

"How do you do that?" Scanlan asked.

"It's not you. It's the birds, bugs, and tree creatures," Jace responded. "When you began breathing hard because you were afraid of being discovered, the air around you vibrated with disharmony. The creatures fled your presence."

"So not to be sensed, I have to not be afraid of being spotted," Scanlan suggested as he slipped down to a spot beside the Archer. "That seems unnatural."

Jace pointed to a bird on a branch. Then he blew out from between his lips. Although the sound was low, the bird took flight.

"The bird, the calm of the forest, and their response to a threat is natural," he lectured. "Being nervous for no reason is unnatural."

Scanlan closed his eyes, calmed his breath, and relaxed. A moment later, a butterfly landed on his arm.

"It's as if I don't exist," he stated. The winged creature flew away and Scanlan acknowledged, "Thank you for the lesson. But why are you here and not at your wedding party?"

"It seems I'm now a member of the Gnātos Tribe and a son of Clan Chief Kentus," Jace answered.

"In these mountains and around the lake, you have power, rights beyond most, and authority. What's wrong with that?"

"I'm half Roman, a nobleman of the Republic, and a former Battle Commander of a Legion," Jace listed. "How am I supposed to go and fight my former comrades?"

"You could leave," Scanlan proposed. "No tracker could catch a Cretan Archer. If I was older, I'd leave."

"It's a cycle of life," Jace revealed. "As a youth, you want to leave home and experience the world. As a man who has witnessed cruelty and done distasteful acts, the desire to stay where I am most at home is stronger than the urge to roam."

"What will you do?" Scanlan asked.

"What choice do I have?" Jace Kasia conceded. "I will fight for my wife, my tribe, and my new life."

***

On the morning of Jace Kasia's wedding, three-hundred and fifty-three-miles south of his cottage, the Senate of Rome completed their daily devotional. They finished early, giving opposing factions the opportunity to bicker.

President Caecina waited for a few arguments to cool before calling the Senate to session. "Please take you seats. Now gentlemen, we've much to discuss."

Following his directions, the antagonists separated and went to their chairs.

"Philip of Macedonia is still on the march," a Senator shouted. "And Villius Tappulus is dancing around and not bringing the Greek to battle."

"Consul Tappulus is pursuing battle and a treaty," Lucius Lentulus replied, defending his co-Consul. "Greece is a difficult knot to untie."

"What about the Insubri?" Cornelius Scipio mentioned from his seat.

"Do you wish the floor?" the President of the Senate asked.

"I do wish to address the Senate," Cornelius assured him.

"The Senate recognizes Senator Scipio Africanus."

Standing, Cornelius looked upward, seemingly ignoring the Senators and his surroundings.

"This morning, I am not thinking of Greece or the crimes of Philip of Macedonia," he said, as if holding a conversation with guests at a dinner party. "This day, my mind is troubled by atrocities closer to home. I weep for the murdered citizens of our Republic. My spirit rages at the thought of Republic women awoken from their slumber only to have spears thrust through their throats. Unable to cry out a warning, or voice their horrors, as flames consumed their homes and their babies. My soul laments the men dragged from their beds and forced to watch their loved ones burn. And then to suffer more as their merchandise was carted off before their businesses went up in smoke. In my fevered vision, I see cruel Insubri spearmen laughing at the misery of the people of Placentia. I again witness flames destroying the trading city. And I hear King B'Yag and his vicious gang of chiefs mocking Rome for our inability to hold the offenders to task."

As if overwhelmed by the images, Cornelius slapped a hand over his eyes and dropped into his chair. Silence fell over the chamber. In the next few moments, Senators grew angry as they replayed his words in their minds. Once the tension was as taut as a bowstring, Cornelius pushed to his feet.

He began to speak when a single pair of hands, clapping slowly and loudly, broke the mood in the chamber.

"Senator Scipio Africanus, what a wonderful rendition of recent history," Marcus Cato exclaimed. He continued the mocking applause. "It was great theater. Worthy of a stage and a performance in a Greek tragedy. Oh, I'm not saying the sack of Placentia wasn't heartbreaking or a slap in the face to our Republic. But the first-hand account, when he was nowhere near the assault, was pure theater. Next, he'll be telling you how only he can deliver justice for the dead."

Senator Cato stopped clapping and sat. Typically, when a Senator countered another, they delivered a concept for the chamber to consider. The sarcastic delivery of Cornelius' purpose stripped Scipio of his carefully planned argument.

Cornelius hesitated long enough for the Senate to wonder how he would handle the interruption. During that period, he stood still until most of the chamber shifted to watch for his response.

"What is good elocution but an attempt to bring your audience to a conclusion," he announced. "I want to thank Senator Cato for helping me keep this speech brief. Yes, I want a Proconsul position and permission to raise Legions. But who better than me? I have the coins to fund the Legions. The experience to train the Legionaries. And a history of victories. Who better to bring the tribe to their knees? Make me a General of Rome and I will punish the Insubri before summer's end."

President Caecina nodded at Cornelius before rapping on his stand. "Can I get a second to authorize Proconsul Scipio Africanus to raise Legions and punish the Insubri?"

"I second the nomination," declared Gnaeus Lentulus, the brother of Consul Lucius Lentulus.

He didn't fool anyone. His second was to keep his brother in Rome and off the battlefield. Since being denied a triumphant parade following his campaigns in Iberia, the word was Lucius Lentulus thirsted after a victory. His brother feared Consul Lentulus would be too rash in his judgement to run a successful campaign. Cornelius was the safe choice.

"Can I get a third to support the motion?"

Another Senator stated, "of course. Who better than Cornelius Scipio Africanus to deliver the gladius of justice to the lawless."

Murmurs of agreement followed the declaration.

"All in favor, raise your hand," Caecina instructed.

While clerks moved around counting votes, Marcus Cato, Titus Crispinus, and Valerius Flaccus huddled with their section.

After looking around, Crispinus warned, "he's going to get the votes."

"He is the hero of Carthage," Flaccus sneered. "And I fear, soon to be our King."

Clerks collected the votes and reported the findings to Caecina.

"The motion carries and the Senate salutes Proconsul Scipio Africanus," the President of the Senate announced. "Two Legions are authorized for the conquest of Insubri. The Gods willing, you will be victorious by summer's end."

***

Elated by the appointment, Cornelius departed the Senate. On the steps, he punched the shoulder of his bodyguard.

"When do we march, General?" Sidia Decimia asked.

"I need to interview for a couple of Battle Commanders and a Senior Tribune of Horse," Cornelius replied. "In the meanwhile, I'll send word to the central Legion to have Optios begin recruiting Legionaries."

"From what I've learned, Insubri territory is heavily wooded," Sidia advised. "Cavalry is less important than scouts and heavy infantrymen in a forest and when crossing rivers."

"Crossing rivers?" Cornelius inquired. "Other than the Po, what rivers do we need to cross?"

"That sir, depends on the season and where the Insubri place their army," the bodyguard answered. "On our side of a swollen river or on the far bank."

"I see what you mean," Cornelius allowed. "So many details to consider and decisions to make. It's almost overwhelming."

"I agree, General Scipio Africanus," Sidia commented. "It's preferable to city life."

"To be planning a campaign again, does feel good," Cornelius granted. "It's where I am most at home, in a camp and on the march."

In high spirits, the General, and his Optio bodyguard, marched from the Senate. Behind Cornelius' back, his adversaries remained together. Their conference centered on one objective: finding a way to prevent the newly elevated Proconsul of Rome from going to war.

Chapter 18 – Power of the Podium

Weeks later, with a sea breeze softening the heat of early summer, Cornelius Scipio Africanus rode around Boar Legion's training ground. Optio Sidia Decimia rode off to the left of the Proconsul, keeping pace but holding back. On Cornelius's other side, Colonel Alapam Terrigenus trotted beside the General. Not far from the coast at Rimini, the

Legion stomped up and down a field that, in any other year, would be under cultivation.

"Colonel, they look good," Cornelius commented.

Almost three thousand heavy infantrymen hammered their shields forward, pulled them back, and struck out with their gladii. Then, in three uniformed lines, the Legionaries stepped forward and began another advance.

"They look good moving straight ahead," Alapam agreed. Then he cautioned. "But put a hoard of Insubri warriors in their way and the Maniples will break."

"What do you need to remedy that, Colonel Terrigenus?" Cornelius asked.

"Forty-eight days of intense training," the Battle Commander answered. "And several skirmishes to season the Legion."

"You can't have six weeks," Cornelius told him. "I can give you is three. Do the best you can."

"Even if I have to put half of them on crutches," Terrigenus assured him, "Africanus Boar Legion will be battle ready."

He saluted and turned his horse, returning to his staff. Cornelius, Sidia, and Legionaries of the First Century trotted away, heading for Africanus Ibex Legion at another drill field.

"He's not wrong, sir," Sidia remarked. "Not only will the Maniples solidify and be better able to react, the river levels will have dropped in six weeks."

"I can't wait six weeks," Cornelius confessed. "If I wait too long, Cato and his ilk will be screaming for my demotion. We should be on the march next week. At three weeks, I'm tempting the fates."

Colonel Causam Belua noted the arrival of the Proconsul. He left his staff and rode to meet Cornelius.

"Good morning, sir," the Battle Commander stated. He offered a salute before asking, "when do we march on the Insubrians?"

"Is your Legion really prepared for combat, Colonel?" Cornelius questioned.

"Africanus Ibex Legion is ready to die for the Republic, sir," Causam declared.

"Colonel Belua, if I might offer a little tactical advice," Cornelius imparted. "You win battles by making the other guy die for his nation. Not by dying for ours."

"What I meant, sir, was we are ready to fight."

"I liked the forty-eight days better," Cornelius muttered. Then with authority, he instructed, "Colonel, you have three weeks to firm up your shield walls and toughen up your Legionaries."

"Yes, sir," Causam Belua confirmed.

As Cornelius and Sidia rode for the headquarters pavilion, the bodyguard proposed, "The Legionaries have good equipment and experience in Greece."

"Equipment is important," Cornelius pointed out. "But none were at Carthage with me. Or in Iberia with Consul

Lentulus. I'm not sure how much fighting they did in Greece."

"You seemed overly worried about what everyone says will be a quick siege," Sidia told him.

"Milan is an ancient city and a stronghold of the Insubrians," Cornelius warned. "Just because we show up at their gates, doesn't mean King B'Yag will come running out with a pen, ready to sign a treaty."

"I guess we'll find out in three week," Sidia proposed. Lifting an arm, the bodyguard pointed at a group of Legion staff officers riding in from the southeast. "That can't be good, sir."

"Let's get to my tent and prepare for the visitors. Maybe hospitality will soften the news."

Putting heels to flanks, they raced their mounts to the stockade and the headquarters of Africanus Legions.

***

Cornelius listened as a guard from First Century challenged the new arrivals.

"State your name and the purpose of your visit, sir."

From outside, a male voice replied to the First Optio. "Praetor Baebius Tamphilus. I'm here to deliver a message to Scipio Africanus."

An instant later, the tent flap opened and a man with a General's helmet under his arm walked into the tent. Behind him came two senior staff officers.

"Proconsul Scipio Africanus, greetings from the Senate of Rome," Tamphilus stated. He crossed the floor and handed Cornelius a scroll. "You are hereby released of command of what going forward will be known as Lentulus Legions."

For as many times as the Senate, or rather specific Senators, had attempted to remove him of command in Silicia, the news while hurtful wasn't unexpected.

"Praetor Tamphilus, may I offer refreshments to you and your staff while I read about my future?" Cornelius inquired.

He didn't wait for an answer. Just waved his hand for a servant to step forward and strolled to the rear of the tent, alone. After breaking the seal, he unrolled the parchment.

***

Cornelius Scipio Africanus, Nobleman and Citizen of Rome,

We trust this message finds you vibrant and in good health. Due to an emergency in Rome, you are directed to remove yourself and your belongings from the Legions. After turning over all appropriate documents and alerting your staff to the change of command, make haste to the Senate for an important vote.

Signed,

Lucius Lentulus

Citizen of the Republic and Consul of Rome

***

"Optio Decimia, pack our bags. It appears the fates couldn't wait."

"Will we be coming back, sir?" Sidia inquired.

"Not before the Legions march," Cornelius answered. He tapped the scroll on his thigh as he approached Tamphilus. "Praetor, there are several things you should know about the Legions and the campaign."

"Proconsul, I've negotiated with Carthaginians and Iberians, and commanded Legions," Tamphilus snapped. "I was warned not to delay your departure with a change of command ceremony. I assume that includes small talk and gossip. Let's avoid those. You can leave at your leisure."

A Praetor addressing a Proconsul in such a manner would normally be a mistake. For Tamphilus to dismiss Cornelius meant the man had powerful allies backing him. Figuring his detractors had laid political traps for him, Cornelius walked away without any acknowledgement of his anger. He would deal with the people behind his recall later.

Once in Cornelius' private quarters, Sidia stopped packing and noted, "You seem bothered, sir. I mean beyond the obvious travesty."

"This scroll," Cornelius told him, "doesn't include my title as a Proconsul or reflect my position as a Senator of Rome."

"What does that mean, sir?" the bodyguard asked.

"I wish I knew, Optio Decimia," Cornelius admitted.

***

Taking advantage of Legion way-stations on the roads, Cornelius and Sidia changed horses often. With little sleep and too many miles in the saddle, they approached the walls of Rome at dawn.

"Cornelius Scipio Africanus and my Optio," Cornelius reported at the gate.

"Yes, sir, we know who you are," the militiaman commented. "You are the hero who defeated the Carthaginian monster, Hannibal. Welcome home, General."

A few paces from the gate, Sidia pointed out, "I'd guess, sir, there's no arrest warrant out for you."

"There is that," Cornelius confirmed. "Let's go to my Villa. We can clean up before going to the Senate. I'm wearing my toga with the purple stripe of a Senator. I want you in your Legion armor."

***

By midmorning, cleaned up but unrested, they entered the chamber. The first thing Cornelius noticed was Consul Lentulus at the lectern. There was no rule against a Consul taking charge of the day-to-day activities of the Senate. He would when it was time for elections of the new Consuls. But during the year, a Consul's job was to work behind the scenes, smoothing out problems, and trying not to offend anyone.

"Sir, where is the President of the Seante?" Sidia whispered.

Cornelius stood at the top of an aisle with his armored bodyguard a step behind him.

"Perhaps he took sick," Cornelius suggested.

Lucius Lentulus had three Senators talking to him at the same time. Being diplomatic, he attempted to deal with one, but that angered the other two.

"I will not be ignored," one of the two shouted. "The new aqueduct should take priority over a stable."

"Why are you listening to that drivel when the roads require your full attention."

Lentulus came close to exploding on the demanding Senators. His eyes bulged and his cheeks puffed out. Before he ruined his political career, the Consul spotted Cornelius, banged the lectern, and announced.

"Hold your concerns," he barked. "Sit down. Domini Cornelius Scipio Africanus has arrived."

The use of Master as his title struck Cornelius as odd.

"Come forward, Domini," Lentulus requested.

To unexpected applause, Cornelius marched to the front of the chamber. Once there, the Consul directed him to turn and face the Senate.

"I nominate Domini Scipio Africanus for President of the Senate," Lucius Lentulus announced. "Do I have a second?"

From an unexpected quadrant of the chamber, Marcus Cato exclaimed, "After his defense of the Senate against the absolutely vile law to allow voluntary exile, I name him a champion of the Senate. And for that reason, I second the nomination."

As complementary as the seconding of the nomination sounded, Cornelius understood. Cato had engineered his removal from command of the Legions and his exclusion from the campaign against the Insubrians. The new position, while exalted, came with a stipulation that Cornelius could not leave the city of Rome.

"I hear a second," Lentulus acknowledged. "Let us vote."

The count took little effort to see the popularity of Cornelius. And Consul Lentulus barely took a breath before declaring, "The Senate congratulates and welcomes Domini Scipio Africanus as the new President of the Senate of Rome."

Cornelius stepped behind the lectern, rapped on the top, and said, "the Senate of Rome will come to order."

***

During the remaining session, President Scipio Africanus discovered a freedom he hadn't realized was possible. His flexibility came from the power of the podium. Any motion he didn't like became a topic for a committee where it could be discussed to death. Or the motion, with the backing of the President, might be elevated to an immediate vote.

When the Senate broke at midday, Cornelius approached Lucius Lentulus.

"Lo Consul, what happened to Domini Caecina?" he asked.

"An opportunity came up and he had to resign," Lentulus answered. "Acreage on an indebted farm became available next to his estate at Casale in northern Campania. He needed to be there to develop the expansion. You should appreciate the venture. The owner was a victim of

Hannibal's rampage through the area. He has debts which forced him to sell the land."

"Hannibal did a lot of damage to Campania. I assume, when Caecina resigned, you thought of me?"

"No, Domini. We went through four rounds of candidates before sending for you," Lentulus admitted.

"Let me guess, Marcus Cato suggested recalling me?"

"He did and he used the same mention of the voluntary exile law and the right of appeal when putting forth your name."

"Cato and his faction don't approve of the idea of new laws, do they?" Cornelius inquired.

"It's not the Roman way, the laws are already on the twelve bronze tablets, and we aren't a Greek democracy," Lentulus mimicked ideals of the faction. "It's their typical reasoning for keeping the Republic trapped in the past."

"Thank you, Consul," Cornelius stated before facing the chamber.

He searched the Senators still there. After thinking of the politics of several, he settled on Sextus Paetus. Then he approached Paetus and invited him to lunch.

***

The afternoon session drew fewer Senators. While the morning assembly was reserved for large important issues, the afternoon typically dealt with mundane maintenance items. Many Senators skipped out, preferring to do business or to soak in the baths. Taking advantage of the reduced number, Cornelius introduced a motion.

"I've been approached by several members of the Senate. They asked me to find a definitive conclusion to the debate concerning changes to the law," Cornelius lied. It was the President of the Senate who drew Senators to the cause, not the other way around. "One change grants citizens of Rome the right to ask for a review of a sentence by another magistrate. And the other change grants citizens of Rome the ability to accept exile in place of execution. From what I've been told, the citizen choosing exile must divest himself of all property in Rome. Can I get a second on the motion?"

One of the few members of his faction to attend the afternoon session, Titus Crispinus, half dozed in his chair. A large midday repast and several glasses of good Roman vino left him groggy and inattentive. He dismissed the motion until a Senator spoke up.

"I second the motion to amend the laws of Rome to elevate citizens of Rome above the masses," Sextus Paetus declared.

Titus Crispinus snapped out of his fog. Waving for an assistant, he instructed, "Go find Senators Cato, Flaccus, and the others. Tell them to hurry while I stop this madness."

"I have a second," Cornelius announced. "All those in favor…"

"Cornelius, I demand that you stop this nonsense," Crispinus shouted.

Cornelius bent far over the lectern as if to get a better look at the speaker.

"Do you have something to add, Senator Crispinus?"

"I demand that you stop this vote."

"Are you the President of the Senate or am I?" Cornelius quizzed him.

"You are."

"And what is my title and name?" Cornelius continued.

"President Scipio Africanus," he reported. While they talked, Titus Crispinus looked around for the rest of his faction.

"That's correct," Cornelius told him before addressing the chamber. "All those in favor of amending the law to lift citizens of Rome above the masses raise your hand."

"I protest this vote and the very idea of the motion," Titus Crispinus called out while waving his arms for attention.

But the President of the Senate, using the power of the podium, ignored his pleas and waited for the clerks to walk the chamber, counting the votes.

"By an overwhelming majority of all those present, the Senate has adopted the right of a citizen of Rome to appeal a verdict. And for a citizen of Rome to exchange a death sentence for exile and the endowment of his property to the state. So sayeth the Senate of Rome."

Marcus Cato and Valerius Flaccus arrived in time to hear the final resolution. They exchanged pained expressions with a distraught Titus Crispinus. Silently, they cursed Cornelius Scipio for his underhanded slap at their faction.

None of them accepted responsibility for denying Cornelius his Legions and a campaign by putting him in a position of authority. Even if they had, they would be wrong. Because the hands that guided the events belonged to Adrestia, the Goddess of equilibrium and balance.

***

While Cornelius thought of other ways to torment his adversaries in the Senate, Gnaeus Lentulus' worst fears came to fruition.

"I'm sending a message to Praetor Tamphilus to advance the Boar and Ibex Legions against the Insubri," Consul Lentulus told him at the end of the session. "I'll be joining them for the attack on Milan."

Gnaeus shivered. His brother was indeed rushing into battle. Whether to gain fame or to wave a victory in the faces of the men who prevented Lucius Lentulus from holding a triumph parade after Iberia, didn't matter. What Gnaeus worried about was losing his brother to a strong and intrenched enemy due to a rash decision.

Act 7

Chapter 19 - Battle Scheme

Two days after the Legions marched from Remini, Insubri couriers arrived at Milan with the rising sun. By midday, King B'Yag's messages to his clan chiefs left the city. Three days later, Samo Kentus stood on a hill, looking down on a thousand Gnātos warriors. His sons, Abbo, Attalus, and Jace Kasia, occupied places of honor at the front of the spearmen.

"The red capes and big shields are on their way to Milan," Samo announced. "If my leg would allow me, I'd be right there with you. But I'm unable to march. In my stead are my three sons. Each is brave and strong. Follow them and come home safe to me, to your family, and to your tribe."

A fleet of boats and rowers, either very young or too old to fight, waited to ferry the warriors across the Maggiore. Once on the east bank of the lake, the warriors marched for Milan. Three days on the trail brought them to the capital. Rather than a solid army waiting for the Legions, they found a disorganized mass of humanity outside the walls.

Moving away from the confusion, the three brothers located an open field. Under the direction of Jace, the spearmen marked off lanes and began to set up their camp.

Only a small group complained about the regulated areas. The leader of the resistance puffed up his chest.

"We know how to camp," Katumaros protested. "Why do you feel the need to get in everybody's business? I'm going to go relieve myself. Care to watch?"

The five spearmen who hung around their big friend laughed.

"The latrine area is out there," Jace directed, indicating a cleared spot beyond the tents. "You're a big boy. I trust you know enough not to foul where you sleep and walk."

Growling his dislike at Jace's manner, Katumaros said, "We know that. But why the broad lanes between tents?"

"If an advance Century attacks us, which way will you run?" Jace asked.

"I wouldn't run. I'm not a coward," Katumaros bragged.

"Neither am I," Jace explained. "The wide lanes give us space to fight. Imagine forming a shield wall and tripping over your giant food bowl."

"I like to eat," Katumaros told him, defending his oversize dish.

The five friends of the big spearman laughed as Jace walked away. Halfway across the camp, Abbo intercepted Jace.

"Let's go find War Chief Brocc B'Yag," he suggested.

Jace vaguely remembered Tasco Brocc, the war chief's son. Although he couldn't recall details, the feeling made him uneasy.

"You two go ahead," Jace volunteered. "I'll stay here and get the camp organized."

"In the spring, we had half as many warriors and only two of us," Attalus advised. He walked from his tent and stood beside Jace. "Brocc acted as if granting us an audience was a distasteful favor."

"And every time we offered a plan, Brocc acted as if we were imposing on his free time. Then if we pressed, he had his personal guards shuffle forward," Abbo related. "This time, we have a thousand spears and three sons of Samo. We will have our say."

"I guess, I'm coming with you," Jace concluded.

Abbo and Attalus hooked Jace's arms and the three marched from the camp.

***

After elbowing their way to the gate and being passed through by the guards, they discovered the streets of Milan contained as much mayhem as they witnessed outside.

"I thought the Legions were on the way," Jace said to Abbo.

After separating to allow a group of armor warriors to pass, Abbo moved next to Jace and remarked, "According to the message from the King, they marched from Remini eight days ago."

"Then we should be staged in front of the walls," Jace told him, "waiting to die like good subjects."

"To die?" Attalus questioned.

"A Legion drills consistently to hold a shield wall," Jace described. "Look around at this mob. A Maniple line will chew through these spearmen until they are full of killing. Then the second Maniple will rotate forward and begin their bloody feast."

"What would you do instead of waiting to die?" Abbo asked.

"Get the Legion to march up the east side of the Lambro River, and ambush them when they cross to Milan."

"All the rivers are running high," Attalus noted. "Crossing is difficult."

"Wait," Abbo said, holding out his arms to stop his brother and Jace. "Why would the Latians come up the east side of the Lambro?"

"War Chief Brocc would need to present an opportunity that a Roman Battle Commander couldn't resist," Jace replied.

"Like what?" Attalus inquired.

"No Battle Commander wants an army behind him," Jace offered. "Show a Legion Colonel a strong enough force and he'll have to cross the Po early."

"You will tell that to the war chief," Abbo directed.

"No. You do it," Jace pushed back. "The less I say the better."

Attalus yanked their arms, and the three walked deeper into Milan.

**

An army of light infantrymen faced a challenge when forced into a defensive stance. While perfect for quick in and out strikes and flanking maneuvers, placing them on walls and stationing them on defensive lines highlighted the weakness of mobile infantry. Compounding the limitations for the Insubri warriors, their commanders came from a hierarchical structure of nepotism and not from merit.

In a large room, warriors and clan war chiefs stood along the walls. The Insubri War Chief sat at the head of a long table with clan chiefs taking up the chairs. Brocc glanced up and noted Abbo and Attalus approaching.

"Will you look at this?" Brocc B'Yag exclaimed. "The Gnātos Clan finally made an appearance. Better late than never."

The latter statement he addressed to the clan chiefs around the table.

"We've brought a thousand spears and three commanders," Attalus told him. "I and my brothers…"

"March south and form a line to defend the walls," Brocc B'Yag snapped, interrupting Attalus. "It's a simple enough order, even you should be able to follow the instructions."

Before they lost their temper, Abbo and Attalus started to back away. At a half-step, Jace's hands pushed into the small of their backs.

"Let's not die in defense of a city that will fall in a day," Jace whispered. "Look at the wall behind Brocc."

A parchment map of the area surrounding Milan hung on the wall. Ten miles southeast of the city and across the

Lambro, a wetland was noted by the words *Caution Swamp*. Beyond the swamp, a nearby town was marked on the map as *Dresano*.

"I don't understand," Abbo admitted.

"Get us assigned to Dresano," Jace insisted.

Before Abbo could say anything, a voice shouted from across the room.

"Come here, Latian Dog," Tasco B'Yag ordered. "And do it on your knees."

Based on the easy going personalities of the Kentus brothers, Jace didn't expect help from them. And the conference room was too packed with Insubri commanders to allow a fair fight. Jace searched for an escape route other than the doorway.

"Sucaria told me about that dog thing," Abbo mentioned to Jace before notifying the war chief's son of his error. "Tasco, if you have business with a war chief of the Gnātos Clan, you need to approach us."

"But do so carefully," Attalus cautioned.

"I don't have to show respect to one of my slaves," Tasco declared while crossing the room. "Get on your knees, Dog."

In a flash, Abbo drew his hunting knife and extended it hilt first. Tasco stopped and eyed the handle.

"Here is a Gnātos blade. Take it if you dare," Abbo offered. Then to Brocc B'Yag he expressed his regret. "War Chief, I apologize for dishonoring your meeting. But if he takes the blade, a Gnātos War Chief will take it back."

"For defending the honor of our clan, we never apologize," Attalus explained. "For spilling blood to defend that honor, we never apologize. For bleeding your son like a cut pig, or exposing him as a coward, we do not apologize. For we are Gnātos Clan."

The room grew silent. Tasco stared at the hilt of the weapon with one arm half raised as if to take the knife. In that instance, Jace understood the War Chief's attitude towards Abbo and Attalus. He wasn't dismissive of the brothers. Brocc just didn't know how to manage men with a well-defined code of honor.

"Father, he is my slave," Tasco protested.

"Didn't you give a Latian Dog to M'anta?" Brocc inquired. "If you gave a slave away, you can't claim ownership later."

"But I," Tasco started to say. He saw the deadly look in Jace's eyes and the defiant expressions on the faces of Abbo and Attalus. Rather than pressing his cause, he said. "Never mind."

Tasco left the room, and Jace thought it was the end of the incident. He was wrong.

"Will no one fight for their honor?" Abbo challenged. "I am holding the knife. Come and take it."

Where the room was silent before, a few grumbled. No one had time for a blood contest.

"Put it away, War Chief of the Gnātos," Brocc requested. "In a matter of days, Rome will take enough of our blood."

Abbo slipped the blade into the sheath and pointed at the map on the wall.

"We will draw the Legion up the east bank," he revealed. "When they cross over the Lambro, and climb wet and exhausted from the river, you can kill them. Think of our battle scheme as a gift from Clan Chief Samo Kentus."

"My father will be pleased that we've invoked the name of Samo Kentus," Brocc stated. "The three of you, come around the table and tell me your plan to defeat the red capes and big shields."

While Jace, Abbo, and Attalus described the trap for the Legions, Tasco B'Yag left Milan. Along with two friends, he headed for the Gnātos camp. If he was going to salvage his pride, Tasco needed to find a way to punish the Clan's war chiefs. Especially the one he knew as the Latian Dog.

**

Katumaros complained the loudest when Abbo instructed the spearmen to pack up the camp.

"We just got here," the spearman whined. "And who willingly crosses the Lambro this early in the summer?"

"Maybe the commander who plans on saving your life," Attalus shot back. "If you want, you can join the spearmen in front of the wall. We'll speak fondly of your memory on feast days."

"No way I'm leaving," Katumaros stated while reaching for his tent. "I'm staying with my clan."

"Then keep quiet and follow orders," Jace told him.

Under his breath, Katumaros grumbled. No one paid attention or heard his repeated threat. "I'll have my revenge. You'll get what's coming to you, Latian Dog."

***

On the west bank of the Lambro River, an Insubri scout looped a rope over his shoulder. Knee deep in the river, he lost his footing and fell. Before he got too far downstream, the men holding the end of the rope pulled him in.

"Not good," he complained. "The river is running too high on the banks."

Jace pushed to the front of the column. He studied the river, took the rope and the loose end, and marched to a big tree.

"A tree can't reel you in," the scout warned.

Jace tied the rope around the trunk and vanished into the trees, heading upstream.

"If he dies," Abbo proposed. "I don't want to be the one to tell Brigid."

"Better you than me," Attalus responded. "What is he doing?"

"No clue," Abbo admitted.

Splash!

Out in the river, Jace appeared. While the river carried him downstream, the Archer kicked and stroked for the distant shore. Near the far bank, a rooster tail of water washed over his head and he slowed. With mighty kicks, Jace moved towards a low-hanging branch. Grabbing the limb, the Archer pulled himself out of the water and onto the shoreline.

"We'll need at least twenty ropes across the river," he shouted.

"We only need a few for our spearmen to cross," Attalus called back.

"They're not for us," Jace explained. "They're for the Insubri running from the Legion."

***

By the next morning, the thousand warriors from the Gnātos Clan and two thousand from neighboring clans camped on the north side of the Po River. The war chiefs from the clans sat around a single campfire.

"A Legion travels like a bug," Jace told them. "They put three rings of scouts out front when the main body is on the march. Acting like antennas, the scouts feel out ambushes or large groups of enemy spearmen."

"They won't need a scout to see us," Abbo mentioned.

The three thousand spearmen had collected wood and built over four thousand fires. Smoke hung thick in the air and clouds of it drifted across the Po River.

"They can't miss the smell of our burning wood," another volunteered.

"We want them to see us and cross here," Jace instructed. "As they march north, we'll cut the Legions off from their scouts and leave them blind."

"How do you know so much about the Romans?" a clan war chief asked.

"I spent a lot of time as a captive in a Legion," Jace lied. "I've seen what they do to tribes that underestimate the red capes and big shields. We need to defend the shore when they come across, but not too well. Give them a fight before running for Dresano."

"It's twenty miles," Attalus said, brushing off the idea. "We can stroll there and stay ahead of them."

"A fully armed and armored Legionary can march twenty miles in a day and still join battle with an enemy before dusk," Jace warned. "Run ahead except for your ambushers. And remember, they need to take the bodies of the forward scouts. It's the only way to keep the Legion blind as to what we have planned at the swamp."

"We will run," Attalus assured him.

***

In the weak light of dawn, Abbo, Attalus, and Jace stood on the north bank of the big river. Not far to the west, the Lambro added its water to the Po.

"I may have misjudged the speed of the Legions," Jace remarked. "They may have passed us, crossed upriver, and be on their way to Milan."

Abbo and Attalus examined the trees and trail across the river. They had no comment until a pair of scouts appeared.

"Lingones Tribe," Attalus said, identifying the scouts. "They're from the east."

"There's no reason for them to be this far west," Abbo proposed. "Unless they're scouts for a Legion."

The pair of Lingones sniffed the air and faced the river. To confirm the presence of an Insubri army accompanying the campfires, Abbo, Attalus, and Jace waved. Behind the three, a war cry rose from three thousand spearmen.

"That'll get their attention," Attalus said.

"Let's be sure the other war chiefs and their spearmen know not to fight too hard," Jace advised. "If the battle scheme is going to work, we don't want the Legion to give up crossing the river here."

The Cretan Archer had no feelings one way or the other about the fate of the Legionaries. They were professional fighters, just as he was a mercenary. But the undertrained warriors of the Gnātos Clan were defending their, and now Jace's, new homeland. His plan was designed to bring as many of the spearmen home to Samo Kentus and their families as possible.

What the Archer didn't realize, behind him in the Insubri army, a conspiracy was under way. Its aim? To be sure, Jace Kasia never made it back to the shores of Lake Maggiore and to Brigid, his wife.

Chapter 20 – My Gift to Rome

Typically, Katumaros enjoyed being in the center of the attack. It gave the big spearman an opportunity to pick on the shorter and less robust warriors of his clan. And later, when he bragged about saving a spearman by countering a spear shaft, or using his shield to defend a fellow tribesman, it didn't matter if his exploits were lies. Being in the center of an assault allowed him to claim, if anyone challenged his assertion, that the action happened on the other side of his shield. He'd browbeat his detractor and explain to the crowd that the skeptic was simply out of position to witness the heroic act.

Counter to his preferred location, in the afternoon, Katumaros guided his five companions to the end of the Gnātos Clan formation. Inserting themselves between their clan and a smaller clan of young warriors put the large spearman between the two clans.

"Why are we here next to strangers?" one of his mates inquired. "They're so few of them, we might as well be on the end of the formation."

"Someone has to help the youths during the fight," Katumaros explained. "Who better than the victor of a thousand battles?"

The five knew the big spearmen and they hung around him for the same reasons weak men gathered around bullies. Some of them to boost their standing in their village, some hoping to get splashed with a dose of his confidence, and several for their personal protection. The one thing they had in common, the five knew he told fibs about his experience.

"A thousand battles?" asked a young spearman from the neighboring clan.

"Why sure," Katumaros stated. "Listen to me and follow my directions and you'll survive this fight."

It didn't take long for the word to spread that the Gnātos Clan had positioned their mightiest warrior between the clans. Surely, the big man was there to stabilize the line and help the young spearmen.

***

As if schools of fish making ripples, the kicks of skirmishers disrupted the surface as they swam the Po River. Spread wide to prevent the Insubri from clustering together and throwing them back into the water, the vanguard of the Legion reached the far side. And then the war chiefs made a mistake. They clustered their spearmen and countered small groups of swimmers. Moments later, realizing their mistake, the Insubri leaders withdrew up the embankment, relinquishing the shoreline to the Legion.

"Get some infantry over there," Colonel Causam Belua ordered. "If they give me a foot, I'll take a mile."

Ibex Legion of Lentulus Legions, first Maniple, held their shields as if the hardwood structures were rafts. They stacked their war gear on the shields in preparation for the combat swim.

"First Maniple go, go," their Centurions shouted. Then, in disgust at what the water would do to the officer crests on their helmets, the Centurions splashed into the Po River.

***

Having backed up the embankment, the Insubri clans set a new defensive line. Attalus Kentus, on the far right, walked behind a section, reminding them to make contact before running away. In the center, Jace Kasia told the spearmen to make a show of defending their line before sprinting north. And on the left, Abbo Kentus reminded the warriors on his side of the same thing.

Allowing the skirmishers to make land and get organized provided a safe zone for the heavy infantry to dress in their armor and prepare for an assault. Before the Legionaries stepped off, Abbo noticed the end of his line drooped down the bank. Not much, but noticeably ahead of the rest of the spearmen. Thinking to address the alignment, he raced to Katumaros.

Knowing the big spearman had a temper and was easily irritated, Abbo whispered, "Straighten this section of the line."

"Sure thing, War Chief Kentus," Katumaros acknowledged. But after Abbo walked away, the big warrior announced to the Clan with the limited number of spearmen. "The war chief said to hold your positions. You're doing great."

***

Stacked in three lines, the Centuries of First Maniple stepped off. The deadly straight lines, big shields, and level spears presented a moving wall to the Insubri. Fifteen paces from the bank of the river, the Legionaries approached the tribesmen. Except on the far left. There, the young tribesmen were shoved back by the initial thrust of Legion shields. Giving ground, they backed away a little.

"Hold your line," Katumaros told the youths. Even as he and his companions stepped back to stay with their clan, the big warrior advised. "Hold. Hold."

From the center, Jace noticed the break in the line and the danger to the young spearmen.

"Abbo, to your left," he alerted his brother-in-law.

With all his focus on the advancing Legionaries, Abbo had missed the separation. Sprinting to the end, he shouted for the young clan to break contact.

"Get back, run," he shouted. As he ran in front of Katumaros, the big spearmen put out his foot and tripped Abbo. In a hard tumble, the war chief rolled into the Legion shields. Scrambling with his fingers and feet digging into the dirt, he fled uphill.

At the center of the Insubri line, Jace watched for first contact, preparing to order the retreat. A bad feeling swept over him. He glanced to his right. Attalus waved and went back to observing the Legionaries as they closed the distance to his spearmen. Then the Archer looked to his left, searching for his other brother-in-law.

***

Pinned to the ground by a Legion spear, Abbo kicked with his legs as he attempted to pull the spearhead out of his side. Through the pain, he remembered the young tribesmen.

In an act of defiance, he bent his head back and ordered, "Run. Run for your lives."

The young spearmen spun from the fight and raced away. The Legionaries laughed, relieved at avoiding a shield wall battle after the tough swim.

"Looks like you caught one of their war chiefs," Optio Meres noted.

"What do we do with him?" a Legionary asked.

While Meres pondered Abbo's fate, another war chief strolled down the hill with his hands up. Although not as tall as the other Gauls, he sported the massive Gaulish mustache that extended down his jowls and covered his mouth. The second war chief stopped beside the injured one.

After a glance at Abbo, Jace Kasia announced, "Congratulations, Thirteenth Century. You've captured two war chiefs of the Insubri Tribe."

Optio Meres might have ordered both of the war chiefs killed, except for two oddities. The newly arrived chief greeted them with the correct number designation of their Century and he spoke perfect Latin.

"Your name?" Optio Meres inquired.

"Colonel Jace Romiliia Kasia," Jace answered. "Commander of Romiliia Legion of Scipio Legions, Carthage."

The bold statement meant Jace was once a high ranking Rome officer but now a Legion deserter. Deciding on battlefield justice, Meres directed, "Kill them and let's get back into this fight."

Three Legionaries drew back their spears.

"There's something you should know," Jace advised.

The combat officer of the Thirteenth overheard the announcement and strutted to his Optio and the out of line squad.

"Hold your thrusts," Centurion Stirpis ordered. The officer walked to Jace and looked him in the eyes. "What should I know?"

"The Insubri have set a trap," Jace warned. He indicated the running tribesmen. "I wouldn't go deeper into their territory with less than two and preferably three Legions."

After a moment to consider the information, the combat officer directed, "Send them to Colonel Belua as a gift from the Thirteenth. That should earn us a reward."

"Make the Battle Commander carry the Insubri War Chief," Meres instructed. "Two of you take them to First Century. And don't take all day doing it."

Jace eased the spear from Abbo's side, pulled him off the ground, and slung his brother-in-law over his shoulder.

"Brigid is going to be really mad at us," Abbo groaned before going limp.

***

Ecstatic at the results of his clever ploy, Spearman Katumaros ran ahead of his companions.

"Legionaries captured Jace Kasia and Abbo Kentus," one of his cronies called from behind. "Did you see that?"

Katumaros slowed his pace and threatened, "Shut your face. No one mentions it until I tell Attalus about the sad turn of events."

It took all of his control to keep from bragging about his part in getting the two war chiefs captured. Later, he would tell Attalus of his brave and selfless attempt to save them. As for the real tale, the big spearmen needed to keep it a secret. A secret he could only share with Tasco B'Yag in exchange for a fat coin purse.

***

"You heard Optio Meres," Stirpis instructed. "Thirteenth Century, let's get back into this fight."

"It just doesn't seem fair," an infantryman noted while cleaning the blood off his spearhead.

"What doesn't seem fair?" Meres asked.

"That we have to go through all the trouble of chasing them down, just to kill them," the Legionary replied.

The lines of Insubri tribesmen were far ahead and moving away quickly.

"If you don't shut up and march," Meres growled at the Century. "All the killing will be done and you'll be stuck digging latrines for exercise."

At a run, the Thirteenth hurried to catch up with the other Centuries of First Maniple. Once connected with the end of the assault line, they settled into a Legion shuffle. None of the Legionaries, their NCOs, or Centurions considered that even though the Insubri were running, the jogging Centuries kept the fleeing tribesmen in sight. And none heeded Jace's warning about an ambush.

***

On the southern bank of the Po River, Baebius Tamphilus sat on his horse, seething at the developments. Across the water, the First and Second Maniples of Ibex Legion, Centuries of Velites, and his auxiliary skirmishers chased the Insubri. Heavy infantrymen of the Third Maniple were wading ashore and dressing for combat. While the Praetor watched, a boat rowed from downstream. In the craft sat Colonel Causam Belua and five First Century bodyguards from Ibex Legion.

"Senior Tribune Calcare, we've driven the Insubri off the battlefield," Tamphilus announced before complaining. "But tell me, how can I capture glory when the enemy is running away."

"Praetor Tamphilus. Before we can mount an effective campaign," the senior staff officer counseled, "we have to get a pair of Legions and their supply wagons across the Po."

"What are you talking about?" Lieutenant General Tamphilus snapped. "Ibex Legion is already in contact. And soon Colonel Belua will personally be in pursuit of the cowardly tribesmen. As their General, I need to be part of that action."

"Sir, I recommend setting up a marching camp across the river," Senior Tribune Calcare suggested. "Once our rear is protected, we can advance into Insubri territory."

"Nonsense, we are not going to wait," Baebius Tamphilus declared. "Are we not Legions of Rome? Send word to Colonel Terrigenus. Have him swim his auxiliary skirmishers and Velites across. He can keep the Boar Legionaries back and use them to ferry the supplies across and to build a marching camp. Will that settle your uneasiness?"

"To a point, General Tamphilus," the Senior Tribune granted.

***

Across the Po River, the boat carrying Causam Belua reached the north shore. He stepped out of the watercraft and observed his Third Maniple marching up the embankment.

"Colonel, a gift from Thirteenth Century," his First Optio told him after consulting with a pair of Legionaries. "They captured two Insubri War Chiefs."

The Colonel barely glanced at the captives. Ever since his selection as the Battle Commander of Ibex Legion, Belua had dreamed of winning a battle. In his haste, he didn't interrogate the prisoners.

"Put them in the boat and send them to Lieutenant General Tamphilus, with my compliments," Belua instructed. Then to his First Century, he directed. "Let's go."

On foot, the Battle Commander, his staff, and bodyguards marched after Ibex Legion. Before following, Legionaries shoved Jace and Abbo into the boat.

"Are you going to be a problem?" the man on the rear oar asked.

Jace checked the wound in Abbo's side. While holding a bandage to stem the bleeding, Jace assured the riverman, "He's in no condition to swim. And I'm not leaving him. So, you're safe."

Newly arriving Legion light infantrymen from Boar Legion shoved the boat off the shore and ran to catch Ibex. The riverman poled the craft into deep water. In broad sweeps of the rear oar, he propelled the boat across the Po. When they reached the south shore, Tamphilus greeted the boat.

"Get them out," the Lieutenant General ordered. "I need to get across."

Jace helped Abbo out of the boat and for a moment, Tamphilus stood in front of the Insubri War Chiefs.

"Who are they?" Senior Tribune Calcare asked.

"Insubri War Chiefs," the riverman answered.

"General, what do you want me to do with them?" Calcare asked.

"Kill them," Tamphilus answered. But he paused, looked into Jace's eyes, studied the Latin face, and changed the instructions. "Send them to Rome. They can be my gift to the Senate."

Senior Tribune Calcare waved over a supply officer as the General climbed into the boat.

"Put these two with the baggage wagons to Genoa," he instructed. "After the detachment collects Consul Lentulus' luggage, the ship can take the war chiefs to the Capital."

The Centurion pushed Jace to get the pair moving.

"Senior Tribute, I've got to tell you something," Jace attempted to speak with the senior staff officer.

The supply Centurion smashed the Archer in the small of his back. After falling to his knees and dragging his brother-in-law down with him, Jace cradled Abbo in his arms. The protective move proved unnecessary. No kicks followed.

"Speak only when spoken to," the supply Centurion informed Jace. "Learn that and your journey south will be much easier. Now get up and move away from the river."

Calcare waved a dismissive hand. "If they give your men trouble on the road, they can beat them. But the Insubri need to be alive and standing when they reach Rome."

"Yes, sir," the supply officer acknowledged.

The General rowed away, and Senior Tribune Calcare went to brief Colonel Terrigenus of Boar Legion. No one bothered to question the Insubri War Chiefs about the tribe's strategy or what waited for the Legion near the hamlet of Dresano.

***

The heavy forest blocked the Centurion's view of the neighboring Century.

"Optio, move us to the left," Stirpis ordered. "We don't want any tribesmen getting between us and the Twelfth."

"Yes, sir," Meres stated before instructing, "Century shift left, tuck us in tight."

The Thirteenth Century moved towards the center. What Centurion Stirpis didn't know, on the far left of the Maniple, the Second Century adjusted to avoid the start of a swamp. They stepped right, squeezing the twelve Centuries of First Maniple into the shape of a bow rather than a maneuverable line. Because the Maniple's Tribunes traveled in the forest and off the road, the two staff officers lost contact with each other. Neither realized the danger of the misshapen formation.

"Enemy sighted," came a call from the Centuries in the center. "Standby to advance."

Without a visual, the Maniple relied on their training. The twelve Centuries tightened their first two lines into a shield wall and the third line stepped back and prepared to throw javelins. In an open field, the formation provided flexibility and the ability to repel the charge of an enemy from any direction. In the forest, and bunched up in the center, the Maniple appeared to be a sacrificial beast, extending its chest to the blade of a priest. Yet, it was still a solid mass of shields and a formidable fighting force, until the Centurions in the center ordered, "Centuries wheel left."

They followed the road, pursuing a horde of fleeing Insubri. Unseen for the moment, the Lambro River flowed rapidly southward. It would become a barrier to any heavy infantryman seeking to escape in a westerly direction, just as the swamp behind them stopped any retreat.

The sudden rotation of the Maniple marched the Second and Third Centuries on the left into the sticky mud of a swamp. On the far right, the Twelfth and Thirteenth Centuries got separated when they circled the hamlet of Dresano. Without realizing their wings had been clipped, the eight remaining Centuries of Ibex Legion's First Maniple continued around until their assault lines faced westward.

When the Legion Maniple faced the Lambro River, newly appointed War Chief Katumaros released his spearmen. Coming out of the trees to the north, the warriors screamed battle cries and struck the side of the formation.

In a desperate attempt to form lines that faced the enemy, the Centurions ordered, "Centuries, to the rear, wheel right. Step back, step back."

The movement brought the eight Centuries around and put their shields in line. But the Legionaries, who survived the initial onslaught, were shin deep in swamp muck and unable to perform even basic maneuvers. As if stationary targets, they fell to Insubri spears and died in the putrid water of the bog.

***

War Chief Attalus Kentus roared defiantly as he led Insubri warriors from the east. They emerged through the trees, catching the Second Maniple strung out and vulnerable. Rushing forward to help the First Maniple, the Legionaries were unable to form a shield wall. Attalus and his warriors swept through the gaps, slaughtering Legionaries. All the while, they yelled about vengeance for Abbo and Jace.

***

Colonel Belua encouraged light infantrymen, coming from the Po, to surge ahead of him and his staff. Proudly, he marched northward to his great victory. But several miles from the river, he began to encounter dead Legionaries and light infantrymen alongside the road. From ahead, wounded infantrymen staggered into view.

"I don't understand," Belua admitted. "I must have sent over six thousand men forward to chase the Insubri. Why are there dead and wounded back here?"

"Sir, it might have been an ambush," his senior combat officer suggested.

"If that's true," Battle Commander Belua remarked. "Where are the Insubri bodies?"

An instant after his question, Insubri battle cries echoed from the woods on both sides of the road.

"Bíois. Bíois."

Chapter 21 – A Pit in The Forum

During the retreat to Rimini, Lieutenant General Baebius Tamphilus remained in the center ranks of Boar Legion. His usual position at the head of the Legions depended on a vanguard of light infantry and scouts. The Legion of Battle Commander Terrigenus had few remaining to protect the Praetor. For two days after the doomed assault, wounded had staggered out of the woods. Terrigenus' remaining light infantry were helping the injured men keep up with the march.

Most of the Legion's skirmishers and Velites had moved north from the Po River. And, like Colonel Belua and his ill-fated Ibex Legion, they never returned from Insubri territory. And so, other than cavalrymen riding on the flanks, Boar Legion moved without the normal screen of light infantrymen.

While the Legion marched steadily but with caution, compared to the four couriers sent racing for Rome, it was a snail's pace. Two Tribunes as witnesses to the massacre and two Centurions carrying scrolls for Consul Lentulus rode south while the Legion marched southwest.

Three days later, when Ibex reached the seaside garrison, the mounted messengers were only two days from Rome.

The third unit dispatched from Boar Legion were the wagons detailed to collect Consul Lentulus' belongings. Slowest of them all, the transports bounced along a rutted route. With mountains looming on both sides, the Legion detachment picked their way along the Trebbia River. The small group was still two days from Genoa when the four Legion messengers reached Rome.

***

Abbo Kentus groaned and jerked away.

"Hold still," Jace scolded.

He finished dribbling vinegar over the entrance and exit wounds on Abbo's side. As he tightened a wrap around the Insubri's waist, Abbo pulled away.

"Maybe you should cut his throat and save the vinegar," Legionary Casus offered.

"Abbo will heal," Jace said defending his brother-in-law, "it's more than I can say for you."

Casus held up his right hand. Although heavily bandaged, the shape revealed two missing fingers. And the dirt and dried blood on the fabric showed neglect.

"I didn't see the blade before it took my fingers," Casus stated. "But I can feel the pain you want to dispense. I'll let it heal by itself."

"If you don't let me continue the treatment, you'll lose the hand," Jace warned, "or maybe the entire arm."

"But it hurts when you cut and rinse it," Legionary Casus protested.

The three other escorts nodded their agreement. All four of the Legionaries had wounds that allowed them to escape the battle. Regulated to baggage detail, they guarded two empty wagons, mules, a pair of teamsters, and two prisoners. To their amazement, one of the prisoners spoke Latin and understood medicine.

"You need to cut away the rot and wash the wound until it's pink," Jace explained. He stepped down from the moving wagon and inquired. "Come on, which one of you heroes is next."

One with his arm in a sling walked quickly to the wagon and hopped on. He swung his legs while Jace removed the sling.

"It never occurred to me how much it hurts to get poked with a spear," infantryman Stridor complained.

"Most infantrymen keep their shields between their bodies and their enemies," Jace offered. He peeled away the bandage, revealing the man's shoulder wound. He poured a little vinegar over the injury before adding. "They don't turn sideways so a spearhead can get behind their shield and under their armor."

"I didn't turn on purpose," Legionary Stridor griped. "Someone bumped me."

"A hand's width more and the Insubri would have taken your windpipe," Jace observed. He slipped the sling over the Legionary's head and tucked the arm through the loop. "As it is, you'll be sore but you'll recover the use of your arm."

"What about my fingers?" Casus inquired.

"Hop on the wagon and let me have a look at that hand," Jace instructed.

After cutting away rot and rinsing the wound, he wrapped the hand with a fresh bandage. Following treatments to the injuries of Casus, Stridor, Ventus, and Poples, Jace settled into a leisurely walk behind a wagon. The trail turned downhill, the river rushed to the sea, and the baggage detachment continued its journey to the harbor at Genoa.

***

In Rome, Lucius Lentulus threw his glass of vino across the room. The glass shattered on the bricks, leaving a wine stain on the wall. Despite the violence, his guest didn't flinch.

"That, Consul, was a waste of fine glass and good vino," Cornelius Scipio offered.

"That was a mild reaction to the mess Baebius Tamphilus made of my Legions," Lentulus grumbled. "He was supposed to wait for me at the Po. Not send an entire Legion to die on Insubri blades."

"I know you want to rush north and punish the Insubri," Cornelius sympathized. "But you've got a more urgent calling right now."

"And what, President Scipio Africanus, is more important than revenge?" Lentulus demanded. "What in Hades is more pressing than reclaiming Roman honor?"

"You said it, honor. More specifically, honoring the dead," Cornelius clarified.

"Funeral games to pacify the citizens of Rome," Lentulus blew out. "Can I get the Senate to pay part of the cost?"

Pushing to his feet, Cornelius replied, "If they were my Legions, I would expect to pay for the games. But since you asked, I'll survey a few Senators to see if the motion would pass."

"You've become quite the politician," Lentulus remarked.

"Not by choice, Consul Lentulus," Cornelius said as he walked to the doorway. "I'd rather be on the march at the head of a Legion."

"In light of the disaster and public opinion," Lucius Lentulus reflected, "so would I."

Two days later, with funds from the Senate and Consul Lentulus, teamsters brought in wagonloads of sand to create an arena in the Forum. And carpenters began constructing temporary stands for the spectators around the fighting pit. As the venue rose from a grassy area between temples, the call went out for criminals under sentences of death, captured tribesmen from Gaul and Iberia, and warriors seeking fame and renown.

Gamblers set up tables in anticipation of round-upon-round of betting. Also drawn by the promise of flowing silver, slave traders hustled to purchase strong bodies. For each quality slave, they would collect a share of the riches by providing gladiators for the blood sport of the funeral games.

***

A slight breeze blew across the beaches of Genoa. Riding the gentle current, the Roman quinquereme *Domina Melpomene* approached the shoreline. Without breaking the rhythm of the flapping sail, the rowers extended one-hundred-and-eighty oars and stroked together before the sailors lowered the cloth. Under command of the ship's officers, the five-banker cut a half circle in the water and backed to the shallows.

"There's your ride," Casus commented.

Abbo leaned against a crutch. While his fever had broken, his side pained him and made it difficult to stand upright. Jace hovered nearby in case Abbo needed help.

Over the weeks they waited at Genoa, the infantryman's hand healed. And thanks to training by Jace, his thumb and two-finger grip on a spear improved, possibly enough to save his job as a heavy infantryman. But the true benefit of the grip, was that it gave Casus the ability to manage a hoe, an ax, and a shovel on his family's farm.

The two wagons and teamsters waited with the four Legionaries and two prisoners.

"We'll be heading for Cremona," Stridor declared. "And you'll be going to Rome."

After pained expressions by the other three Legionaries reminded him that Jace and Abbo were prisoners, he lowered his head and clamped his mouth closed.

Oarsmen pushed the five-banker onto the beach and one of the infantrymen called up to the steering deck. "We're here for the Consul's luggage."

"No Consul on board," a ship's officer replied. "We're here for strong men with the ability to fight."

A ramp dropped to the beach and a moment later, a Ship's Centurion and the First Principale walked to the shoreline. Behind them, an Optio and a squad of Marines marched from *Domina Melpomene*.

"What are you four doing?" the first officer asked.

"Sir, we're assigned to deliver these prisoners to the ship and to collect the Consul's luggage," Legionary Ventus answered. "And take it to the Consul's headquarters at Cremona."

The First Principale pointed to Jace and directed the Marine Optio. "take him. Leave the cripple. Better yet, sell him to a slave trader."

After delivering the instructions, the ship's officers marched down the beach, heading for Genoa. The squad moved forward to split Jace from Abbo. Jace braced, ready to resist being separated from his brother-in-law.

"Optio," Ventus and Poples said at the same time.

"What do you two want?" the NCO asked.

"Jace nursed us back to health," Poples told him.

"Because of him I can use my hand," Casus stated.

"And I can move my arm," Stridor added while swinging his arm around. "We own him and he's very attached to Abbo."

"What do you want me to do about it?" the Optio questioned.

"Take them both," Ventus suggested. "Abbo is healing quickly. Whatever the First Principale has planned, he'll be ready."

"What the first officer needs are strong men to participate in funeral games," the Optio told him. "Men capable of fighting and bleeding for the Legionaries of Ibex Legion."

"Then take them both," Casus insisted. "We are members of Ibex. Let them both bleed for us."

The other three nodded their confirmation of the assertion. After thinking over the logic, the NCO ordered his Marines, "take them both to the holding area."

"Thank you," Stridor offered.

"Don't thank me. I should thank you for your sacrifice. The reports from the battle at Insubri are terrible. It must have been Hades."

Casus held up his hand, displaying the missing fingers.

Moments later, Casus, Stridor, Ventus, and Poples watched as the prisoners were led away.

"If we can locate cargo headed to Cremona," Poples suggested, "we can make a profit on the trip back."

The four stood silently for a moment before Ventus mentioned, "We didn't tell the Optio that Abbo and Jace are Insubri war chiefs."

"I figure fighting as gladiators will be rough enough," Stridor divulged. "Why add to their misery?"

"Agreed," Casus and Poples confirmed.

The four Legionaries turned and strolled to the wagons. Their minds occupied with finding loads to transport to the north.

At an empty section of beach, Jace and Abbo were directed to sit on the sand.

"Stay there," the Optio directed. He left one Marine to watch the prisoners and took the other nine to Genoa.

"*Domina Melpomene*," Abbo read. "What does it mean?"

"It's the name of the warship," Jace answered. "*Domina Melpomene* means Mistress of Calamity."

"Sounds like my sister," Abbo said with sadness in his voice.

Jace found himself unable to say anything.

***

The temporary arena acted as the northern point of a triangle that included the Temple of Vesta and the Temple of Castor and Pollux. Wooden stands had been constructed on four sides with passageways for attendees between the seats. A holding pen for the fighters was built to the northeast and a shelter for the guards with parking for the burial wagons sat off to the northwest. Body removal had to be quick during summer to prevent the smell of death from ruining the ambiance of the games. Spilling blood might be sacred and a way to speed the souls of the deceased on their journey to Hades, but no one wanted a too real reminder of corpses and rotting bodies.

Traffic along the Via Della Salara increased since the carpenters placed the first boards. Citizens, freemen, and slaves stopped at the sandpit to reflect on the reason for the funeral games.

"Or they have a morbid fascination with killing," Cornelius offered.

"Not as morbid as one might think," Lentulus proposed. They walked to the gladiator pens, where the Consul pointed to the preparation area for the fighters. "After searching for gladiators, I'm coming up short for three days of games. Either murderers are taking the summer off or they've curtailed their activities until after the games."

"Now who is being morbid?" Cornelius remarked. The two men strolled through one of the passageways and stopped at the edge of the sand. "I received word from Ostia that two 5-bankers had arrived with fresh meat for your sacrifices."

"Why do I have the feeling you don't like watching men fight," Lentulus confessed.

"It's not the fighting," Cornelius told him. "It's the lack of strategy and the inevitability of the outcome. It's static and always ends the same way. No self-respecting General would willingly march his Legions into the narrow confines of a round battlefield."

"Afraid of being bested in combat?" Lentulus asked.

"Afraid of being unable to retreat to a stronger position," Cornelius countered.

***

A hundred male slaves, all fit and furious at their situation, shuffled through the streets of Rome. After two days of hiking from the docks at Osita, they were tired, irritable, and hungry. In the middle of the herd, Abbo Kentus limped along Via Della Salara. Although the Insubri war chief didn't grumble, he shared the angry sentiment of the slaves. Beside him, however, Jace Kasia walked with a bounce in his step and a smile on his face.

"Doesn't this make you angry?" Abbo asked his brother-in-law. "If I ever get home, I will kill Katumaros. That trip wasn't a mistake or a slip. He intentionally dropped me into those Legion shields."

"Why would he do that?" Jace questioned.

"I don't know. Unless Tasco B'Yag wanted revenge on me for Attalus and I challenging him in front of his father. He could have paid Katumaros."

The smile fell from Jace's face and he clinched his fist. He would leave Katumaros to Abbo. But Tasco B'Yag would answer to the Cretan Archer if Jace and Abbo managed to get out of Rome alive.

From the sides of the road, Legionaries shouted at the crowd of potential gladiators, "Stay on the road. If you run, we will hunt you down. And you'll see your last sunrise from the top of a cross."

"I guess we stay on the road," Abbo mentioned.

"There is nowhere else I'd rather be," Jace stated to Abbo's dismay.

Sixteen miles from the sea, and across the city of Rome, the gladiators arrived at the Forum. Few had ever been to Rome, and the sight of all the temples around the Forum overwhelmed them.

Instead of looking around, Abbo focused on the structure in front of them.

"What is that?" he asked.

"The sand pit in the Forum," Jace replied, "is the arena where we will die. Or depending on the Fates, where we will thrive."

Near the stands, their Legion guards instructed, "spread out and grab a piece of grass. That's your home for the funeral games. Sit down and you'll be fed. Resist and you will die."

A Centurion marched to the front of the slaves.

"I need bodies to dig latrines," he announced.

Jace stood, reached down, and pulled his brother-in-law to his feet.

"Why do you want to help them?" Abbo whined.

The combat officer counted out five men and waved them forward.

He added, "for the extra work, you'll receive extra rations."

Jace bent to Abbo and whispered, "That's why we will dig. You'll need your strength for the fighting."

Act 8

Chapter 22 – Fighting Circle

Consul Lentulus and Senate President Scipio Africanus discussed the trials of building a new Legion as they circled the sand. After noticing the arrival of the slaves for the games, the two Romans climbed to the top of the stands and gazed down on the ninety-five gladiators.

"A quarter of them appear as if they'll drop from exhaustion at any moment," Lentulus observed. "They won't provide much entertainment."

Cornelius studied the strong ones and added, "and the rest appear ready to eat the weak. I bet at every meal the lions take the food from the hungry ones. And thusly, Consul, the weak will get weaker."

"If these games are going to be successful, all the fighters need to be fed and watered," Lentulus stated. "I guess we could save the weak ones for day three."

"You'd dangle them like sacrificial meat in front of vicious lions?" Cornelius questioned. "Maybe we should split them into two groups. Over feed one and keep the rest on normal rations."

"Suppose we fight the underweight ones against the weak ones on day one," Lentulus proposed. "The fights would be evenly matched and crowd pleasers. The best would move forward to face the bigger and stronger fighters on day two."

"It does keep the fights even," Cornelius said without emotion. "If any gladiator match truly is even."

"I take it you won't be attending the funeral games," Lentulus guessed.

"Not for all the silver in every purse at the betting tables. As I pointed out, I don't like the battlefield."

After another look at the gladiator pool, the Roman noblemen turned from the slaves and descended the levels of benches.

***

From behind the gladiator preparation building, Abbo Kentus glanced around the structure.

"There are two men in togas with purple stripes on the seats," he reported.

From down in the trench, Jace lifted up a basket of dirt.

"The purple stripes mean they're Senators of Rome. Probably the sponsors of the games," he informed Abbo. "Here, take this and dump it."

"It really is a wonder," Abbo mentioned as he lifted the basket.

"What?" Jace inquired. "The city of Rome."

"I've seen paved streets and temples. It's the way they sloped the bottom of the trench to meet the sewer pipe," Abbo explained. "And the clay tiles they'll use to line the bottom. It is truly the finest latrine I've ever seen."

"Just wait until they release the water while you're using it," Jace teased. "Your backside will feel as fresh as a field of lilies."

An Optio appeared from around the building.

"You two can talk later while you eat," the NCO instructed. "For now, how about you dig?"

Jace ducked down and hoed up another layer of dirt, while Abbo carried the basket to a mound of loose soil. Confused by the reference, Abbo couldn't remember ever feeling as fresh as a field of lilies.

Later, the five men on the work detail cleaned up and went to the main group of gladiators. Before they reached the grassy area, the Optio headed them off.

"You're assigned to that area," he directed, while pointing to another location.

Abbo whispered, "they have all the slight men grouped together."

Jace smiled and nodded at a row of cook pots.

"Looks like the Romans are fattening us up for the slaughter," Jace commented.

"How did we end up with the sheep?" Abbo asked. Then he thought for a couple of steps and added. "Never mind. Don't answer. I'm hungry."

***

On the first day of the funeral games, a few attendees arrived early. Filling in the lower tiers, they claimed what some would argue were the best seats. Best being defined as proximity to possible blood splatter, the visceral sight of specific cuts from spears or blades and the details of a face, grimacing in defeat or in death. For those benefits, the lower benches provided the thrills.

Yet, the questionable part of the positions came with drawbacks. The food and beverage venders were not prepared to begin servings at sunrise. The betting booths lacked the parchment sheets for odds and names. Nor had the men who took bets come with their fat coin purses to entice the gamblers. And capping off the negatives of being there at sunrise, priests of Rome stood in the center of the arena and droned on about their Gods.

When the ball of the sun topped the horizon, the middle tiers filled with new spectators, and the last priest took to the center of the sand.

"The blood spilled today will benefit the souls of the departed," a priest of Bellona exclaimed. He pulled a knife, held the blade over his head, and slowly turned in a circle. Sunlight reflected off the sharp steel, sending rays across the faces of the attendees. "Our Goddess of War, Bellona, is uniquely situated to value the sacrifices of these gladiators. And so, I offer this for the Goddess."

With those words, the priest sliced his forearm. Holding the appendage out, he allowed drops to fall, providing the first blood to bless the arena.

***

In the gladiator preparation building, Optio Herminia pointed at the weapons rack while shoving a trio of fighter to the head of the line.

"Give these three spears," he directed the Legion armorer.

The Legionaries in the building braced. As the slaves or the condemned were armed, no one cared how they became the entertainment, the Legionaries lifted their shields for protection against a rebellion. Order would be maintained before the games at the tip of the gladii.

"Give the next three short swords," the NCO instructed.

Spears against swords meant the Optio Herminia was picking potential winners and losers. The next three fighters shuffled forward to accept their swords. At the end of the trio, Jace Kasia bumped the gladiator ahead of him.

"Take your sword and move off," he snarled. Angry, the man spun around. But rather than finding another thin man, he faced the broad chest of an Archer. Adding an insult on top of the rude behavior, Jace directed. "Clean the dirt out of your ears, Iberian, and get your sword."

Barely controlling his temper, the man from Iberia took the sword, confidently swiped the air with the blade, and left the building. Jace accepted his sword and followed.

***

Outside, Legion infantrymen lined the pathway to the arena.

"Who wants to go first?" Centurion Flere inquired.

The short Iberian used his sword to point at Jace.

"I want to bleed him," he declared. "Better yet, give him to me and my tribesman. We'll scatter his blood across the sand."

One of the thin fighters with a spear stepped over and stood beside his fellow Iberian.

"I see the balance," Flere offered. "You three follow me."

His observation wasn't wrong. The Archer stood taller and was much broader than the Iberians. But they were two men, and Jace was one. Plus, they had a spear. When the four reached the center of the arena, the crowd whispered that the Gaul, with the long mustache, would die.

"Drawn from the west, we have two fine specimens of Iberian tribesmen," Flere announced to the crowd.

"The Gaul should present his throat and spare himself the embarrassment of being slaughtered," a spectator taunted, "and us the toil of watching him die quickly."

As if to confirm the observation, Jace attempted to rest the sword on his shoulder. But he lost his grip, and the weapon fell to the sand. In the stands, boys rushed up and down, taking bets. Most were against the Gaul.

"And opposing them, we have a vile creature from Insubri," Centurion Flere told the crowd.

Although Jace looked Gaulish with his tied back hair and full mustache, upon confirmation that he was Insubri, the spectators shouted insults and jeered. The officer waited for them to settle.

"And so, for the men of Ibex Legion, the Senate of Rome and Consul Lentulus present these funeral games," the Centurion shouted. "Citizens of Rome, you are here to witness the spilling of sacred blood in their names."

Flere marched to the edge of the sand and turned to face the combatants.

"Anyone who refuses to fight," he warned, "will be gutted and left to die with their intestines piled on their chest. Now fight."

Confusing to the crowd, Jace picked up the sword but remained bent over. Dragging the tip of the blade, he drew a circle in the sand.

"What's that?" a heckler asked.

"Maybe he's a witch, and the circle will keep the spearman and the swordsman out," another proposed.

Jace moved to the center of the fighting circle and encouraged, "Come and reclaim your honor, Iberian."

The swordsman walked to the circle and looked at the line. As if afraid that his foe might be a witch, the Iberian used his foot to erase the line. The crowd and the spearman watched in silence.

During the removal of the line, Jace stood absolutely still. With a desire for revenge and to punish the Gaul, the Iberian paced three steps into the fighting circle.

In a flash, Jace gripped the blade of the sword by the tip and flipped it end-over-end. Spinning in a blur, the weapon flew at the Iberian. The thin man jerked backwards a step but stopped. The sword buried its tip in the sand between his legs.

Laughing with relief, he looked down. During that break in concentration, Jace leaped high in the air, curled into a ball, and extended his leg. As if leaping from a ledge, Jace Kasia's heels hammered into the Iberian's head. The thin man fell to his knees, his sword dropping to the sand.

Jace snatched up both weapons before kicking the Iberian in the face. After the thin man flew out of his circle, the Cretan Archer redrew the erased part of the line.

Back at the center of his fighting circle, Jace held out both swords and informed the spearman, "It's your turn, Iberian."

Screaming at the turn of events, the audience roared its approval of the bout. Although many complained about losing the coins, they had bet on a sure thing. On his hands and knees and wobbly, the thin man gushed blood into the sand from his nose and mouth. Spectators cheered the spilling of sacrificial blood.

When he finally collapsed, two Legionaries ran to him. They grabbed his arms and pulled the Iberian away.

Satisfied with his plan to get two swords, Jace thought he only had the spearman to contend with before he retired for the day. Unfortunately for the Archer, the Centurion wanted to see a swords fight. Angry at the stunt, he sent the other swordsman onto the sand to show his displeasure. The crowd, on the other hand, erupted in full voice to show their pleasure at the addition of another fighter.

***

The spearman shuffled left while the swordsman approached from the right. Jace responded to neither threat. Statue like, he waited in the center of his fighting circle.

"Close the distance and fight," Centurion Flere ordered. "Get on with it. Fight."

From the stands came the chant, "Get on with it, fight. Get on with it, fight."

Compelled by the noise and his nerves, the spearman lowered the shaft and ran at Jace. Joining the attack, the swordsman fanned his blade in circles, as if to confound his target. It was difficult to tell if the target was confused because Jace stood stock-still.

But when the spearman stepped over the line and into the circle, Jace stepped towards the man. He swung both swords: one on a flat plain that impacted the spearhead, and the other in a slashing move that severed the fingers on the spearman's forward hand.

Blood gushed, soaking the sand, and the stands rocked as the attendees screamed and stomped their feet.

The spearman dropped his shaft and bent forward to cuddle the raw nubs. Jace rolled his body over the injured man's back to escape the spinning blade of the swordsman. On the other side, he landed on his feet and came to a guard position.

"You should have stayed beside the spearman," Jace offered.

With his left sword, he cross blocked and stopped the spinning blade of the swordsman. Next, Jace kneed the injured spearman into the swordsman's legs. Stepping forward while putting all his weight behind his sword, the Cretan Archer ran the blade through the swordsman's collarbone and into his chest.

While one man died, and the other cried, Jace Kasia threw them outside his circle. Then calmly, he redrew the lines where they were scuffed.

"Come out of the arena," Centurion Flere directed. To the last pair of spearmen, he ordered. "Get onto the sand and fight."

Jace placed the blades under his arms and raised his hands to show his palms were empty. As he walked out of his circle, four Legionaries passed him on their way to clearing the arena of bodies.

"Centurion. Can I keep the swords?" Jace asked.

"We'll hold onto them until your next fight," the officer replied. "But yes, you can use them again."

"Can I sharpen them?" Jace added.

"Would you also like a jug of vino and a roasted pig?"

"If they're available, yes," Jace responded to the sarcasm. "But really sir, I'll settle for a whetstone."

"Tell the armorer I said to let you sharpen the swords," Flere allowed before inquiring. "Where did you learn your Latin?"

"A few years back," Jace answered, "I did some scouting for the Legions in Iberia."

But the Centurion had stopped listening. His attention was focused on the inactivity in the arena and the bored silence of the crowd.

"Get on with it. Fight," Flere directed the spearmen. "Or I'll come out there and gut you both."

***

A break in the fights at midday allowed the attendees to use the public latrine, place bets, or buy beverages and roasted meats and vegetables. While the activities varied, one topic was on everyone's lips.

"When does the circle warrior fight again?" they asked.

To the dismay of the attendees, the answer came back, "You'll have to wait until tomorrow to see the Gaul fight again."

The afternoon bouts featured another Insubri. While he won his fights and spilled blood for the deceased Legionaries, Abbo wasn't as dynamic as Jace. Even when the gladiator fights ended for the day, the crowd still buzzed about the Gaul, who fought in a circle.

***

Once Cornelius Scipio settled in for the evening and the household guards took responsibility for the Senate president, Sidia Decimia left Villa Scipio. Blocks away, the aroma of baked goods drew the bodyguard into a storefront.

"I don't remember you keeping your ovens hot this late in the day," Sidia remarked.

"It's not a typical day," the baker told him. He handed over a round of bread. "As a matter of fact, it's highly unusual. But my sellers at the Forum sold out and I had to begin baking to restock their carts."

The top of the loaf glistened from a light brushing of olive oil and sparkled with a dusting of salt. Sidia broke off a piece and admired the olives and oregano leaves baked in the dough.

"General Scipio was at the Forum yesterday," the bodyguard remarked before taking a bite.

"So was I," the proprietor reported. "It's like any normal set up for funeral games."

"What's different?" Sidia inquired. He took a bite and chewed the savory bread.

"One of the gladiators draws a circle in the sand," the baker answered. "And he stands in it, daring the others to come into the circle and fight."

"He's presenting a stationary target," Sidia summarized. "It's not the best strategy. What are people excited about?"

"Any fighter who crosses the line into the circle is quickly and brutally beaten," the baker stated. "Tomorrow, the stands will be packed early."

Sidia handed over a coin for the bread and left the shop. A block away, he stopped in mid-stride.

"A Cretan Archer fighting circle?" Sidia Decimia questioned.

After thinking for a moment, he attempted to discard the idea. Continuing to his living quarters, a villa supplied by Cornelius Scipio, Sidia attempted to get the concept out of his mind.

Chapter 23 – In One Fate

Jace spent the evening sharpening and cleaning not only the pair of swords he claimed, but an entire rack of blades.

"Nice work, Insubri," the armorer complimented him.

"How nice?" Jace inquired.

"What are you getting at?" the Legionary questioned.

"If I did such a good job," Jace suggested, "perhaps you'll give me a shield."

"Tomorrow is day two of the games," the armorer told him. "Every fighter will get a shield. What happened to you wanting two swords?"

"I still want the two swords and a shield," Jace explained. "But not the big shield. I want the small one that fits on my forearm."

"No one else wants that piece of wrist jewelry. It's yours."

"A word of advice, armorer," Jace offered as he handed back the whetstone. "Tomorrow, bet on me winning."

"You won't be facing the lightweight guys," the armorer noted. "The fighters tomorrow are as big as you or bigger. And they'll have big shields while all you'll have is a tiny one."

"And two swords," Jace reminded him.

He left the gladiator preparation building and went to find Abbo.

***

The rising sun illuminated full stands and crowds blocking the passageways.

"Sir, we have the eyes of Rome on us," Optio Herminia proposed.

"I noticed important Senators and poor shop owners sitting together," Centurion Flere responded. Then he scanned the spectators on the ground. "The barbarian has fired the imagination of the city with his circle. I don't want anyone getting inside our barrier, disrupting our operation, and bothering the gladiators. We need them fighting in the arena, not where we have them bedded down."

"I'll increase the perimeter guards," Herminia promised. "And with your permission, I'll send to the garrison for more infantrymen."

"Do that," Flere confirmed. "Anytime legislators are forced to sit with shop merchants, the area is overcrowded. The Goddess Manea can't be far behind with her blessing of chaos."

"Centurion, you can depend on us," Optio Herminia swore. "A riot will not disrupt the funeral games."

"You can say that," Flere cautioned, "but we can't hold back the citizens of Rome. Any more than we could hold back the waters of the Tiber during spring flooding."

Herminia saluted and went to organize the guards. Left alone, Centurion Flere watched as more people arrived and shoved at the backs of those already standing shoulder-to-shoulder. What worried him were the few who pushed through and wedged themselves into the stands.

"Goddess Manea hear my prayer," the Centurion uttered. "Give me two days of peace to finish the games. And I'll sacrifice a bull to you."

Then he had a thought. If the Gaul was killed, the enthusiasm would die, and the overcrowding would fade back into the city streets and plazas.

***

The morning passed with Abbo, facing two different adversaries in single combat. Cheering greeted the blood sacrifices he extracted.

"Come off the sand," Flere instructed. He eyed the bleachers and those standing in the grass. If anything, the crowd had grown while waiting for the other Gaul to enter the arena. Abbo strolled by and overheard the Centurion speaking with a Legionary. "Go tell Optio Herminia to arm two more gladiators. I want the Insubri dead before lunch."

It took all of Abbo's will to keep from rushing to Jace. As he neared those waiting to fight, he dropped his spear.

"The Centurion wants you dead," Abbo whispered while bending to retrieve the shaft.

An infantryman spotted the Insubri and barked, "You there, keep moving."

Jace nodded at his brother-in-law to let him know he understood the warning. Acknowledgement was the only thing Jace could do. He couldn't very well resign his position as a gladiator.

"Insubri, get into the arena," Flere commanded. As Jace crossed the grass, the Centurion addressed two Greeks with spears and light infantry shields. "Kill him quick and you'll get extra rations. And tomorrow morning, I'll let you sleep in."

The Greeks were thieves from Corinth and had worked the roads to rob guarded Roman merchants. They understood intimidation and weapons. Before crossing the grass, the two adjusted their shields and talked for a moment. Their fight started with mental combat and planning. Before they even reached the arena, they wanted the Insubri to think about defending against a tightly coordinated attack.

After the conference, the two strolled leisurely across the grass, heading for the arena. Well trained, they linked shields and rested their spears on the top of the barrier.

The formation presented Jace Kasia with a short wall of hardwood topped with iron spearheads. One strategy to defeat them involved Jace running around the arena until one of the Greeks lagged. Once separated, he could take them down one at a time. Or, as Jace had done the previous day, stand still in the center of his circle and wait for them to arrive.

***

Screams of anticipation, shouts for revenge, and calls for the betting men to come to a section and take wagers, greeted the arrival of the circle warrior. Alerted by the vocal mayhem, Sidia Decimia raised up on the balls of his feet. From the back of the spectators and over the heads of the crowd, he noted the gladiator's long hair, tied back to keep it out of his face. And when the man turned, the mustache hid his lips and the long handles of the mustache obscured his jaw line. But the nose and flashing eyes left no doubt as to the barbarian's identity.

"It's Jace," Sidia gushed.

"What?" a man in front of him asked.

Overjoyed at seeing his cousin alive, the big Hirpini grabbed the citizen and gave him a hug. Festival booths had sprung up to serve the masses at the funeral games. They forced Sidia to circle around the lines of people waiting to buy food, beverages, or religious items. Once clear of the obstructions, he sprinted to the gladiator preparation building. When he arrived at the compound, a pair of Legionaries lowered their spears and blocked the entrance.

"Sorry, Optio," one informed him. "No one except Central Legion personnel are allowed in. We've had too many citizens attempting to get close to the gladiators. And a few drunks who want to fight them."

With passions running high, Sidia appreciated the reasons for isolating the fighters.

"Who is managing the games?" he inquired.

"Centurion Flere, commander of the Thirty-First."

Sidia's heart dropped. He had hoped for a junior officer. But Flere was Third Maniple and he commanded a Century of veterans in the middle of the assault line. Flere wasn't going to be easily convinced, but Sidia had to try.

"Ask the Centurion if he will grant me an audience," Sidia requested.

The Decanus of the squad guarding the perimeter marched across the small compound. After saluting his

Centurion, the squad leader started speaking. But a roar from the attendees and a wave of Flere's hand delayed the conversation. In the arena, the two spearmen had reached the edge of the Insubri's circle.

***

Hundreds of stomping feet and pumping arms rocked and swayed the bleachers. Pegs in the wooden stands snapped from the torque or were squeezed out by the twisting beams. Unaware of the instability, the spectators continued to violently express their excitement.

From the middle of the arena and the center of his circle, Jace Kasia studied the two Greeks. He was looking for signs of a specific character trait.

***

In a harsh trial years before, Jace learned about the attribute.

"In every group, be it a pair, a foursome, or a pack, one will attack you first," Zarek Mikolas lectured. "It won't be the bravest, or the smartest, or the one with the best maintained gear."

Young Jace Kasia stood in a knee deep depression. The hole wasn't the problem; it was the slithering snakes, crawling over his feet and between his legs. Shaking in fear and terrified, he barely heard the words, let alone understood their meaning.

"Master Archer," Jace stammered, "what does that have to do with these snakes?"

Balkan whip snakes, dice snakes, cat snakes, and leopard snakes swirled around the bare legs and feet of the boy.

"Reptile, animal, or man, they all share one trait," Mikolas said before inquiring. "Have you identified it yet?"

Jace closed his eyes and focused on taking even breaths. In the dark, the images of the snakes faded, and a calmness settled over him. Then he realized what was missing.

"The most afraid will attack first to cover their fear," Jace guessed.

"Find the snake with that trait," Zarek Mikolas instructed, "and remove him from the pit."

Slowly, to avoid agitating the others, Jace located the one coiled and ready to strike. In a quick grab, he snatched up the frightened reptile and tossed it out of the pit. As if the boy wasn't in the hole any longer, the remaining snakes calmed.

"If I remove the frightened enemy," Jace questioned, "will that end the fight?"

"Of course not," Zarek Mikolas replied. "The fight begins when you remove the frightened adversary."

***

The pair of gladiators stepped over the line of Jace's circle. Tremors in the fingers of the Greek on the left, and the rapid pulse of the arteries in his neck, identified where the attack would begin. Jace jerked right and the two spears shifted as did the pair of shields. The move caused the more afraid of the pair to step ahead of his partner.

"Thank you, Master Mikolas," Jace thought before he dropped and rolled to the left.

At the spear and shield of the Greek on the left, Jace grabbed the forward wrist. Pulling as he pounded his feet into the man's shield, Jace launched the Greek into the air.

Using the man's weight to jerk him over a shoulder and to his feet, the Archer faced off against a single adversary.

On the bleachers, the crowds stood and stomped their appreciation for the maneuver. The second Greek glanced around Jace to see if his partner would be rejoining the fight. It appeared he wouldn't. Not from being thrown or suffering a hard landing, which he did. The injured Greek wouldn't be fighting that day because as Jace pulled the man with his right hand, the Archer stabbed him with the sword in his left. Bleeding, the Greek climbed unsteadily to his feet. Blood spurted out and ran down his leg. The sight drove the spectators to new heights of frenzy.

Jace retrieved his second sword and swung the pair in a figure eight while stepping to the edge of his circle.

"He's a bit hot headed," Jace offered.

"He always has been," the Greek said before charging forward.

A spear and a shield should have been enough to drive the Archer out of his circle, if not enough to stab him through the chest. Neither happened as the Archer parried the spear with one sword, stepped in close, and used the other to stab over the Greek's shield. The blade sank into the man's neck and Jace released the hilt. Before the gladiator fell to the sand, Jace caught him and freed his sword. Next, the Insubri tossed the dying man out of the circle.

As if a single-throated monster, the citizens of Rome thundered a terrifying cry. At first, the people in the other stands, the Legionaries, and the gladiators assumed it was a response to the circle warrior's victory. Not until a complete section of the bleachers crashed, resembling flat bread with tiny broken figurines embedded in the crust, did anyone recognize the cry as one of panic.

High on Mount Olympus, the Goddess Manea laughed at the havoc and folly of the panicked humans.

For a moment, Jace considered running into the mob and escaping. But he couldn't leave Abbo. Resigned to staying with his brother-in-law, the Archer marched to the line of shields protecting the compound, the gladiator preparation building, and the sleeping area for the combatants. The shields parted, Optio Herminia met Jace and turned him over to a pair of Legionaries. They escorted the Archer directly to the sleeping area where Abbo waited.

When the bleachers collapsed, people showed what was in their hearts. Some ran away out of fear. Others looked for ways to profit from the tragedy. And the last and largest group, raced to help the injured. Sidia Decimia joined the rescuers.

Centurion Flere never saw Jace return from the arena. He was too busy securing his area and then sending Legionaries out to help uncover bodies and free those trapped under beams and corpses.

***

By late afternoon, the rubble was cleared, the lumber stacked, and the bodies removed. Flere was about to begin an inspection of the gladiator area when Senate President Scipio and Consul Lentulus arrived in a carriage.

"Centurion, what happened?" Lentulus asked as he climbed down.

"That Insubri gladiator happened, Consul," Flere replied. "He excited the minds of some Romans to the detriment of all."

"Does he have a name?" Cornelius inquired.

"We don't take the names of sacrificial animals, sir," Flere advised. "It's unusual for one to stand out in the arena."

"Do you think this slave should be put on trial for provoking a riot?" Lentulus asked.

"No one wants him in front of a magistrate facing a civil charge," Flere replied. Then he assured them. "Tomorrow, he'll die on the sand and Rome will return to normal."

"Suppose I told you his name is Colonel Jace Romiliia Kasia from Scipio Legion in Africa?" Cornelius inquired.

"It wouldn't matter, sir," Flere pointed out. "He was condemned to the arena. If anyone frees him, citizens will riot in the streets. Romans want to watch him fight and bleed."

"How can you know all that?" Cornelius demanded.

"It's simple, sir," Flere told him. "The betters have taken in a fortune in gold, both for and against him. If he's removed from the games, everybody loses."

"And if he stays in the games?" Lentulus asked.

"He'll die and make half the gamblers very happy. And the rest, poorer by half," the Centurion replied. Flere noticed Optio Decimia behind Cornelius and asked, "Did you want to speak with me?"

"Not anymore, sir," Sidia told him.

"If you'll excuse me," Flere requested. "I need to check on the gladiators. Then get my Legionaries busy rebuilding the bleachers. It won't be as high, but it'll seat attendees for the closing day of the games and be safe."

"Thank you for answering our questions," Lentulus offered. As Flere marched away, the Consul turned to Cornelius. "Mister President, the only way I can see you getting your Battle Commander out of a death sentence on the sand is to put him up on a cross. In one fate, he goes down fighting. In the other, he suffers for several sunrises before expiring."

"To avoid rioting, I'd have to charge him with vanishing before a battle," Cornelius commented. "No one could argue that being injured is a capital crime."

"Sir, it's Jace," Sidia remarked. "Surely you aren't going to crucify him."

"You have nothing to worry about," Cornelius assured his bodyguard. "I don't know of any crime he's committed. At least one serious enough to remove him from the arena."

***

Lieutenant General Baebius Tamphilus arrived in Rome the following morning. All that was on his mind was saving his career. Even as he traveled to the Senate, Tamphilus considered words that would justify losing an entire Legion. And what excuse he'd use to mend the rift between Rome and her allies caused by the loss of so many auxiliary troops. By the time he entered the Senate Chamber, he knew what he would say.

"The Senate recognizes Praetor Baebius Tamphilus," Cornelius announced from the dais. "Come forward and report on your operation against the Insubri."

Friends of Colonel Belua and relatives of noblemen and farmers killed under his command sat with their arms folded. Their hands balled into fists.

"I tried to stop Colonel Belua," Tamphilus lied. "But the Battle Commander of Ibex ordered an advance. We needed to build our marching camps for security, and probe ahead. But Colonel Belua commandeered a boat, crossed the Po River, and pursued the Insubri force. I admit, it's a tragedy. If I could return to that day, I'd strip off my armor and swim across the river to physically restrain the Battle Commander."

"It's your testimony that Colonel Belua disobeyed orders?" Consul Lentulus questioned. "That he ignored proper Legion procedures and blindly advanced into enemy territory?"

"That's correct, Consul," Tamphilus confirmed. "I knew there was trouble when he sent the two Insubri war chiefs over to me as a gift. It was obviously a sign of megalomania."

The idea of a Colonel becoming tyrannical and disobeying orders gripped the Seante. They feared a king and the first step to a royal ruler was an out of control Legion Battle Commander. However, while the Senators recoiled at the idea of a leader with uncontrolled power, Cornelius Scipio Africanus focused on another part of the Praetor's speech.

"Two Insubri war chiefs?" he asked.

"Yes, sir. One of his Centuries captured two war chiefs," Tamphilus replied. "Belua sent them to me. I assumed he had questioned them to gather intelligence. Being angry, I passed them to my supply officer for transportation to Rome."

Cornelius turned to Lentulus.

"Consul, did you receive a pair of Insubri war chiefs?" he asked.

"The only Insubri that came from the north recently," the Consul informed Cornelius, "are the pair that are fighting in the arena."

"And I was…" Tamphilus started to say. He stopped when Cornelius hammered on the dais.

"Senate of Rome," Cornelius proposed, "I make a motion that Jace Romiliia Kasia, a former Colonel in Scipio's African Legion be held for trial. The charges being aiding an enemy of Rome. Desertion of his Legion while in contact with the Carthaginian army. And being an accessory to murder of Ibex Legion and allied forces. Can I get a second on the motion?"

Everyone knew Colonel Kasia was a favorite of Senate President Scipio. Thus, it was no surprise when the Senators hesitated. The chamber waited for a few moments before a commanding voice called out, "I, Senator Marcus Cato, move to accept the motion. And I do so wholeheartedly."

Before Cornelius could ask for a second, Titus Crispinus sealed Jace's fate. "I second the motion."

"The motion carries," Cornelius declared. "The Senate of Rome hereby issues an arrest order for Jace Romiliia Kasia. Optio Sidia Decimia, you know the culprit by sight. Gather a squad. No, wait. Make that two squads and bring the accused before the Senate of Rome."

Chapter 24 – Send for the Accused

Jace deflected the sword stroke with the buckler. Then he spun around, passing cleanly through the path where the sword blade would have traveled. The eluded spear thrust pierced only dust. And the shaft, during a side sweep, hit the swordsman at the same moment the Archer ran his sword into the man's ribs. A push on the injured swordsman toppled him into the legs of the spearman. Without space for a stroke, Jace leaped onto the spearman and pummeled him to the sand with the sword.

At the victory, the crowd forgot about the previous day's tragedy. They stomped and jumped up and down with elation. Much to Centurion Flere's delight, the rebuilt bleachers held. But the outcome of the mismatched fight provided him an equal amount of consternation.

After waiting for the Insubri to throw the injured men out of his fighting circle and redraw the line, Centurion Flere complained, "can someone please kill that Gaul. Give me two more gladiators for the arena. Hold up. Give me three fighters. This has to end."

The selected trio of warriors had witnessed the effects of Jace's fighting style and knew victims of his work. They linked shields and marched across the grass as if approaching a Legion assault line. Yet, it wasn't a shield wall with armored infantrymen, but a single man with a small shield on his forearm and a pair of swords in his hands.

"When he goes down, run out there, and get his body off the sand quickly," Flere directed a pair of stretcher bearers. "Don't give the crowd a moment to consider rushing the arena to collect souvenirs."

"Yes, sir," the bearers confirmed.

Forgetting the spectators, the stands, and the compound, Flere concentrated on the arena. As the three gladiators approached Jace's fighting circle, the crowd bellowed and stomped, creating a deafening racket. It's why Centurion Flere didn't hear the young Tribune approaching from the rear. Or why the twenty Legionaries and the Optio running by caught him off guard.

"Centurion Flere you are to read this scroll to the crowd," the staff officer instructed. "After your announcement, we will remove Jace Romiliia Kasia from the funeral games."

"Who is Jace Romiliia Kasia?" Flere asked, forgetting Cornelius' comment from the day before.

But he didn't need a reply. The answer was obvious from the twenty Legionaries who surrounded the Insubri and the Optio. The Sergeant stood talking with the infamous warrior who fought only in his circle.

***

"Cousin Jace, you are in big trouble," Sidia proposed.

"More than this?" Jace asked. He pointed at the three gladiators standing outside the ring of heavy infantrymen and the hushed crowd.

"Far more, I'm afraid," Sidia assured him. "I'm to escort you to the Senate to stand trial for capital crimes."

"Cousin Sidia, I need a favor," Jace requested. "There's a Gaul name Abbo Kentus. He needs to come with us."

"He'd die easier in the arena," Sidia suggested. "But if you want company while you examine rooftops as you die, I'll have Lucius get him."

"Senior Centurion Lucius?" Jace asked, thinking the officer was his former senior combat officer.

"It's not him. His son was elected as a Tribune last year," Sidia informed Jace. "He's a good officer even though he's young."

Jace and Sidia stopped talking when Centurion Flere marched through the ring of Legionaries. His presence sent howls of confusion through the attendees. Sidia left to speak with the Tribune while Flere held up the scroll.

"Your attention please," Flere announced. He pointed a finger at Jace. "Who we thought was an Insubri warrior is in reality an Insubri war chief."

From the third tier, a heckler shouted, "In that case let him fight and die in the arena."

A chorus of voices echoed the sentiment.

"That was the plan until we discovered that the Insubri war chief is also a Legion deserter," Flere explained.

"More reason for him to die on the sand," another heckler stated. Again, the suggestion was picked up by vocal supporters.

Flere lowered his head. He was accustomed to giving orders to Legionaries. Being put in the position of answering to an unruly mob threw him off.

"Ignore them, Centurion Flere," Jace coached. "Push through to the end of the scroll and be done with it."

"Why should I take advice from you?" Flere demanded.

"You're a combat officer and a good one, I gather. But you aren't a politician," Jace explained. "As to why you should listen to my recommendation. Keep reading."

A flash of anger settled the Centurion, and he focused on the mission.

"By name, Jace Romiliia Kasia was the Battle Commander of a special wall breaching Legion assigned to Scipio Legions Africa," Flere read. Out of curiosity, he looked in Jace's direction to see if he recognized any sign of a Legion commander. But all he could identify was the long hair and full mustache of a Gaul. The Centurion continued with the charges. "Kasia vanished before the battle of Zama and reappeared as a tribal war chief for the Insubrian army. It can only be assumed that Colonel Kasia had gone to the Insubri for shelter and assisted them in planning the murder of Ibex Legion. As such, he is being held over for trial by the Senate of Rome."

Angry shouts greeted the Centurion as he rolled the scroll.

"Take him away," Flere directed the escort squads. Then to his Century, he added. "Get me three more gladiators on the sand. And hurry."

At the compound, Tribune Lucius, Sidia Decimia, and Abbo Kentus waited for Jace and the squads.

"To the Senate?" Jace inquired.

"To a domus owned by an absentee owner," Sidia answered. "President of the Senate Scipio Africanus said a condemned man should be groomed and shaved and dressed properly before being sentenced to death."

"He doesn't leave a lot of room for doubt," Jace mentioned.

"You know General Scipio's tactics," Sidia offered. "He is precise and decisive and usually gets what he wants."

Abbo fell in beside Jace as the detachment turned onto Via Della Salara and marched for the house.

"Wouldn't we be better off in the arena?" he inquired.

"Possibly," Jace admitted. "But a sword is a shortcut where the law is open to arguments. And in this case, I feel better pleading my cause than in fighting a line of gladiators. Especially, the last one in line."

"Who is the last one in line to fight you?" Abbo asked.

"You, brother-in-law. The last two to fight in the arena would be us."

"Brigid wouldn't like that at all," Abbo noted.

***

Smaller than the other homes in the neighborhood, the footprint however, allowed for the usual number of rooms around an atrium. The peaceful residential neighborhood provided a sharp contrast to the bleachers and blood stained sand in the Forum. The Legionaries were distributed around the domus while Sidia, Tribune Lucius, Jace, and Abbo entered through the front door.

"Nice house," Jace remarked when they passed through the entrance and emerged in the courtyard. "Who lives here?"

"I do," Sidia answered. "When I'm not needed by the General. I'm sort of the caretaker of the property."

"That settles the who. Now, why are we here?" Jace inquired.

In the courtyard, two men waited beside a tub of water.

"To get a shave and a haircut," Sidia replied. "After a much needed bath."

"The funeral games care only for what's inside the body of a gladiator. They aren't worried about the outside."

To confirm the comment, Sidia and the two men sniffed. Jace stripped off the soiled linen armor and the dirty tunic, then stepped into the tub.

"Can I borrow? Rather, can I have one of your tunics?" Jace asked as he settled into the water. "I don't suppose you'll want it back after a period of hanging on a cross."

"Appropriate clothing has been provided," Sidia told him. He marched to a storage room while one of the men scrubbed Jace's back and washed his hair. By the time the servant rinsed the soap from his eyes, Sidia stood holding a set of familiar armor.

"That's my ceremonial armor and helmet," Jace remarked. "Where did you get them?"

"General Scipio had all of your baggage shipped from Carthage and stored in the domus."

"My hunting bow?" Jace asked.

"It's there along with your hooded doublet, arrows, and your war bow."

Jace stepped from the bath, and the servant began oiling and scraping his skin. On a table, the barber prepared his steel razors and bronze shears. During the entire process of bathing and oiling, Tribune Lucius walked along the edge of the courtyard in slow, steady laps.

"Tribune Lucius, how is your father?" Jace inquired. He sat beside the barber as the man began clipping away the oversized mustache. "Is he still climbing and drawing?"

"After the defeat of Carthage, my father left the Legion and began studying law," the young staff officer replied.

Sidia inhaled as if building his courage before mentioning, "Jace, Tribune Rete Lucius, by order of Senate President Scipio, is your trial speaker."

"Your father, Rete, is a wise man. He gave me good council when we landed in Africa," Jace offered. "I assume you apprenticed for the law under him."

"No, sir," Rete admitted, "I was more interested in being a Legion officer. Had I been a year older, I would have been with Ibex Legion during the Insubri operation."

A shiver ran down Jace's spine. His speaker couldn't be any more hostile to him than a dead Ibex Legion staff officer resurrected to curse him.

"There is a legal consultant names Porcius Laeca," Sidia said, intending to bring a little hope to his cousin. "But he's out of the city. A messenger was sent to request his presence in the Senate. But he's in Albano Laziale participating in a trial. It may take another day for him to reach Rome."

"What was that you said about General Scipio?" Jace emphasized each word. "His tactics are precise and decisive. And he usually gets what he wants."

"It does appear the General wants you up on the wood," Sidia said, validating the conclusion. "Maybe he has something in mind."

"An undisputable guilty verdict," Rete Lucius offered before resuming his laps around the courtyard.

Once Jace was shaved and bathed, Abbo washed but refused the shave. His proud Gaulish mustache and long hair would remain untouched.

Although the undersized domus lacked a pool in the courtyard, the tub served the purpose. And when compared to sleeping outdoors on the grass at the Forum, the surrounding kitchen, bedrooms, dining room, lavatory, and storage rooms felt palatial.

The evening, the last of their lives for two of the men, drifted by on platters of food and good wine or fruit juice.

"I've no complaints about the hospitality of this inn," Jace Romiliia Kasia announced while looking up from the courtyard at the stars. "It's the hefty fee for checking out that bothers me."

***

"What bothers me," Cornelius Scipio Africanus announced as he looked down from scanning the ceiling of the chamber, "is the delay due to legalities."

The morning session had sped by with sacrifices and talks about the success of the funeral games. One bone in the Senate's fish dish, the case of Romiliia Kasia lingered as if it was a fisherman's catch left out in the sun to rot.

"I move for a quick crucifixion," a Senator suggested.

"Based on rumor and circumstantial evidence, I can't disagree," Cornelius told him. "However, on what grounds would the Senate of Rome execute a citizen of Rome? Would the record show the Senate as if a King pointed the finger of doom at a citizen and declared him a dead man."

To emphasize his theory, Cornelius extended an arm and his index finger. Then he pointed at specific Senators, lingering just long enough on each to make them squirm in their seats.

To end the display by the Senate President, Titus Crispinus asserted. "We need a trial to put this business behind us, once and for all time."

"If you insist," Cornelius snapped. "Titus Crispinus has made a motion to bring Jace Romiliia Kasia to account for the capital crimes of desertion in the face of an enemy of Rome. Taking up arms against a Legion of Rome as an Insubri war chief. And the murder of Ibex Legion by planning an ambush. Can I get a motion to accept?"

"For the crime of treason, I move to accept the motion," a Senator shouted.

"Hold on," Cornelius warned. "If you reduce the charges to one, such as treason, the guilty party could walk free with a slight majority of votes."

"I've changed my acceptance," the Senator stated. "I move to accept the original motion."

"Can I get a second?" Cornelius asked.

On the right side of the chamber, Marcus Cato spoke to his faction.

"What is Scipio doing?" he whispered.

"It appears he's sealing the fate of one of his Battle Commanders," another Senator answered. "Could be a political ploy to strengthen his next move."

"That's what I'm asking," Cato complained. "What is Scipio doing?"

"Colonel Kasia has been with Scipio since the disaster at Lake Trasimene," Valerius Flaccus recalled. "If he is cleaning out old associates, he must be building a coalition with newer, more powerful allies."

"Who are they?" Cato asked.

On the left side of the chamber, a Senator responded to Scipio, "I second the motion."

"We will now vote on the motion. All in favor?" Cornelius requested. The motion to try Jace Kasia passed almost unanimously. The President of the Senate ordered. "Send for the accused and his speaker."

Act 9

Chapter 25 – The Law of Rome

In a reversal of roles, one transformed from a Legion staff officer to a legal speaker and the other from a gladiator to a Legion commander. Rete Lucius wore a blue toga and Jace Kasia had on his ceremonial armor with a white combed helmet under his arm. Together, the two marched down the aisle and stood in front of the Senate of Rome.

"Rete Lucius, by what authority do you accompany the accused?" Cornelius asked.

"The law provides for a speaker to act as a voice for the defendant," Rete answered. "If he requires elegance in telling his tale, I am available."

"And what is your relation to the accused?" the President asked.

"None. I have no relation to Jace Kasia," Rete disclosed. "To be precise, sir, I have personal animosity towards the man."

"As does everyone in this chamber based on the current evidence," Cornelius told him. Next, he addressed Jace. "Battle Commander Jace Romiliia Kasia, former Colonel of Scipio Legions Africa. You stand accused of desertion in the face of an enemy of Rome. Taking up arms against a Legion of Rome as an Insubri war chief. And are culpable in the murder of Ibex Legion by assisting in the planning and ambush. How do you plead?"

The chamber fell silent. Some expected Jace to confess and beg for mercy. Others assumed he'd loudly protest his innocence. But none were ready for his reply.

"It's all true," Jace informed the Senate of Rome. "I left my command in Africa and journeyed to Insubri. There I met and married a clan chief's daughter. Along with her two brothers, I assumed the role of a clan war chief. However, my part went beyond assisting in the planning of the ambush. The entire defensive operation was my idea."

"Then you confess to all the charges?" Cornelius inquired.

"President Scipio Africanus, I confess to no such thing," Jace revealed.

Senators shouted for his immediate execution while others complained that he should have been left to die in the arena. But a few called for quiet, so they might hear his reasoning for such monstrous deeds.

Cornelius pounded on the dais and chastised the chamber. "Need I remind you that this is a legal trial. And no matter how evil and abhorrent the acts, the accused is a citizen of Rome and of noble birth. We will conduct the prosecution with restraint and dignity. Proceed, Colonel Kasia."

At the use of Jace's rank and status, a new thunderstorm of protests rolled across the chamber.

"A traitor doesn't have status in Rome," one sneered.

"He wears the uniform he disgraced," several Senators pointed out.

Cornelius held out both hands to still the dissidents.

"While my heart, like yours, suffers from the disrespect, Battle Commander Kasia has never been downgraded or relieved of his command," Cornelius explained.

"We'll soon remedy that," a Senator shouted.

"As would be fitting, by the end of the tribunal," Cornelius told the Senator. Then he focused on Jace and allowed. "You were saying?"

"I left my command in Africa because I was knocked addlebrained by a thrown spear. Then taken prisoner by Tasco B'Yag. I might say, against my will. But for a period, I had no will, nor idea of who I was. It was he who transported me to Insubri Territory."

"Have you any proof of the fantastical tale?" Senator Cato demanded.

"Are there any Senators who are physicians?" Jace asked.

Several raised their hands. Jace spread the short hairs on his scalp and exposed the hole in his head. Then he went to the doctors for a confirmation of the surgery and the scars around the hole where fragments of skull bone had been removed.

"President of the Senate, we have examined the defendant," one physician announced. "It is our expert opinion that Kasia suffered massive trauma to his cranium. Confusion and memory loss is to be expected in such cases.

Further, we believe his being alive and aware shows the hand of a God in his survival."

"I will not allow this trial to diverge into a discussion of the divine," Cornelius stipulated. "Colonel Kasia, please proceed."

"As I said, Tasco B'Yag took the shell of my being to Milan," Jace stated. "There he mistreated me."

"Can you show signs of that?" challenged Senator Crispinus.

Jace held up his left hand and displayed the ring finger and the small finger on the hand. Both were twisted, and the joints swollen, signs that the fingers were not set properly after being broken.

"Before Tasco B'Yag, I was a Master Archer," Jace told the Senate as he attempted to fully close the fingers on the hand. No one asked about his skills in the arena with a sword in his left hand. Taking advantage of the lapse, Jace lied. "Now I can barely hold a hunting bow to feed my family."

Senators mimicked his misshapen hand and its reduced motion. Rapping on the dais brought their attention back to the front of the chamber.

***

"The Senate acknowledges the two injuries," Cornelius professed. "But neither are an excuse for joining the ranks of an enemy and teaching your Legion drills to a barbarian tribe."

"Mister President, I never taught Legion drills to the Insubri tribe," Jace advised. "My training was limited to the Gnātos Clan and only for specific individuals. And I never lifted a blade, a shield, or a spear against any Legionaries or auxiliary forces."

The Senate chamber vibrated with a sympathetic note after Jace's testimony. Breaking the mood, Cornelius growled, "but you did plan, and in your own words, refine the ambush where Ibex Legion was butchered. Explain that."

The aggressive tone snapped the mood of compassion in the chamber. And for the first time, Jace Kasia hesitated. In his mind, he prepared his next argument. But in his heart, he hurt from confusion. The General, who he had served so loyally for so many years, seemed determined to see him nailed to a cross.

"Here, in my tale, I am going to blame the Battle Commander of Ibex," Jace proclaimed. After the incendiary remark, he waited for the storm of disagreements.

During the silence, an old Senator told him, "Praetor Tamphilus already explained Colonel Belua's impetuous nature. You just tell us your side of the story, Colonel Kasia."

The use of his rank and the acceptance of the other Battle Commander's error freed Jace of his stress. He just might pull this off and ride home to his bride.

"Brocc B'Yag, the war chief for the Insubri Tribe, ordered the clan to set up our defensive line south of Milan," Jace described. "I've been a Legionary and know the power of a Roman infantryman. And I didn't want the clan to face certain annihilation."

"What did you do?" a Senator inquired.

"I convinced Brocc to let us cross the Lambro River and leave the defense of Milan to another clan. There we would lure the Legion across the Po River," Jace answered. "My plan was to guide the Legion up a narrow road to where the wagon trail bent just before reaching a crossing in the Lambro River. My plan showed the Legion executing a flank maneuver. To Brocc, I explained the Latins would wheel around and advance towards the riverbank. My clan would then charge out of the forest and hit the Legion lines broadside, trapping the infantry between the road and the swamp."

"No Battle Commander would advance his Legion into that terrain," a Senator uttered in disgust. Then he lowered his eyes and said. "But one did, didn't he?"

"This trial is a farce," Marcus Cato exclaimed. Jumping to his feet, he offered. "Jace Romiliia Kasia is obviously a traitor. In light of his excuses, believe them or not, he is nothing except a barbarian lover. For that alone, he should be stripped of his citizenship, lashed, hobbled, and sent to the slave market."

Voices, both agreeing and dissenting, bellowed for attention. Before Cornelius could gain control of the Chamber, a Tribune, escorted by Sidia Decimia appeared at the top of an aisle.

"Tribune Laeca, come down and consult with your client," Cornelius told him.

Still at the top of the aisle, Sidia took a moment to salute before marching away.

"I will have order in the chamber," Cornelius yelled. He glared at the disgruntled Senators until they settled and sat. "Porcius Laeca is a legal scholar, as many of you know. He was requested by Jace Kasia as a legal authority. While they talk, allow me to remind you of the villainy of the defendant. Because of his plan, as improbable as it sounds, Ibex Legion marched into the trap. Legionnaires, Velites, their Optios, Tesserarii, Centurions, and Tribunes, died brutally in the woods of the Insubri. Wives weep, children miss their fathers and uncles, and mothers cry at dawn when they look at untended fields. Untended because the farmers are dead because of Jace Romiliia Kasia."

Nerves grew taut and the faces of the Senators appeared a stern as granite.

"Tribune Laeca, do you have anything to add," Cornelius inquired.

"Not at this time, Mister President," the legal expert replied.

He returned to speaking with Jace, ignoring the happenings at the dais.

"Senate of Rome, we will now vote on the guilt or innocence of Jace Romiliia Kasia. I will cast the first vote. Guilty, and I propose the death sentence," Cornelius informed the Senate. "All those in favor of the death penalty, raise your hand."

Clerks walked the chamber counting votes. Once done, Cornelius called for the not guilty vote. Moments later, the head clerk delivered a piece of parchment to the President of the Senate.

"The Senate of Rome has reached a verdict," Cornelius announced. "Jace Romiliia Kasia, the chamber finds you guilty. You will be..."

"President of the Senate," Porcius Laeca called out. "A point of order, if you will, sir."

Frustrated at being interrupted, Cornelius waved the piece of parchment at the Tribune. But he didn't scold the legal expert.

"You have a point of order?" he asked.

"Indeed, I do. According to a new law, voted in last spring, a citizen of Rome may avoid a sentence of death by surrendering his property in Rome and voluntarily going into exile," Laeca explained. "My client, Jace Romiliia Kasia, wishes to sign over his domus to the state and leave Rome forever."

"So states the law of Rome," Cornelius acquiesced. "Jace Romiliia Kasia, you will retire to your domus and await a magistrate to finalize the exile."

As Tribunes Porcius Laeca and Rete Lucius, and Jace Kasia walked up the aisle, Marcus Cato roared from his section.

"Scipio, you set that up," he bellowed. "This entire affair was you using the Senate to get your man freed."

"Senator Cato, I appreciate your passion," Cornelius told him. "But if you ever want to be recognized by the

Senate while I am President, I suggest you sit down, clamp your lips shut, and keep your ugly opinions to yourself."

His faction pulled Cato to his seat before he could do any more damage. Questioning the honesty of the President of the Senate was, for a period, political suicide.

"I have attempted to be fair in the trial of a trusted Lieutenant," Cornelius confessed. "If anyone witnessed me being partial to my Battle Commander please see Consul Lentulus and register a complaint. If not, this matter is closed."

Chapter 26 – One More Favor

The thick substance in the copper pot bubbled. As it melted, the raw aroma of rotten pelt drifted through a corner of the courtyard.

"I didn't know you had a house in Rome," Abbo remarked.

Jace stirred the hide glue and admitted, "neither did I."

With a brush, he put a fine coat of the glue on his old war bow.

"You're lucky Optio Decimia handed me the sales document when I arrived," Porcius Laeca explained. "Without property to surrender, the law wouldn't apply."

"And right about now," Abbo offered, "we'd be watching the sunset from a cross."

"That you would be," Laeca confirmed.

A servant opened the front door. Cornelius marched through the entrance and proceeded to the courtyard. Sidia, a man in magistrate robes, and a scribe with a wheeled cart, followed the President of the Senate.

Jace set down his brush, stood, and braced. Abbo Kentus and Tribune Laeca did as well.

"General Scipio Africanus welcome to my home, I guess," Jace ventured. "A house I didn't know I owned."

"A few years ago, Colonel Kasia, you gave me a price for going on a dangerous mission," Cornelius remarked. "Do you remember?"

"There were so many, I can't remember details," Jace admitted. He reached up and touched the hole in his skull. "As much as I do recall, some memories evade me completely."

"You told me the price to hire a Cretan Archer at that moment was a house in Rome," Cornelius told him. "You never stayed in the city long enough to claim your payment."

"It's a nice house," Jace observed. "Too bad I have to give it to the government."

"Tribune Laeca. Please consult with the magistrate and scribe to assure that the documents are correct," Cornelius directed. "I have stipulations beyond the legal for Jace and the Insubri."

"Yes, sir," the legal expert acknowledged.

Once he was at the table with the scribe and magistrate, and out of hearing range, Cornelius told Jace, "Don't worry about the house. I'm buying it from the state before the public sale. Like you said, it's a nice house."

"Sir, you didn't send the Tribune away to brag in secret about your real estate investments," Jace remarked. "Is there something else on your mind?"

"Next summer, I'm marching across the Po River and capturing Milan for the Republic," Cornelius answered. "You can doubt me and prepare to battle my Legions. But Colonel Kasia knows my record of conquest."

"I remember that very well, sir," Jace stated.

"Good because the price of you two riding out of Rome depends on your oath," Cornelius informed them. "Swear to me the Gnātos Clan won't take up arms against me and you'll ride out with a letter of safe passage from the Senate of Rome."

"And if we don't give our oath?" Abbo asked.

"There are worse fates for my enemies than fighting in an arena," Cornelius answered. "For instance, being sent to the slavers and assigned to work in a mine."

"We Insubri enjoy our mountains and freedom," Abbo submitted. "As the son of Samo Kentus, Chief of the Clan, I give you my oath that the Gnātos Clan will not take up arms against you."

"Jace?" Cornelius asked.

"As the son-in-law of Samo Kentus, Chief of the Clan, I give you my oath that the Gnātos Clan will not take up arms against you."

"Now that we've settled that, let's go sign some documents," Cornelius directed. "My wife is holding a gala this evening and there are some newly rich merchants attending. They want to fund a Legion. Maybe I'll call it Owl Legion, named after Minerva, the Goddess of Commerce."

On the table, the scribe had placed duplicate documents. One would go into the records of the Senate of Rome, and the other would travel with Jace Kasia. At the top of each sheet of parchment and written in large letters were these words: Salvation of Exile.

"General Scipio, if I might ask one more favor," Jace requested after signing the documents.

"If it's within my power. What do you want?"

"There's a boy in Arona I'd like to adopt," Jace explained. "While I'm forbidden from ever visiting Rome, it would be nice if Scanlan had standing if he decides to visit the city in the future."

"It's not a difficult task for the President of the Roman Senate," Cornelius assured him. "Scribe, write up an adoption agreement."

Chapter 27 – The Currency of Courage

Thirty days after riding through the gates of Rome, Jace and Abbo rode a boat to the western shore of Lake Maggiore. High on the slopes, the homes of clan members were visible between the trees. Approaching the shore, they passed between familiar stilt houses. Children followed their progress by running along the boards overhead.

"I never thought I'd see this sight again," Abbo confessed. "But your courage brought us home."

"It was more a life of hard training and rough living that brought us back," Jace told him. "I can tell you, I was more afraid than at any time in my life."

"You. Why?" Abbo inquired.

"For the first time, I had something to live for and a place I yearned to return to," Jace replied. "I never realize home was the true currency of courage."

Once the boat touched the muddy bank, they took their packs and bundles and hiked up the slope.

"What are you going to do about Katumaros?" Jace asked.

"The days grow shorter and the nights longer," Abbo stated. "One night, he will simple cease to exist. And if asked, I will claim to know nothing about his disappearance."

***

Jace Kasia climbed the pathway to his cottage. As he hiked, far below, the waters of the lake reflected the sun and a cool breeze announced the coming of winter. Smoke from the fireplace combined with the aroma of fir trees. They flooded his senses with awe. Believing, for the moment, the scene was the most picturesque thing he's ever witnessed, Jace dropped his bundles on the porch and opened the door to the cottage. One look inside, however, changed his opinion of true beauty.

"Jace," a startled Brigid choked out.

"Stay right there," he instructed. At his pack, he unstrapped his war bow and carried it inside.

Glowing, Brigid stood beside a crackling fire with a confused expression on her face. Her eyes followed Jace as he crossed the room to the fireplace. Slowly, for it was the last time he would use it, Jace Kasia hung the war bow above the mantel. Then he reached out and wrapped one arm protectively around her shoulders. With the other, he gently placed the hand over her distended belly.

"My father was exiled from Rome before he and my mother died leaving me an orphan," he whispered in Brigid's ear. "I swear to you and my child, I will never leave you for anything."

Brigid shifted her face and looked into his eyes. Next, as she leaned into his lips, she whispered, "welcome home, Cretan Archer."

The End

A sample of Allies, Spies, and Conflicts

#1 in the new series *Provinces of Rome* by J. Clifton Slater

Chapter XXX – The Roster

"We already have an experienced crew," the Naval Scheduler informed him. He pushed the identity parchment back across the table. "Go try a civilian shipper. King Phillip of Macedonia won't have to fear you for a few years. Come see me when you have more experience."

Scanlan Saltare fumbled, lifting the parchment from the table. While retrieving it, he scrutinized the scroll, the list of names, and the placement of the oarsmen. In addition to the substance of the Scheduler's list, he studied the handwriting style of the Centurion.

"We are done here. Move along," the officer directed.

Scanlan stepped away from the recruitment table, but he didn't leave the area. Instead, he walked along the pier, looking down on the beached warships. If any had been named *Eagle*, he would have targeted that warship for a rowing position. But *Accipiter de Pax*, the Hawk of Peace, appealed to him as a close second.

From the end of the dock, he faced out to sea. There, to the east lay the Adriatic Sea and his future. To the west was his home and bitter feelings for his clan and the Insubri Tribe. After lingering for a while, Scanlan walked back towards Classis.

The town of Classis catered to the Eastern Roman Fleet, which explained the crowds of oarsmen, Legion Marines, sailors, and carpenters. Once on the street of sail makers and other shops supplying equipment to the warships, Scanlan headed for a three story structure.

"Excuse me," he questioned the guard at the entrance to the administration building. He licked his lips and held his eyes downcast as if he was extremely nervous. "I've come to see someone called the Scheduler. I'm told he's on the second floor. In the northeast corner."

"You've been given wrong information," the guard chastised him. "First off, the Scheduler is down on the dock. Second, his office is on the third floor, and it's in the southeast corner so he can see the harbor. You aren't too bright are you?"

"What?" Scanlan asked while letting his mouth hang slack.

"Nothing. Move along," the guard ordered.

As if afraid he'd bump into someone, Scanlan slouched away from the doorway. At the corner of the building and blocked from the guard's view by the crowd, he squeezed into a narrow alleyway. After extending his arms to measure the distance between the three story admin building and its two-story neighbor, Scanlan Saltare returned to the dock.

He'd keep the Scheduler under surveillance until the Centurion finished his day.

***

The coming night was pushed back by lamp light from windows of shops where workers toiled, restaurants where diners lingered over platters of food, and pubs where sailors hovered over pints of beer and wine. But as the sun dipped below the horizon, the streets of Classis grew dark. As if synced to the setting sun, the Scheduler appeared in the doorway. He nodded to the guard, left the Naval admin building, and hurried down the street.

Scanlan waited until the lamp light created easily avoidable pools of illumination. Then he eased out of the recess where he'd spent the early evening. At the corner of the building, the youth squeezed into the narrow alleyway.

The first step was always the hardest. He extended one foot and planted it against the wall. Next, he leaned back onto his shoulder blades braced against the two-story building. Then he lifted the other leg and pressed the wall behind him with his hands. In an awkward crawl, Scanlan Saltare scaled the walls. Once near the roof of the neighboring building, he lifted a hand, grabbed the tiles, and allowed his legs to drop. For a moment, suspended by the fingers of his left hand, he dangled above the alleyway. But a twist turned him to face the wall and a reach got him purchase with the other hand. A hard pull launched him to the roof.

Crouched and scanning, Scanlan checked to be sure he was alone. Then a leap across the gap and a grab onto the windowsill placed Scanlan at the third floor of the admin building. A tap on the shutters opened them, allowing him to climb through the window. Not by chance, it was the southeast corner.

Conveniently, a scroll marked *Accipiter de Pax* lay on the Scheduler's desk.

After unrolling the roster for the *Hawk of Peace,* Scanlan struck a flint and by weak candlelight, he uncapped an ink container. After dipping a pen, he wrote his name on the ship's list in a perfect copy of the Scheduler's writing. He waved the scroll to dry the ink before rolling it and placing the document on the desk, exactly as he found it.

***

Shortly after dawn, the rowing officer of the *Accipiter de Pax* unrolled the scroll and began reading off names. Part way down, he announced, "Scanlan Romiliia Saltare."

"Here, Second Principale," Scanlan responded.

"Bow section. Sort out your seating with the lead rower," the ship's second officer instructed.

"Yes, sir," Scanlan confirmed.

He lifted his bag and walked up the ramp of the quinquereme. In his mind, he thought, the great adventure has begun.

Scanlan had no clue just how prophetic was his thought. Eyes were watching him. Looking down from the third floor of the admin building, two men observed the youth as he strolled up the ramp.

At the east window, the Scheduler glanced at the older man standing next to him.

"How did you know he'd find a way onto that five-banker, Tribune?" asked the officer in charge of staffing warships.

"There's only one Romiliia family," the staff officer replied. "Any son of Lucius Jace Romiliia Kasia must be a special lad. I needed to know how special."

"And your evaluation?"

"Could you pick his writing out from the names you wrote?"

"No, he matched my handwriting to the letter," the scheduler admitted.

"He's apparently that special," replied the head of Naval Planning and Strategies for the eastern fleet.

***

Scanlan Saltare was soon drafted into the murky world of espionage. Partially because of his adopted father's reputation, but also for his unique talents. A set of skills that elevated the youth above other spies and earned him the code name: Nightjar.

Welcome to 198 B.C.

The end of the sample

Author Notes:

Thank you for reading the tenth and final book in *A Legion Archer* series. In *Salvation of Exile* the Cretan Archer, Lucius Romiliia Otacilia Jace Kasia, finally found a home. And while Proconsul Cornelius Scipio Africanus would fight in the wars for Greece and command Legions against the Insubri, he will be a minor character in the next series.

Hopefully, you will join me in the historical adventure in the *Provinces of Rome* series, book #1 *Allies, Spies, and Conflicts*.

Now let's separate fact from fiction for *Salvation of Exile*:

Porcius Laeca, Tribune

Until 199 B.C., a citizen of the Roman Republic had little recourse when sentenced by a magistrate. Although the law championed by Tribune Porcius Laeca is complicated, at its core was a citizen's right to an appeal, including the right to choose exile over a death sentence. You can learn more by researching *Lex Porcia*. Tribune Porcius Laeca was assisted in getting the laws written and passed by legal scholar Sextus Paetus, known as The Clever.

The Battle of Cremona

Lieutenant General Hamilcar, one of Mago Barca's commanders, remained in the Po River Valley when Mago fled Italy. He gathered disgruntled tribes in 200 B.C., and looted then burned the town of Placentia. After crossing the

Po River, the army of Gauls besieged Cremona. Caught by surprise, the regional Governor of Cisalpine Gaul, Praetor Furius Purpureo, needed far more troops than his garrisons to put down the attack. Consul Aurelius Cotta extended him the authority, authorizing Purpureo to command Legions. After a forced march, Praetor Furius Purpureo engaged the rebellious tribes. According to Historian Livy, during the battle, Hamilcar died along with tribal leaders, and 35,000 warriors were killed or captured, 70 clan standards were seized, and 200 wagons of plunder recovered. Fear of another Hannibal heightened the emotions of Rome at the attacks. When Furius Purpureo emerged victorious, it caused a celebration. And it was warranted as his Legions defeated an army almost twice its size.

Jace's Symptoms

I used the medical description of *vascular intracranial hypertension* to give Jace Kasia his symptoms as the Latian Dog: Chronic headaches, progressive visual deterioration, blurred vision, and deficiencies in key areas of memory, learning, visual and spatial skills, concentration, language, and executive functions (coordination of cognitive abilities and behaviors).

As far as Jace's surgery, the actual process of treating a head wound is more complicated than simply drilling a hole in the injured person's skull.

Trepanation

The term means borer or auger, and it describes a surgical procedure in which a hole is drilled, or scraped, into the human skull. Archeologists have evidence of holes being made in skulls for medical purposes from as early as 4,000

B.C. The purpose of trepanation was to release the pressure of built up blood from the brain after an injury. More sophisticated than scraping a hole, the *terebra serrata* was an ancient tool for trepanation. Consisting of a brass tube with a serrated end, the surgeons would roll the tube between their hands to drill a hole in a patient's cranium.

We don't know how many patients died because doctors drilled into the Dura, the membrane around the brain. Or how often the membrane was damaged and blood seeped into the cranial cavity. No matter how many failed, we have skulls with precision holes to attest to the widespread use of trepanation throughout history.

Traveling from Credaro to Arona

The rivers Jace and Sucaria crossed, moving east to west are the Serio River, Brembo River, Adda River, Bevera River, Lambro River, Seveso River, Olona River, and Ticino River. If you search a map of the Lombardy Region of Italy, you can roughly follow the path of their travels.

Clan Names

We know from Livy's History of Rome, after The Battle of Cremona, the Legions captured seventy standards. We can only assume each standard represented a segment or a sect of a tribe. Unfortunately, we don't have the breakdown of the Insubri. I prefer clan as the designation for smaller family groups within a tribe.

Arona

Gnātos in Latin means born or son. The Gnātos Clan in *Salvation of Exile* is purely fictional, however, Arona is a real location. And while not the home of a clan chief, as far as we know, the huts on log piles on the edge of Lake Maggiore are historically accurate.

Wedding Ritual

I mixed historical rituals to create the wedding of Jace and Brigid. Because I couldn't find any articles about the Italian Gauls or the Insubri Tribe's wedding ceremonies, I reverted to ancient Roman-Latin elements.

Sextus Pompeius Festus (Festus) was a Roman writer from 2nd century A.D. He claimed Roman brides wore a hairstyle known as *senibus crinibus,* which loosely translates to six locks of hair.

The 1st-century B.C. Roman poet Ovid referenced a celibate spear. This spear in his writings instructs his female audience to, during the wedding ceremony, let a *hasta recurva*, arrange their virgin locks.

Festus also mentioned that ancient Roman brides wore a piece of headgear called the corolla, a crown made of herbs, flowers, and foliage personally handpicked by the bride.

And for the actions in the wedding ceremony, I was inspired by modern historian Mary Beard. She writes about the middle of any transformative ritual. For instance, from single individuals to a married couple, there is a point in the ceremony where the participants are neither single nor married. I found the idea of a middle point interesting and used the elopement as the transitional period.

Cornelius' Election

History reveals the complicated personality of Publius Cornelius Scipio Africanus. On one hand, he enjoyed the notoriety and acclaim of his victory over Carthage. On the other, Cornelius wanted to get back to a legion and onto a new campaign.

Out of fear that Cornelius would win more battles and collect enough glory and fame to declare himself King of Rome, his detractors concocted a unique ploy. In 199 B.C., they elected Scipio Africanus as the President of the Senate. The position prevented Cornelius from leaving Rome and assuming control of a legion.

Gladiator Games

Public gladiator games in 200 B.C. were rare. Called funeral games, the blood sport had a dual purpose. The spilling of blood on the ground was believed to help a deceased soul get to Hades quicker. And the games provided a popular pastime for the citizens of Rome.

The games of the era were held at the Forum, known as that time as the Comitium. They built a temporary facility for seating and viewing the fights. Arena in Latin means sand, desert, grit, ring, or theater. The meanings are appropriate for the public spectacle.

While Cornelius organized public games to honor his father and uncle, we have no records showing that funeral games were held for the dead Legionaries killed by the Insubri in 199 B.C.

Baebius Tamphilus

Praetor Baebius Tamphilus marched legions over the Po River with the intentions of punishing the Insubri Tribe. According to the Senate of Rome, the Insubri were guilty of rebellion and breaking treaties. Plus, the acts of looting, burning, and murdering citizens of the Republic when the Gaulish tribes destroyed Placentia.

Livy, History of Rome part 32

"...Tamphilus rashly invaded the territory of the Insubrian Gauls and was cut off with almost his entire army; he lost more than six thousand seven hundred men..."

I'm suspect of Livy's number of dead. There are few historical references to the defeat, other than his, and no notable battles are associated with the massacre. A legion at the time consisted of 2,880 heavy infantrymen and at least an equal number of light infantry and calvary. Livy's number of dead equates to the loss of a legion and a half. Yet, Praetor Baebius Tamphilus escaped punishment and went on to a successful career, suffering little humiliation and no ostracization. In *Salvation of Exile*, I settled on a loss of a reinforced legion.

Victory of the Insubri

The ancient city of Milan would have been the target of the legions. It held the government and housed the royalty of the tribe. For the Roman commander who captured Milan, the rewards and glory would go far in advancing their political career. Reference: Milan was *founded around 590 B.C. under the name Medhelanon by a Celtic tribe belonging to the Insurbes group.*

Constructed on a plain between the Olona, Lambro, and Seveso rivers, the city offered a hard target for Praetor Tamphilus. To my way of thinking, a direct attack route in would have given the sixty-seven thousand members of the legions an escape route. My thoughts, as reflected in

Salvation of Exile, meant the Insubri army offered a better target. Perhaps a gathering of warriors to draw Praetor Tamphilus away from Milan. His intention would be to clear his flank before laying siege to the Insubri capital.

Lucius Lentulus

The Consul in 199 B.C., and the absentee General of the devastated legion, did ride north. After relieving Praetor Tamphilus, he began recruiting Legionaries for new legions. Despite his efforts, before he could march on the Insubri and get revenge, Lentulus was recalled to Rome. With his co-Consul in Greece, Consul Lucius Lentulus was charged with organizing the elections of 198 B.C. The selection of two new Consuls, and a slate of civil servants to manage the Republic, took precedence over a field command.

***

I loved researching and writing *A Legion Archer* series and from your response, you also enjoyed the historical exploits in the ten books. If you appreciated *Salvation of Exile,* consider leaving a written review on Amazon or Goodreads. Every review helps other readers find the books.

I welcome emails and reading your remarks. If you have comments, e-mail me.

E-mail: GalacticCouncilRealm@gmail.com

To get the latest information about my books, visit my website. There you can sign up for my monthly author report. In every newsletter, I start with an article about ancient history before giving you updates on my books.

Website: www.JCliftonSlater.com

Other books by J. Clifton Slater

Provinces of Rome series, unfolding adventures as Rome turns its attention to the Greek city-states and the influence of Macedonia.

#1 Allies, Spies, and Conflicts

A Legion Archer series, set in the backdrop of the 2nd Punic War

#1 Journey from Exile

#2 Pity the Rebellious

#3 Heritage of Threat

#4 A Legion Legacy

#5 Authority of Rome

#6 Unlawful Kingdom

#7 From Dawn to Death

#8 The General's Tribune

#9 When War Gods Battle

#10 Salvation of Exile

Clay Warrior Stories series, set in the backdrop of the 1st Punic War

#1 Clay Legionary

#2 Spilled Blood

#3 Bloody Water

#4 Reluctant Siege

#5 Brutal Diplomacy

#6 Fortune Reigns

#7 Fatal Obligation

#8 Infinite Courage

#9 Deceptive Valor

#10 Neptune's Fury

#11 Unjust Sacrifice

#12 Muted Implications

#13 Death Caller

#14 Rome's Tribune

#15 Deranged Sovereignty

#16 Uncertain Honor

#17 Tribune's Oath

#18 Savage Birthright

#19 Abject Authority

Gygax Odyssey series, historical fantasy set in 607 B.C.

Based on a story passed down from Ernest Gary Gygax, the co-creator of the board game *Dungeons & Dragons*.

(Co-written with Luke Gygax)

#1 The Gygax Odyssey

#2 Wrath of the Cyclops

Printed in Great Britain
by Amazon

Salvation of Exile

A Legion Archer
Book 10

J. Clifton Slater